PIPER J. DRAKE

DEADLY TESTIMONY

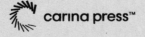
carina press™

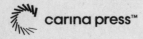
carina press™

Recycling programs
for this product may
not exist in your area.

ISBN-13: 978-1-335-01311-8

Deadly Testimony

Copyright © 2018 by Piper J. Drake

This edition published by arrangement with Harlequin Books S.A.

® and TM are trademarks of the publisher. Trademarks indicated with
® are registered in the United States Patent and Trademark Office, the
Canadian Intellectual Property Office and in other countries.

www.CarinaPress.com

Printed in U.S.A.

To Patty, who introduced me to the hotel that provides a goldfish to keep travelers company

DEADLY
TESTIMONY

Chapter One

The people standing between Isabelle Scott and a hot bath needed to move. Immediately. Or violence would occur.

However, the event she'd been covering as private security had just ended and she wasn't technically on the clock at the moment so she wouldn't be paid for the violence. Nor would she have a convenient justification should legal repercussions ensue.

So she'd try to be patient with the four men managing to block the way to both elevators of the hotel. As she approached, she assessed the situation automatically out of habit. The four of them weren't friends, per se. Actually, three of them looked to be surrounding the fourth and the poor bastard was backing right into the wall between the two elevators. He was obstructing her access to the button she needed to call her ride up to the ninth floor and she'd be damned if she was going to take the stairs if she didn't have to.

Not that she had a problem with stairs in moments of necessity. Stairs were a lot safer than elevators in certain situations and there were times when making the choice to step into the elevator was basically the equivalent of entering a kill box.

She drew her brows together in a scowl. Not the line of thought she wanted to end the night with and, allowed to go further, those kinds of memories would result in nightmares. No thanks.

"Look, fellas." She tried to pitch her voice for politeness. Pleasantry? One of her former teammates, Victoria, was better at it than she was. But she wasn't the ruffian Victoria liked to say she was, in teasing. Well, not completely. "Could you please step aside?"

There. Victoria would've been proud.

One of the three threw a hostile glance over his shoulder without taking time to get a real look at her. "Walk away, bitch. Go get a drink at the bar or something. This'll take a few minutes."

Lizzy clenched her jaw.

The bar was crowded and she wasn't in the mood for a drink. After heading up security for a private party for eight hours and watching important people schmooze with others of equal or greater "status" in a wine-infused corporate boondoggle, all she wanted was to soak out the tension of the day and get some sleep. Maybe order room service. Their client had reserved a block of rooms for the security detail as part of this particular engagement and she'd been looking forward to putting the hotel's hot water heaters to the test.

Her plans aside, the three men closing in on the fourth had the kind of build and stance that stood out in a hotel full of less rough-and-ready corporate types. These were men of physical action. From the less than perfect fit of their suits and the way the fabric of said suits draped oddly over their forms in a few strategic places, she was guessing they were hired help and armed. Very out of place and definitely moving on the fourth with a predatory intent.

The remaining man was about six foot, give or take an inch with his dress shoes. His suit was properly fitted across broad shoulders and an athletic build. He had a well-defined jaw and high cheekbones. Sharp intelligence was evident in his dark eyes as he took in everything around him, darting around to each of his aggressors and beyond them looking for exit routes.

His pale complexion was not unusual for Seattle in early spring. But in combination with his facial features and thick, stylishly crazy hair, his skin tone was a characteristic of East Asians as opposed to Southeast Asians, who were a few shades darker in skin tone throughout the year.

She'd guess he was Korean as opposed to Chinese. Taller than most Asians and in better shape than most people in general. But it wasn't going to do him much good against three opponents of equal or larger size unless he had the kind of training to handle multiple aggressors. The kind of training she had.

And if he did, he'd have stepped out of the situation by now.

Isabelle sighed. No wingman or cavalry coming to his aid. He needed help but it wasn't forthcoming. This was not going to resolve in the next thirty seconds and that was all she was willing to wait. Besides, she couldn't leave a person alone to face odds like these. She'd been on her own in these situations plenty of times and it'd never been fun.

"Gentlemen, get out of my way."

Humor and interest sparked in the Asian man's eyes. He understood English, apparently. Seattle being a major city for travelers, it was always good to note rather than assume a listener could understand the conversation. Especially if she might have to advise him to take action.

The hulking goon who'd originally spoken to her turned then. "What did you say?"

Maybe the English language, or conversation in general, wasn't goon number one's strong point.

"Get. Out. Of. My. Way." She put some steel into her voice this time. No need to increase volume when intensity works better.

Beady eyes narrowed at her as goon number one flexed his thick fingers into a meaty fist and released them. Threat clear.

Ah, well. Intonation could work on people with more neurons firing inside their heads. She might not have a whole lot of stature going on at five foot four, but her new friend should've at least spared a moment to ponder that maybe a woman in a black suit with white dress shirt and an earbud hanging over her collar from a wire might mean something.

He was a thug dressed in a monkey suit.

She was a much higher pay grade.

He advanced on her and made a grab for her arm. She saw it coming with plenty of time to react, rising up on the balls of her feet and keeping her limbs loose in anticipation, her joints relaxed to maximize her range of motion. As his left hand reached her upper arm, she stepped forward slightly with her left foot to meet him and seized his wrist from the inside, her thumb pointing downward. Swinging her hips and right leg around so her butt lined up with her attacker's forward leg, she bent her knees briefly and hip bumped him to rock his weight upward. She completed her move with a full upward body-twisting motion, throwing him completely over her and onto his back.

She wasn't entirely heartless though. She kept a hold on his arm to prevent it from breaking or dislocating as he fell. It'd been known to happen when a person was caught by surprise. And judging by his yelp midair, he was definitely surprised.

The man didn't get thrown by a person almost half his size all that frequently, maybe. He should experience it more often though. It'd make him a better fighter.

He crashed down on the very hard, cold marble floor of the elevator lobby and she turned to address his companions. They were just beginning to respond, their postures open with their surprise as they started to reach for their weapons.

Not the wisest decision for either of them. Her position was easily within most people's reactionary gaps—the distance needed between a person and an attacker to have the time to react to an aggressive attack. She'd allowed the first man to make a move against her because she needed a reason to cite self-defense but she preferred to take her fight to her opponents.

He'd started it. She'd finish it.

She covered the ground between her and the nearest man standing with a slide step, landing in a Bai Jong or ready stance and immediately lashed out with her rear leg in a powerful front kick directly to the man's chest, then instantly drew her leg back to return to her stance. The air left his chest in a whoosh and he stumbled backward into the wall behind him.

Pivoting to face the third man, she struck with a hooking kick as she came around, catching his gun hand and sending his weapon clattering to the floor. He didn't have time to react as her other leg swept up in a high round-house and caught him on the side of the head. The man remained standing for a second, clutching the side of his head, then toppled over.

Three opponents, all downed and barely groaning.

The entire altercation took less than ten seconds. She leveled a stare at the only man left standing. He prudently kicked the fallen handgun to one side, well out of reach of the downed men, and pressed the elevator call button for her.

"Thank you." The elevator opened immediately and she stepped inside without turning her back to him.

There was a faint smile playing on his lips and one eyebrow was raised as if he had found something incredibly interesting. She scowled at him. His smile widened.

"Believe me." His voice had a rich, sensual quality to it. It hinted at intimacy he had no right to and a lot of naughty things. "The pleasure was mine."

As the elevator doors began to close, police jogged up to him, huffing with effort. "Mr. Yeun. We can't guarantee your safety if you don't cooperate with us and stay where we can protect you."

Isabelle was curious. Especially as she caught snippets of them arresting the downed men just as the very slow doors finally closed all the way shut. But the call of a hot bath was stronger than curiosity.

She was done for the night.

Her phone rang and she reached out with unerring accuracy, snagging it from the nightstand. "Scott."

Damned thing was sturdy enough not to break under a pounding or from being thrown so she'd learned to grab it as quickly as possible to shut it the hell up. Even if she wasn't quite awake yet.

"Morning, Lizzy. You were involved in an incident with the police." Gabe's voice came through, crisp and businesslike, maybe mildly amused.

She breathed in through her nose and out in a sigh.

Gabriel Diaz was her superior in the Safeguard Division, newly formed within the Centurion Corporation. He—and two other people who had made up their fire team—was one of the few people she allowed to use her childhood nickname. They'd spent time in the field, survived enough combat situations to not bother counting anymore and, in general, trusted each other with their lives.

Currently, she wanted to end his.

"What time is it?" She refused to look at a clock. The hotel's heavy curtains were doing a fantastic job of blocking out daylight and she had planned to sleep in this morning.

"Oh-eight-hundred." There was definitely amusement in Gabe's voice. The bastard. "Are you with company?"

The face of the very attractive stranger by the elevator last night flashed into her mind.

She grunted and sat up. "Negative."

There'd been police, as Gabe so cheerfully reminded her. The hot guy would've had complications in joining her for the evening. And while she had no issues with law enforcement in general, she did not want them parked outside her hotel room door advertising to the world she had company. Multiple deployments in the military gave her a preference for discretion. She'd rather forego fun times than have her choices in off-duty entertainment subject to misogynistic judgment.

"Then you can tell me about it." He obviously didn't have a snooze button.

As commanding officers went, Gabe was a good one. But aside from admitting whether their conversation could be overheard or not, she wasn't prone to give him insight into her love life either.

Fortunately, he wasn't asking about it. Police. He was asking about police.

"Technically, I was involved in an incident and finished before police arrived on the scene." She could've stuck around to answer police questions but she really hadn't overheard anything before she'd decided to clear her path to the elevator. "Looked like a shakedown or similar disagreement. One of the men attacked me and I defended myself. When he was neutralized, the other two engaged. I eliminated the threats with nonlethal force. Then I entered the elevator and came up to my room."

Gabe was taking notes on her story as she related it. He'd craft it into an even more diplomatic statement if needed. "No worries, Lizzy, the police aren't interested in questioning you or involving you in the charges for those men. They had some interesting history, more than enough to keep the police busy without needing to talk to you. Especially when it was determined you were a Safeguard resource on-site for an unrelated contract."

"Then why did you wake me up?" she growled. If Gabe was using her nickname, they weren't being formal so she didn't have to be polite.

"Because seeing you in action can be inspiring." Gabe remained unfazed. If anything, he sounded downright cheerful. "And in this case, it lined up another contract for you."

She growled again without even trying to verbalize anything intelligible.

"Now, Lizzy, when you're good and people are impressed, there isn't any sense in being irritated about the cause and effect." This time he actually chuckled. "If you give people a demonstration of what you can do, can you blame them for wanting your services?"

She clamped her mouth shut, refusing to rise to the bait. More often than not in the past year she'd had to deal with chronic instances of underestimation. Clients looked at her and didn't believe she could be effective as personal security.

When she'd been active duty, she'd spent a decent amount of time proving herself. In the service, soldiers did as ordered and they worked as a team if the mission was to succeed—and in more cases than she wanted to remember, if they were going to survive—so people learned to trust her. She'd carried her own weight. The men and women who'd served with her had come to respect her for it.

Civilian clients didn't tend to react the same way. The past year with the Safeguard Division had been smattered with a fair share of clients looking for big, burly bodyguards and not willing to believe little Isabelle Scott was capable of defending them. Or, and this bothered her somewhat less, she wasn't the image they were going for when they'd decided adding a bodyguard to their entourage was the most trendy accessory.

Still, she had her pride to consider and she preferred to be on assignment as opposed to working the administrative side of things or training recruits over at the Centurion Corporation facilities just outside Seattle. She was too on edge to train, and she needed the active assignments to help burn off the deep anger still inside her.

Maybe she'd been looking for the scuffle last night. Just a little.

She sighed. "What do you want, Gabe?"

"You've been requested for an assignment. Specifically. And both the US Marshals and police are more than happy to coordinate with you." Gabe snorted. "I need you to get to the office in the next hour to meet the client and coordinate with his assigned protection."

"If he has a marshal and police…" She didn't want to finish the question she had at the tip of her tongue. Full respect to the city's finest but there were instances where augmenting a police detail with private military contractors was advantageous. It was unusual, but not unheard of. Well, this would be a first for her working with a US marshal but she could imagine instances where it'd happen.

"This is by request of the client and he's paying for this with his personal funds. You won't be on the government's or city's payroll."

Wasn't that interesting?

She'd had a good long bath last night and a decent night's sleep. Curiosity was winning this morning. "I'll be there at the top of the hour."

Chapter Two

Kyle Yeun was no stranger to corporate environments, and yet, admittedly, he'd never overseen projects of a military nature, whether they were government or privately resourced. So when he arrived at the offices of the Safeguard Division in downtown Seattle, he'd been expecting something…more outdated. A renovated warehouse, perhaps, or a stuffy windowless set of offices all in psychologically approved standard shades of beige. The city had been around awhile, after all.

Instead, the Safeguard Division was located in a relatively new corporate center. They had taken over an entire floor of a six-story building, maintaining an extremely wide-open office space. Not a conventional cubicle to be seen. Instead, there were clusters of comfortable chairs and table spaces to encourage collaboration. Privacy pods lined the interior wall to accommodate sensitive discussion, but the walls were all glass for complete transparency. Presumably, they were maximizing the natural light coming in from the floor-to-ceiling windows offering breathtaking views of Elliot Bay, Puget Sound and the Olympic Mountains depending on which side of the building one was standing.

Each of those pods and some of the larger conference

rooms seemed equipped with up-to-date videoconferenc-ing equipment. Scattered across the floor, a few employ-ees were working on laptops. There were even standing workstations and treadmill desks scattered here and there. For mercenaries, they presented a high-tech and, yes, so-phisticated atmosphere. One conducive to creative think-ing and group collaboration. Perhaps most surprising to him, it was welcoming for all that it was mostly empty.

He couldn't remember the last time he'd been in a corporate office environment with similar ambience, at least not with his most recent employer.

"Where is everyone?" He spoke out loud to no one in particular. The deputy US marshal and two plainclothes police officers sitting with him glanced in his direction but didn't immediately offer commentary.

Someone, however, did. "Safeguard Division is rela-tively new, Mr. Yeun. Most of our permanent resources are out in the field. It is also Sunday."

An impressively built man stepped around the cor-ner, the one blind corner anywhere near where they were seated.

Kyle stood smoothly as his combined US Marshal and police escort scrambled to their feet. All of them were trying to appear unfazed but none of them had heard the man approach. Maybe it was the open layout of the premises. Kyle had expected to realize someone was approaching—see or hear something—but this man had caught them all unaware.

Having used similar tactics to put colleagues off bal-ance in high-powered boardroom meetings, Kyle had to respect a well-executed play.

Tall, dark, the epitome of quietly dangerous, the man was dressed in a simple black collared polo and black slacks. He held out a hand. "I'm Gabriel Diaz, current lead here."

Kyle took the offered hand and shook it. The man's grip was firm and sure without the accompanying effort to squeeze too much. Gabriel Diaz was not a man with something to prove.

"Thank you for seeing me outside of normal business hours." If such things existed for people who conducted their sort of activities. An offshoot of a private contract organization specializing in personal security, these people were still mercenaries regardless of how impressively they presented themselves.

Kyle, on the other hand, was *the* proof against his former employer and he needed allies like these Safeguard people.

Diaz lifted a shoulder in a nonchalant shrug. "Our line of work rarely keeps the Monday through Friday, nine to five, hours. Why don't we take one of the pods over here? There are white noise generators to keep our conversation private."

Kyle proceeded in the indicated direction without waiting for his escort.

One of them, Officer Austin, cleared his throat. "Surprised to see facilities so open to appreciating the view outside."

Diaz smiled but there wasn't a lot of humor in the man's eyes. "We like having clear view on all approaches to the office building. The exterior windows are Thermopane, of course, and blast-resistant. The interior pods are fitted with ballistic-resistant glass in case of unfortunate, unforeseen occurrences. For us, line of sight is incredibly helpful."

Austin harrumphed. "Business must be going well."

"We do all right." Diaz pulled open the glass door to the pod and ushered them in. "Our parent organization, the Centurion Corporation, was willing to invest in these facilities. As I said before, the Safeguard Division is new."

Deputy Marshal Decker remained a quiet observer throughout. But then, he tended to be a man of few words in Kyle's experience over the past forty-eight hours. Officers Austin and Weaver didn't comment further as they took seats on either side of Kyle.

Of course not. Neither of them had revealed personality to speak of over the past several weeks since he'd entered witness protection. And they were both more than minimally put out when he'd insisted on additional security. He'd registered concerns to their superiors at the Seattle PD and the Office of Enforcement Operations responsible for the administration of coordinated US Marshal and local enforcement. Decker hadn't offered a reaction.

Kyle was not planning to play poker with the man. Ever.

To be honest, Kyle had gone so far because he'd been rattled. There'd been warning signs after the initial appearance at court, escalating to significant threats after the preliminary hearing. None of it could be directly traced to his previous employers, but there weren't many others with the resources to find him after he'd entered witness protection. Last night's incident had proven standard safety precautions were obviously insufficient. He was certain there were representatives on the local police force with both the intelligence and sense of humor to be exemplary guardians but, thus far, he'd yet to meet them.

So when he'd encountered someone who might fit his specifications, he'd immediately tracked her down. It hadn't surprised him at all to find she was attached to a mercenary group. The price tag associated with her services as personal security had been enough to raise even his eyebrows though. The Seattle police department had collectively choked. The OEO had expertly evaded addressing the fees.

"You did mention how new your organization was, yes." Kyle crossed his legs at the knee, not a posture most men adopted in the United States but Gabriel Diaz didn't blink. Interesting. Perhaps he'd done business internationally. In Kyle's experience, body language common to Europe or the Middle East or Asia could make those unfamiliar with it uneasy. "You also mentioned that most of your resources were out in the field. I had the pleasure of witnessing one in action just last night. Were you able to contact her?"

"We'll want a statement from her." Weaver sat forward. The woman was brusque at best, and no-nonsense.

Kyle could respect that in a woman but there was no humor left in her. She'd made a career for herself but she'd shown him very little joy in what she did. Cooperating with her was boring at best, unfortunately irritating most of the time.

Diaz raised an eyebrow. "It was my understanding that the Seattle police department didn't need a statement from Safeguard in regard to the incident last night. My resource was on contract to augment the personal security of a guest at the hotel in question and dispatching potential disruptive elements was within her purview."

Kyle tuned out the next few minutes of police administrative red tape. As far as he was concerned, it fell into the too-long, didn't-listen category. What mattered was when the corner of Diaz's mouth lifted in what was thus far a rare hint of a smile. Conversation ended, in Diaz's favor, apparently.

"If we could return to the main point for being here, I'm requesting the services of your resource. Specifically, the woman I saw last night." He didn't know her name. Luckily, she'd been the only female contracted to augment security at the hotel last night and all of the extra security had been supplied by the Safeguard Division. Amazing how much information the pretty little assistant to the hotel manager had provided with just a few minutes of flattery.

"Seattle PD is not responsible for the costs." Austin crossed his arms across his chest.

"Yes, yes. The OEO passed on the stance for both the US Marshals and local enforcement." Kyle waved a hand in dismissal, aware of the way the gesture caused the good officer to turn red in the face. The man probably had been warned to ensure this expense didn't hit the Seattle PD's budget. Fortunately, a good project manager in the private sector easily commanded a six-figure salary. And Kyle had been very good at his chosen profession for a very long time. "It is within my means to foot the bill personally and I made it clear I would in exchange for coordination between the US Marshals, police and this organization. Until last night, my esteemed police escort might have scoffed at the idea, but the three men this woman so readily dispatched in under ten seconds—I timed her—were a step above the usual muscle sent to keep a normal witness from testifying. At least to my understanding. And your own commanding officer broke the news to me that they'd had orders to kill me, if possible."

He'd dabbled in investment. Finance was a mental exercise for him and he'd made sure he had more than one nest egg tucked away. This expenditure, however costly, was most definitely warranted.

He wanted to live.

"If you'd stay put, you wouldn't be caught out in the open by these people." Weaver shifted in her seat, leaning forward and turning her body to face him.

"They knew my room number. I'm not certain it would have been better to have been caught in the hotel room by them." The public nature of the confrontation had delayed the use of firearms. Otherwise, he could have been very definitively dead before he'd had any sort of chance to call for help. Grim determination made him set his jaw and return the officer's glare. "As it was, I was heading back when they accosted me and the two of you were unreachable at the mobile phone numbers you so thoughtfully insisted I have on speed dial. I'm lucky the Safeguard operative was coming off duty and headed for the elevators."

To be honest, the striking woman had completely distracted him as she'd approached. He'd lost a few valuable seconds where he could have tried to slip away when she'd started conversation. Instead, she'd been forced to engage and he counted himself lucky to witness the beauty of the entire altercation. Fast, decisive, and then she'd gone on her way without a single care for acknowledgment.

He'd been impressed. And not much in this world impressed him in a good way anymore.

Austin let out a tired sigh. "Either way, we've agreed

to coordinate with your resource, Diaz. Is she available or no?"

Diaz slid a tablet out from under one of the side tables and logged in. He presented it to Kyle. "Here's our standard personal security contract, adjusted based on the requirements and background information you provided during our phone conversation earlier. I'd like to be sure we have the details in place by the time she arrives."

"What's her ETA?" Weaver asked.

"Before noon. Considering her temper, I'd suggest we complete any adjustments to the contract before she gets here." Diaz tipped his head to the side briefly. "Patience isn't one of her favorite virtues to practice."

"Not a compliment to your staff." Weaver glowered.

"Oh no." Diaz held up a hand to stall further criticism. "I didn't say she wasn't good at it. In fact, she may be one of the most patient operatives I've ever worked with, given the correct circumstances. It's just not her favorite to put into practice."

Kyle snorted and spared a glance at his glowering escort. "Join the party. What is one of her favorite virtues, then?"

Diaz didn't hesitate. "Wrath."

Chapter Three

Isabelle rolled her eyes. Diaz knew she was watching the feed from the pod. She always stopped in at his office first thing on entering via the back employee entrance on the opposite end of the building from the reception area.

And he'd left her a concise note: *Watch and decide by 1200 hrs.*

Her lead was nothing if not concise. She honestly thought if it couldn't fit on a Post-it note, it probably had too much fluff for his standards of communication.

His message, though, could have a couple of meanings. She had a major decision to make when it came to continuing to take contracts through Safeguard. But Diaz wouldn't give her a deadline with only a couple of hours' notice on that.

No, this was about this specific contract and this particular client. Which was fine. But she still had a bigger decision to make. The reminder was there, in the note, and the way he'd decided to word it. Otherwise he'd have just said, "Watch. Let me know."

It would've been a few words shorter.

Connected to the lead's office was a small briefing room with multiple screens to support videoconference with multiple locations. It was one of the only dark rooms on the premises. A thin film laminate of rodlike nanoscale particles was suspended in a liquid between two pieces of glass for each windowpane making up the walls of the briefing room. When the switch was off, supplying no voltage to the walls, the suspended particles simply floated in a random pattern for one hundred percent opacity. Dial up the controls, applying gradual levels of voltage, and the particles aligned to allow light to pass through for variable levels of transparency on the walls.

The technology was fairly impressive. But for the most part, the briefing room remained opaque and private.

So she'd stood in the briefing room and watched the feed from the pod as Diaz continued to discuss things with Mr. Kyle Yeun. Diaz had also thoughtfully left her a tablet with intel on Mr. Yeun. Basic background check.

On the screen, her potential client leaned forward and started studying the contract. He scrolled through the electronic pages, using the tablet's touch screen with ease. "I assume this contract is executable immediately?"

Diaz answered in the affirmative. Neither police officer attempted to read the contract. The US marshal was maintaining standing position almost directly under the video camera and could probably read the contract upside down on the tablet if he chose. She couldn't see his eyes, so she had no idea whether he was focusing on the contract or the approaches to the pod through the glass walls.

As it was, the man she was here to meet, and possibly begin guarding, was one hell of a speed-reader. Or he didn't care about the particulars.

"The language in your contracts is refreshingly clear and concise, Mr. Diaz." Yeun delivered the compliment in a somewhat distracted tone, his attention still on his reading. Well, he was indeed reading the fine print, then. Fast.

Quite the type A personality was Mr. Yeun. Born in Korea and arrived in the US at a young age with his father and mother, he'd taken advantage of the American school system and every opportunity for advancement. Scholarships for college and internships in the summer. He'd managed to build himself a successful career in fairly short order. Hell, his basic credit check showed him to have excellent credit too. She'd be willing to bet he'd tucked a nice parachute for early retirement.

Even his voluntary testimony in the civil and criminal actions against his former employer spoke of efficient practicality. Whether he was driven by moral and ethical standards wasn't indicated in the depositions. He'd negotiated a deal with the district attorney for immunity, so he wouldn't be going to prison or hit with the hefty fines potentially associated with whatever case this was.

However, the exact nature of the case was suspiciously redacted. A company name stood out in the case though—Phoenix Biotech. Since she'd both encountered the company before and come out of it singed, she wasn't surprised the case was so covered in black marks.

Diaz had pulled up what could be found on public record and she'd read it later. For now, she had the basic information she'd require to decide. She was more focused on watching Yeun and his witness protection. The tension between each of them was not at all good. She couldn't fault Yeun for wanting someone with a personal investment in his safety, even if it came from monetary obligation.

The remaining question was whether she'd be willing to take this job solo. Yes, she'd be coordinating with the US marshal deputy and two police officers but she wouldn't have another Safeguard operative at her back.

Centurion Corporation had their resources assigned to squadrons, each squadron comprised of four to five fire teams. Each fire team was a four-person team. She'd been a part of a fire team since she'd left active duty with the US military and signed on with the Centurion Corporation. A half dozen fire teams, including hers, had moved over to Safeguard but they were still stretched a bit thin with the current contracts.

It'd been a long time since she'd worked alone for as long as this assignment would take though, with no one to watch her back. The only reason she had the last time had been because things had gone sideways. The days it'd taken for her to reach safety again still played out in her nightmares.

Yeun chose that moment to stand up, stepping around Officer Austin to pace the interior of the pod as he continued to read. The other man hadn't given ground, per se, but he'd sat back in his seat to let Yeun by with a roll of the eyes.

Isabelle was going to guess Yeun had a habit of pacing. Something he'd have to stop if she did take over his personal protection. Especially in front of any transparent glass, bullet-resistant or no. What a marksman couldn't see, he couldn't attempt to target.

Yeun himself was easy on the eyes. But the way he tended to twist his mouth into a frown irritated her. Most of his commentary since they'd entered the pod had been patronizing with a dash of arrogance. The man had attitude and he was on every last nerve of either one of his police escorts.

That was what was making her pause. Oh, she could be professional. She didn't have to like the person she was protecting to do her job well. In fact, it was much less complicated if she didn't like the person. On most of her contracts, she managed a convenient neutrality in terms of what she thought of her client.

But if the man had soured his police escort over the past few weeks, they'd be a pain in the ass to work with from her perspective too. There was no way she could walk into this on their good sides. Coming here hadn't been their idea and they were not happy.

Austin had his arms crossed and Weaver was impatiently tapping her fingers against her knee. Both of them were shooting antagonistic glances Diaz's way.

Fun.

She pulled out her smartphone and texted Diaz. On screen, he glanced down at his phone. "For a basic testimony, it seems standard witness protection procedures would be more than sufficient." Diaz nodded to the US marshal deputy, Austin and Weaver in turn. "Our services are generally retained for private concerns where the police are not involved."

Yeun paused in his pacing and looked up at Diaz. She did like that the man at least maintained eye contact when he was going to address people. "I would've thought so too. Last night's incident shook my faith in the police force somewhat."

"Now, wait a minute." Austin sat forward and stabbed a finger in the air, pointing at Yeun. "If you would do as you're told, there wouldn't have been an issue last night."

Repetitive argument was going to get tiresome too.
It was always an exercise in perseverance when she had
to deal with the same gripes, defensive commentary and
complaints over and over again. Hell, it generally meant
she was going to have to consistently reinforce the logic
behind every move she made for this mission to both the
protective detail and her actual client.

Ugh.

Not that she hadn't dealt with it before but she didn't
exactly approach those situations with happy anticipation either. She'd established herself in any number of
teams throughout her military career wading through
this kind of bullshit. What she needed was a reason to
willingly walk into it now.

"We've covered that." Yeun apparently didn't bestow
the favor of direct eye contact on everyone. Currently,
not Austin. "I do not believe the outcome would've been
as definitive if those men had come up to the hotel room
you all had stuffed me into. At the very least, they'd have
been much quicker about threatening me with firearms.
I believe you mentioned each of those men was armed
and they didn't seem to have qualms about drawing their
weapons."

True. The men the night before had walked with the
confidence of having an employer who'd get them out
of whatever legal trouble they got into as a result of
their dirty work.

"At least down on the lobby level, they were hesitant,"
Yeun pointed out. "They were conscious of onlookers."

But he'd endangered innocent bystanders. It was a
craptastic risk to take.

"Either way…" Yeun handed the tablet back to Diaz.
"I felt my life was in danger. They were not going to

stop at an intimidation tactic. And none of us anticipated there'd be this kind of effort to keep me from testifying."

Man had a point there.

"The police force is very busy and last night's incident isn't quite enough to convince them of my assessment of the situation. The US Marshal Service follows a minimal force required doctrine which leaves Marshal Decker here working with us alone in the field." Yeun returned to his seat and looked directly up at the camera. At her. "I'm willing to take action to protect my own interests. If I'm being paranoid and the extra layer of protection is not necessary, it's only my budget impacted. I think it's worth the investment for peace of mind."

Reasonable. Logical. From what she'd seen, there was no particular reason to turn it down apart from a distinct lack of enthusiasm for working with these particular personalities. And that was why she should. There was a job to be done and she hated backing away from anything just because the team might not welcome her. She texted Diaz to let him know she'd take the contract.

Leaving the briefing room, she left the dossier on the table for the time being. She'd ask Diaz to send her the electronic version via encrypted email to study later.

She strode down the length of the office floor, exchanging nods with the one or two other Centurions working in the office today. As she approached the pod, Yeun saw her through the glass and rose.

He beat her to the door and opened it to let her in. "It was also more than worth it to meet you."

Her dark eyes fastened on him, her gaze coldly neutral. "Seriously?"

Absolutely.

Her hair wasn't drawn back in the tight bun at the

back of her head today, but it was still caught up in a serviceable ponytail. It gave her a severe look, accentuating her sculpted features. Hers was an elegant beauty, though it wasn't delicate. She held herself with perfect posture and everything about her spoke of strength and assurance.

Trite as it might seem, once he'd encountered her he'd been driven to see her again. Meet her formally. There were few truly interesting people in this world and in less than a minute, she'd proven incredibly fascinating. He'd have spent at least as much as her signing fee just to find her. Had spent as much on the occasional discreet escort.

This woman though, she was a different type of dangerous and he'd decided it was in his best interest to combine his fascination with the expediency of his need for augmented protection. He also figured it'd be prudent not to suggest services other than those specifically outlined in the Safeguard contract for personal security.

He had a strong sense of self-preservation.

The possibilities though, they were crossing his mind at speed now that he was face-to-face with her again. She possessed exceedingly kissable lips.

"I haven't thanked you yet." He did his best to keep his gaze locked with hers. No wandering. She'd already proven she reacted rather violently to rude behavior. "Miss?"

She considered him for another moment and he honestly wondered if she'd walk right back out of the room. Instead though, she glanced at his escort and gave each a nod. "Isabelle Scott. I was heading up the security detail last evening for a prior client."

Yes, an up-and-coming socialite in the area. The man

had hired Safeguard because private security added to his image. It hadn't taken long to find information about him and find out who he'd hired. Hotel staff loved to chatter about the higher profile customers. Apparently, the man's only complaint was that the head of his security team was unfriendly and unnecessarily abrupt.

From where Kyle was standing, he could understand where the man's commentary was coming from but if Kyle made an educated guess, he'd bet the man had tried to blur the line between business and pleasure and Miss Isabelle Scott made no time for idiots.

"I was fortunate you were there." He gave a sincere smile, not something he did often. "Your timing was excellent."

She grunted.

Not a sound he heard from a woman often but somehow, coming from her, it wasn't harsh. It…reminded him of his mother. He grinned.

Her gaze sharpened. "Something funny?"

Where Officer Weaver's toughness translated to a coarse outward personality, Isabelle Scott's strength had a predatory edge to it. Pinned by her current ire, he did experience some trepidation.

But he only smiled wider. "Not funny. No. I'm just impressed."

She blinked. There was no commentary to acknowledge his compliment but he thought he saw a hint of a dusky rose blush to her cheeks through her bronze complexion.

"Normally, Centurions don't work solo." She glanced at Diaz and then at the marshal and officers. "But this contract doesn't seem to need more than one operator to augment the current protection in place and we're not in the practice of charging a client for redundancy."

Confidence. Maybe a defensive edge to her tone. More and more interesting with every moment.

"Centurions? I thought this company was called Safeguard." Austin probably tried to sound critical but he only succeeded in grumbling.

It was Diaz who answered. "We're all still a part of the Centurion Corporation, Officer. Safeguard, as a specialized division, may have resources rotate in and out from other postings within the Centurion Corporation. Besides, what would you call us, Safeguard-ians? None of us uses a war hammer."

"Okay, we got it. Centurions." Weaver cut off whatever retort Austin was going to give and the two glared at each other.

That was part of the tedium of having the two of them assigned to Kyle's witness protection. The only time they weren't taking shots at each other was when they were mutually annoyed at him. The fun of it wore off after the first few hours. Their commentary got repetitive.

After weeks of following their directions, sitting in substandard hotel rooms and eating horrible fast food, Kyle had reached the end of his tolerance. It'd taken everything he'd had left to convince them to allow him to stay in a decent hotel for the past few nights and after last night's incident, he was likely doomed to return to awful accommodations if he left it to them. No. He couldn't, wouldn't, go on with so little control over his situation.

This act, hiring a person with a vested interest in keeping him safe, was his way of taking control back. And preserving his sanity.

Kyle crossed his arms over his chest and leaned back

against the wall. When Isabelle's gaze returned to him, he addressed her, "I'm open to whatever expertise you'd like to share."

Her brows drew together. "Protecting you is our business now. Per the contract, you follow my instructions. You don't and you're exposed. Maybe dead, if your concerns are correct. I still get paid. But I prefer for my clients to survive and be referenceable."

He noted she didn't say her clients had to be happy and chuckled. "At least our preferences are in alignment."

Tiny muscles in her jaw tightened beneath her smooth skin and irritation flared in her dark eyes as she caught the innuendo. He was pricking her temper. It was probably not a good idea, but too often he was extremely entertained by indulging bad ideas. Riling up Isabelle Scott was going to be an exceedingly fantastic bad idea.

"I'm going to need some time to talk with the marshal and officers here." She lifted her chin in the direction of the still-seated escorts. "Then I'll decide what changes you're going to need to make."

That stopped him. They'd already taken him from his home and halted his search for employment. His life was on hold for this trial. "What changes?"

"Depends on what you've been doing up until now." Isabelle shrugged. "Then we alter your pattern."

Kyle opened his mouth to ask more but Diaz rose in a smooth economy of motion. "I'll take Mr. Yeun to my office to finish signing. You can pick him up there."

Isabelle nodded.

"Now, just wait a minute." Kyle wrestled with his own anger, an unfamiliar feeling. "This is going to go in accordance with—"

"No, Mr. Yeun, it's not." Isabelle's flat statement cut over him before he could gain momentum. "If you want me protecting you, then you are not calling the shots. I'm the expert in this. Not you. And I intend to use my expertise to keep you safe. That includes not allowing you to run around leading the rest of us by the wallet. You are not the person in charge from the moment you sign that contract."

Chapter Four

Think tank, that was what these new offices were supposed to be.

At the moment, Lizzy wanted to curl up in one of the hidden quiet cubbies and block out the rest of the world.

Okay, there were only a few of those cubbies tucked away behind the main office area and they were specifically for employees who became too overloaded too fast to take themselves home or someplace quieter. The cubbies weren't just equipped with white noise. They were designed to give a person solitude, time to get their shit together, before they lashed out and became a danger to the people around them.

Friends and family were safer when the Centurions had an environment to handle those moments.

The missions they'd gone on overseas and the combat situations they'd seen left their mark. Lizzy was no different. And they were all good to go as long as they had the means to see to their own sanity. Call it self-care. Call it mental management. Whatever. It worked and this was one of those places designed with their particular histories in mind.

A normal, civilian workplace might have quiet spots

or they might not. But the people around them wouldn't necessarily understand.

Sometimes ex-military returned home and made new lives for themselves. They remade themselves and put their experiences in the past. Others didn't, couldn't, wouldn't. Whatever. So they went into the private sector, joined organizations like the Centurion Corporation. And they found a sort of balance in the structure it provided. Not civilian life. Not military service.

But in her case, she was torn. Part of her wanted the rest and quiet.

The other part of her wanted to find a good brawl.

Instead of seeking out the quiet rooms, she headed to Diaz's office. He and Kyle Yeun were seated in the armchairs in the corner. Huh. Apparently, Diaz liked Yeun. Otherwise, the two of them would be seated across from each other trading minimal discussion over Diaz's desk.

Diaz had seen her through the glass and given her a tiny nod. She opened the door to the office without knocking.

"Mr. Yeun, if you'll return to the waiting area you saw when you first entered, you'll find your police and US Marshal escorts there." Diaz stood and offered his hand. "Lizzy will be joining you momentarily to take you to your new safe house location."

Yeun shook Diaz's hand without hesitation, then turned and gave her a smile. "I'll await Lizzy's company with pleasure."

She scowled. Both the smile and the commentary were sincere but the delivery was too polished and laden with innuendo. No need to encourage it. In her experience, even if it was intended as friendly at first, the man was fishing to see if more attention would be welcome.

Much better to shut that shit down before it got too irritating.

Yeun hesitated a moment, then apparently realized she wasn't going to give him more of a response. Instead of looking put out, his smile only widened further and he took himself outside.

Both she and Diaz stood watching him until he reached the reception area. There wasn't a direct line of sight, but if a person had a habit of using reflective surfaces to take note of what was going on around the corners, every part of the office space was visible from Diaz's desk.

It required really good eyesight. Which she had.

And Yeun was in possession of a really nice ass.

Diaz chuckled. "Interesting guy."

You betcha.

"Is there a reason you care?" She dumped herself into the armchair Yeun had just vacated, noting he'd left it warm. Normally that creeped her out but currently she wondered if the guy had a fever or if he just ran hot.

"He's a businessman." Diaz shrugged. "Not our usual type of client though. He's not going for the political angle or the socialite status. Obviously has money. Prefers to spend it on what interests him."

She snorted. "Women. Luxury junk. Food and booze."

Assumptions. And not kind. But then again, she wasn't inclined to overestimate people. They were less likely to disappoint that way.

"Background check says yes about the women." Diaz was matter-of-fact about it. "But all discreet escort services and no black marks regarding him as a patron. Not even diplomatic commentary."

Meaning he hadn't used money to smooth over any

issues that would've otherwise earned him red flags in an escort service's point of view. Every escort service kept track of their customers. They might not share those records—in whatever unofficial form those took—with authorities conducting an investigation, but they might share with other information gathering personalities. And Diaz was building up a network of intelligence as part of Safeguard Division's internal assets.

"So he's not abusive and he pays up." Good to know. She wasn't going to judge the man for his choice in company or whether he paid for it.

"He does have expensive taste in cars and material items." Dry tone there. "Also frequents some of the most expensive restaurants in town."

Travel enough and people like her and Diaz didn't tend to keep much in the way of things. Good food, on the other hand, was something worth spending on as far as she was concerned.

"There are worse things." Yeun sounded like a normal guy, actually. She might've been less inclined to take a bullet for him if he turned out to be a horrible person. "Obviously, he's done something to be on the naughty list in the corporate world though."

"White-collar crime, and more than naughty. Anything involving Phoenix Biotech has more serious repercussions. That organization has serious funding and is involved in way more than cutting-edge research." Diaz sat in the other armchair and looked out the window, his gaze unfocused. A few months ago, they'd gone right into one of Phoenix Biotech's facilities to extract a kidnapped woman—the younger sister of Diaz's now-significant other, Maylin Cheng—and Diaz had barely come out of it walking. "It's a slippery slope. A person starts out just with overlooking an email here, deleting an email there. Nothing intentionally wrong, per se. Then things slide into more questionable territory and they find they've dug themselves a hole."

"Some of those corporate types do things they know are illegal and assume money and a good lawyer can get them out of it." Maybe her comment came across a little sharp. But she'd met plenty of those during the social climber party she'd covered last evening.

"And we'll get to know who those types are." Diaz shook off his brooding and leaned forward in his chair. "We're in shady territory here. We don't know what to expect with Phoenix Biotech involved but they are willing to kidnap and kill their resources to accomplish their quarterly business goals. Keeping Kyle Yeun alive to testify against them in this case isn't going to be easy."

"Bring it on." She wasn't boasting, even though she liked a challenge. To be honest, she was spoiling for a fight and Phoenix Biotech tended to hire the kind of personnel who could give her a real one.

Diaz gave her a neutral look and continued without calling her on it. "Private security is going to be like this from here on out. The more we know, the more we can accept contracts on the right side of the law and maybe even help some people who otherwise find themselves in too deep for redemption."

She raised her eyebrows at him. "This is starting to sound like one of those television shows Maylin watches."

Diaz chuckled at the reference to his significant other. "The concept is worth considering. Most important thing I'm trying to keep in mind as I establish Safeguard is making sure we're still doing the right thing. It means we need to make informed decisions and I need people smart enough and with enough of a moral compass to continue making them out in the field."

Oh. Here it was.

"I'm going to need to know soon, Lizzy." Diaz was serious now. "Harte has a new fire team for you, with a commanding position if you want it. You could go back into active duty with the squadron in Centurion Corporation. Or you could officially be assigned to Safeguard Division."

"Not an easy decision." She kept her tone light but making the choice was anything but.

Diaz didn't even pretend to be fooled though. "You've had a lot of time to prove your point, Lizzy. You had your time in the military. You've been a tactical asset to the Centurion Corporation. All along the way, you've proven to the people in your teams and the clients we work for how valuable an asset you are. I'm asking you to start becoming a strategic part of this organization."

"You think I'm ready." She didn't bother making it a question. She was, in terms of skill set and experience. No need to hear Diaz confirm it to validate what she already knew about herself.

"I think you're dodging it."

Yup.

Diaz sighed. "And trust me, I don't blame you. But there are ways to burn off those anger issues of yours besides going out on the high-adrenaline, high-risk missions. Last night wasn't just a good deed."

No. She'd been spoiling for a fight. Otherwise, she'd have called the police and run interference until they could arrive on the scene. This wasn't some faraway place. Here, on domestic soil, she was technically as accountable as any other US citizen when it came to the consequences of disturbing the peace.

There'd been a high probability Diaz would've had to come bail her out of jail when she'd made the decision to get into a physical altercation. And she hadn't cared.

"Fortunately," Diaz continued, "you happened on a lucky situation."

"Lucky for Yeun." The man was sitting comfortably slouched in the reception area, watching his police escort pace. For a person too restless to stay put in a hotel room, he was showing a lot of patience here. Probably because he was here on his own terms, pursuing something he wanted. "We could just keep him here for the next few days until his trial."

"Negative." Diaz cut the air with one hand. "We're not a safe house. None of the facilities are intended for overnight stay, much less something longer. Plus, this is a joint operation. It'd raise the question of why the man isn't being kept in protective custody on police premises or elsewhere in government facilities."

Point. She had no desire to sit around at a police station for hours, much less days.

"It's a good opportunity for us, actually." Diaz sat forward, resting his elbows on his knees.

The motion drew her attention to him and his rare smile was there. He had surprisingly white teeth. Maybe because none of them smiled all that often. Well, except Marc. He smiled all the time, around a mouthful of food.

"You plan on expanding on your thought there?" She crossed her arms. Whatever this was, she wasn't absolutely sure she wanted to know.

"Part of Safeguard Division's longevity is going to rely on the contracts we acquire." Diaz glanced in the direction of their guests and back to her. "Building a good working relationship with police and US Marshals would be an advantage. I'd rather work with them when the situation calls for it."

Relations with local authorities were a major factor to consider in any mission. They could be a big help or could become a dangerous risk. She could see where Diaz was going.

"They don't seem too eager about working with me."

"Consider it a stretch for your diplomacy skills." Diaz grinned. "Come out on the other side of this in one piece and maybe we'll have established a solid precedent for working together in the future."

"Huh." She'd stay noncommittal on the idea.

Commitment was part of her problem.

It was easy when she was responsible only for herself.

"I'll be going silent for the duration." It was her preferred mode of operation. It should be a simple couple of days. If anyone was trying to find Yeun, they wouldn't get his location from any intercepted communications between her and Safeguard.

They could take precautions against it, of course. Their technical expertise was some of the best. But the tricky thing in their business tended to be the knack their fellow mercenaries had in one-upmanship. There was always someone coming up with something better.

The only way to be sure there was no information leak was to have no communication at all.

Diaz nodded. "You know our schedule. Make contact if anything goes out of the ordinary."

"It's what I do."

"Yes." She'd tossed it out as an old joke. Diaz was serious though. "It is. For a few hours or a night. You excel at the short solo missions, even have issues with authority. It's time to quit thinking of those points as badges of honor."

She bristled, defensive. "Don't go all big brother on me."

"Consider it constructive feedback from your commander," Diaz shot back. "We've worked together a long time. If there's anyone I can send out solo, it's you. If you can manage a mission in three or four hours, you can do the same over longer assignments. We both know it. But it's time to acknowledge the fact that you don't like taking responsibility for other people. You won't take a team for longer than a few hours."

"I can work in a fire team long-term." Well, she'd done well in Diaz's fire team. There'd been plenty of others where they could function but they'd never gelled as a group.

"And you used to be able to lead one." Diaz had access to her file. He also knew her background. "Lead and pair with a spotter within the same team."

She ground her teeth and didn't respond.

"Most shooters work with a spotter." He stood after a moment and walked over to his desk. "Whether you go back to the main Centurion Corporation with another fire team or stay here, it'd be optimal for you to be willing to partner up again, Lizzy."

"Victoria and Marc are partnered. You lead." She counted out her team members on the fingers of one hand. "Me as a solo distance shooter worked fine. It could in another fire team too."

There was a chance. A small one. Theirs had been a particularly good combination. It'd take a long while to grow into the same sort of comfortable rapport with a new team.

"Or we could continue to give you specific contracts." Diaz leaned against his desk. "There are good lead positions where you could provide cover from a distance and have eyes on the site without being down on the ground. Harte has several contracts where you'd come in handy."

They didn't just want surveillance. The Centurion Corporation followed a particular moral code, but it didn't mean all the work they did was particularly virtuous. Taking on more jobs as a lone sniper meant she would be further focusing her skill set toward a narrower field. Eliminating specified targets.

Assassinations.

"This is a good time to decide where you want your career to go, Lizzy." Diaz had lowered his voice to a quieter tone. "You're good at what you do now."

"I can be good at anything I decide to do." It came out before she had the chance to consider. It was an automatic defensive response. Because Diaz wasn't quite right about something he'd mentioned earlier. She still had a point to prove.

It might not be to him. Definitely wasn't anything she needed to demonstrate to Victoria or Marc or any of the people currently with Safeguard.

No. She'd just spent so long proving to anyone who came anywhere within her sphere of influence that she was who she was, she wasn't exactly sure what to do now.

Diaz was right. It was time to move on to the next

step. She had no idea what direction it would be in. So she did what came easy.

"First things first." She rose from the armchair. "I've got a job to do."

Chapter Five

"You can't be serious."

Isabelle hustled Kyle Yeun into the small apartment when he stopped in his tracks at the door.

Over the past couple of hours, they'd taken a circuitous route out of Seattle before swapping cars and coming back into the city. It might've seemed ridiculous to some but if Yeun was being followed, convincing anyone watching him that he'd left the city for a few days was ideal. Officers Austin and Weaver had followed in a separate car at a distance along the same route while Marshal Decker had made visual contact at preplanned touch points along the way.

One big, coordinated road trip.

In the meantime, one of the Centurion Corporation trainees had already cleared the apartment and prepped it. Marshal Decker had also come ahead to clear it and had gone to his unmarked vehicle out on the street to take up a stationary position a few blocks up Pike Street.

Officers Austin and Weaver would remain mobile, driving a circuit of the streets around the location watching for unusual activity.

The trainee remained waiting in the apartment for their arrival. She nodded to him as he passed them to leave, handing her the keys to the apartment. She pocketed those and locked the door, throwing the two dead bolts.

"Fridge should be stocked with basics." She moved through the apartment, inspecting everything for herself while Yeun remained standing in the middle of the main room.

The trainees from the Centurion Corporation facility outside Seattle were on point, usually military veterans only in need of training in the procedures specific to their particular private military contracting outfit. And she was certain Deputy Marshal Decker had gone over every inch with his own discerning eye. But she still liked to go over everything personally. When working solo, even in coordination with other organizations, she'd learned to check every detail herself.

"This place is a dump." Yeun didn't bother with more complicated vocabulary.

She tossed her duffel down next to the armchair in the corner of the small main room. "It's clean, there are no bugs and it isn't anything like the places you've been choosing to stay in over the last forty-eight hours. There's plenty of hot water and the water pressure is better than a lot of the older hotels in the area. What's to complain about?"

Yeun's eyes flicked in the direction of the bedroom and back to her. "You're telling me that's a king-size bed in there."

Not a hint of innuendo in either his tone or his posture, but hell, her own brain had supplied a few interesting thoughts. The man was too attractive for his own damned good.

"You're sleeping alone." And there would be no debate

there. Not with him, not with her own libido, no matter how long it'd been since she'd last scratched that particular itch. "You can make do with a queen. The sheets are fresh. No one's bled on them."

"Generally, blood on the sheets isn't the organic matter I'm concerned with when I'm faced with questionable accommodations." Yeun's mouth stretched into a wry grin.

Of course his charm factor amped way up with the change in his expression. She fought against smiling in return. No sense in encouraging him.

For all his complaining though, he appeared much more relaxed than he had back at the Safeguard offices. Fine lines around his mouth and between his eyebrows had disappeared, replaced with much better humored laugh lines at the corners of his eyes. Apparently, peace of mind made a huge difference for him.

He'd unbuttoned the collar and top button of his pristine white dress shirt, as well. Somehow he'd gone from polished businessman to stylishly business casual with just the two buttons. She wasn't exactly sure how he achieved the effect but figured it had as much to do with his posture as the clothing he was wearing.

She liked his business casual look better. It was just a step away from rumpled.

Nope. None of those thoughts would lead her to wise actions. Not a single one of them.

"Not a worry here. There's no television but I brought a tablet. We've created a sock-puppet account for you on a couple of the streaming video sites so you can watch movies without anyone realizing it's you." She pulled a tablet out of her second bag and held it out to him. "I'll have a portable hot spot turned on most of the time for you to access Wi-Fi but I need your word of honor you won't try logging in to any of your online accounts. No email. No websites. Nothing you've ever registered for or created a log-in user name and password. You'll be surfing the internet via proxy server to avoid traceability."

He raised an eyebrow at her. "You'll trust me?"

She stared at him. "I'll be watching you to save you from your own stupidity. The minute you go back on your word, access to Wi-Fi and the tablet stops. You can stare at the ceiling for entertainment."

He snorted. "Understood. While I think I could do so for a few hours, I'd appreciate the option of video entertainment after a while."

"It's only a few days until the court hearing." She settled an earbud in her ear and activated the comm on the secure channel shared by Deputy Marshal Decker and Officers Weaver and Austin. "Scott here. We're about as settled as we're going to get."

Yeun adopted an uninterested expression and went into the bedroom to get a closer look.

Decker's voice came across the comm, his tone soft. "Decker here. I'm in place with eyes on the street."

"Weaver. We're circling the block." Weaver spoke at a slightly louder volume and the mic picked up some residual background noise that sounded like music in the car. She and Austin were the mobile response unit, easily able to move directly to action because they weren't parked at all. That meant they had to take a circuitous route around the block or surrounding streets fairly continuously for periods of time.

"Decker here. Marshal Nguyen would like to have a few words with you." The inflection was slightly different. Strained?

Isabelle frowned. "I'm not leaving my post."

Definitely not within minutes of arriving at the safe house.

"This will be brief." Decker's voice took on a tone of reassurance. Which was creepy because thus far, he'd been a study in how to be neutral.

She huffed and told him where she would be shortly. Stepping over to the bedroom, she rapped her knuckles on the doorjamb twice before entering.

Yeun stood there, in the process of pulling a plain white T-shirt over his head. The majority of his torso was exposed and the man was a fantastic example of lean physique. Muscles rippled over his chest and lats. His abs were flat and sculpted in the kind of six-pack that made her want to run her tongue over them. And then there was the defined V of his hips leading the way down to...

"I'm stepping out to get a snack. You want coffee? Hot chocolate?"

He must've frozen when he heard her knock, but he finished pulling on the T-shirt. Tension she'd refused to admit was building eased a fraction once he'd covered up all those tempting muscles. He gave her a raised eyebrow look again and there was amusement in those eyes. "I can't remember the last time I had hot chocolate."

She set her teeth. "It's a thing. Does that mean you want some or no?"

"I'll take a cup of coffee, please. Dark as you can find with one raw sugar." His mouth stretched into a lopsided grin. "And maybe a small cup of the hot chocolate. It's been long enough, I wouldn't mind giving it another try."

"I'll be about fifteen to twenty minutes." She started to back away, realized she was retreating. So she stopped. "You know the drill. Throw the dead bolts behind me.

Don't answer the door for anyone. I'll text you to let you know when to open the door for me. Stay away from the windows and definitely don't open them."

He didn't bother with a response but he glanced down at the bed.

She followed his gaze and saw a pair of jeans laying there. Good grief, she'd caught him midchange. She raised her gaze back to his and there was real laughter in his eyes now. He placed his hands at his waist and started to undo his belt.

"Come lock the door behind me first. Then you can finish changing." Points to her for keeping her voice steady and firm. Still, she had been the one to walk in on him, even if he hadn't closed the bedroom door or gone into the bathroom to change. "I am sorry I interrupted you."

"Not at all." He might've stopped the process of taking off his suit pants but he'd left the belt unbuckled. "Thank you for offering to get coffee. I don't suppose a hot entrée is forthcoming as well?"

Isabelle sighed. "There are sandwich fixings and ramen noodles here for today. We've got easy access to plenty of food choices within the next couple of blocks. So why don't I just get your coffee this evening and tomorrow I'll see about hot takeout. Deal?"

Professionally speaking, even five minutes was more than she wanted to spend away from her client the first day. Knowing he had already left his handlers when they'd trusted him to remain in his room the night before made her loath to trust him to stay put now. Contract or no.

Personally, putting some distance between her and him seemed like a very wise idea. Her libido was coming unhinged and she needed to get her head back on straight. Stepping out for this meeting was her compromise.

Yeun, for his part, sighed but held his hands out from his sides. "I'll make a sandwich but the coffee better be good."

She grunted and swung a small backpack over her shoulder. "Good coffee is subject to the drinker. Lock the door behind me."

Isabelle stepped out on the street and headed down Pine Street about a block or so, then turned on Post Alley to disappear into one of the small restaurants. She emerged with a different jacket on and her hairstyle changed, thanks to the addition of a small scarf. A few pieces of chewing gum stuffed in her cheeks changed the shape of her face.

Tromping back up the street the way she'd come, she passed the entrance to the apartments and headed into the chocolate and wine store just a few yards up the street.

The decadent scent of chocolate wafted to her from every direction. She bypassed the display case of hand-made truffles from various chocolatiers around the city and made her way toward the back of the small shop.

A small bar was set up, manned by a tall, thin girl with her dark hair held back by a handkerchief. She had a few random piercings and a ready smile. Her posture was relaxed and friendly, a reflection of the atmosphere of the entire shop.

A man was already sitting at the bar with his back to the wall, a tiny espresso cup sitting on the bar at his elbow. He was dressed in dark, nondescript clothes. His skin tone was golden brown and his hair was clean cut.

She approached, studying the specials listed on the sign just past his head as she took in his appearance. Shorter than average height, but she'd bet he was in shape. He'd have to be as a US marshal.

"Can I get you something?" the young girl asked cheerfully.

Isabelle gave her a smile and her order. To go.

"You sure you don't want to have a seat?" The girl offered, waving a hand to the other three stools in front of the bar.

"No thanks." Isabelle shook her head. "I'm out to stretch my legs anyway. Take your time."

"Okay. Feel free if you change your mind." A co-worker entered the shop then, and caught the girl up in chatter about what to wear for a concert that night as she went about fixing the drinks.

Perfect.

"Good to meet you, Miss Scott." The man murmured to her quietly, taking a sip of his espresso.

She nodded. "You wanted to chat?"

"Won't take you away from your client for too long. He has a tendency to get bored and wander off." Nguyen's delivery was dry, maybe irritated but he did a good job of keeping it out of his tone.

"So I saw." It was safe to figure anything Decker knew, Nguyen knew as the senior US marshal oversee-ing the handling of Yeun as a witness.

"This is the OEO's first coordination with the Safe-guard Division, and with Centurion Corporation as a whole." Nguyen didn't put his espresso cup down, in-stead nursing it.

She didn't blame him. The coffee and espresso were

good here. Though the hot chocolate she'd come for was even better.

"It is, however, not my first time working with the Centurion Corporation," Nguyen continued. "With that in mind, I will say I am looking forward to setting this as a precedent for positive cooperation in the future."

"I'm sure my lead will be glad to hear that." Isabelle rolled her shoulders inside her jacket. This wasn't anything he couldn't say directly to Diaz. "There's a point here, isn't there?"

Nguyen's eyebrows drew together. "Just giving you context so you'll take the next thing I have to say seriously."

Isabelle kept her face blank. "Noted."

"It's our hope this will be an extremely simple job for you." Nguyen sipped more espresso, purposefully slurping the liquid. "It might not be."

Isabelle grunted. "I glanced over the public records for this case."

Nguyen nodded. "Could be straightforward. Insurance fraud. Illegal dumping of hazardous materials in navigable waters. Or…it could be more complicated. Either way, our mutual friend is the pivotal testimony to prove it happened at all."

Interesting.

"Why not put more marshals on the case then?" Because, generally, mixing up resources from this many different sources was a clusterfuck. Federal oversight, local law enforcement and private sector didn't tend to play well in the same sandbox.

"I was going to until Yeun requested to contract with Safeguard." Nguyen shrugged. "It's his personal funds and I know the quality of the resources coming out of your parent corporation."

Isabelle took an intuitive hop of logic. "And why increase your resources when the client is willing to do it himself? You do have the minimal force doctrine to keep in mind."

"Exactly." Nguyen placed his empty espresso cup on the tiny saucer. "I do have an interest in making this joint effort successful where others may not. This could remain extremely simple or it could quickly become a bad situation. I wanted to advise you to keep a clear line of sight in every direction."

Isabelle's attention sharpened at the statement. While he could be saying it to just about any person in her line of work, it meant something more to an operative with her specific skill set. The question was whether he was privy to it.

Nguyen placed a card on the bar and stepped off the stool. He turned to face her as he straightened his shirt. "I'd like you to feel free to call me directly if you have concerns or need immediate assistance."

Then he walked out of the store.

Isabelle stood there, peripherally aware of the two employees behind the bar chatting about logistics of a boyfriend picking one of them up directly from work. There'd been several messages in the exchange and she'd need to think on them a bit more.

Nguyen was senior enough not to come out and say anything direct. He'd left her with hints and the seeds for her to consider the possibilities and come to her own conclusions. She needed a bit more information though so, for now, the important things to keep in mind were the warning of the possibility for complications and the invitation to contact him. Directly.

Generally, such a situation didn't speak highly of trust in the man in the field. It didn't surprise her not to be encouraged to go to the local law enforcement resources involved but excluding Decker as well was notable.

"I'm so sorry to keep you waiting," the girl gushed, rushing over with a set of to-go cups in a tray. "Your orders are fresh and hot though, I made sure."

Isabelle thanked her and tipped her, then started toward the front of the shop. Eyeing a couple of the displays, she snagged some specialized provisions for the days to come. Hopefully she wouldn't need them but if she didn't get them, she had a sneaking suspicion she'd regret not being prepared.

Chapter Six

Kyle was entertained enough by Miss Isabelle Scott's reactions to actually wait patiently in the apartment for her to return. Besides, twenty minutes was hardly long and he'd appreciated her giving him a time frame at all. Something neither the officers nor the deputy marshal had bothered to provide him.

It remained to be seen whether she would keep to the given time frame.

In the meantime, he made himself a sandwich. He was pleasantly surprised to find a fresh-baked loaf of bread, presliced and waiting. On first glance, he'd expected it to be from a well-known French bakery in Pike Place Market but the label was handwritten instead. Home-baked? There were also good quality deli meats, again fresh sliced. And a variety of cheeses both sliced and spreadable. The refrigerator had not been stocked with standard supplies from a chain grocery store. There was also Irish butter and Italian sea salt infused with white truffle. Even a jar or two of what looked to be homemade preserves with a handwritten label across the seal. Someone with a palate had supplied them with items to put together a decent repast.

He'd have to look into who supplied Safeguard with their catering. The person, or Isabelle, had good taste.

Spreading out the fixings, he set about making himself a sandwich. He also wrapped up everything again but left it all out so Isabelle could easily put together her own. He'd have made one for her but he didn't know her tastes yet and wanted to see what she made for herself. Besides, observing her had proven a definite pleasure.

She was exceedingly expressive when conversing with him. Or perhaps he'd exaggerated his perceived difference between her stoic professional demeanor with the officers and deputy marshal and her somewhat startled reactions to him. With the others, she'd tended to set her jaw in a stubborn way. As if she was preparing to take on any pissing contests to come her way, and they were a certainty rather than a possibility.

He wasn't sure if she'd noticed the difference in her own behavior yet, but he was hoping she would allow it to continue. Otherwise, she'd be every bit as boring as every other person assigned to protect him.

And really, he couldn't afford to be bored. It'd lead to too much thinking about things he couldn't take action on until after this entire mess was behind him.

The phone she'd left for him was on the table. She'd asked him to leave his personal electronics back at the Safeguard offices. However inconvenient, the precaution was understandable. He had the critical information he needed for the next several days at least. Never would he admit the twitch he experienced, habitually reaching for his smartphone.

He glanced at the screen of the loaned phone to quickly scan the incoming text from her and moved to the door. As she'd instructed, he stood to the side rather than in front of it and listened for her.

"Here." Her voice whispered through the door, just loud enough to be heard.

He undid the dead bolts—really, why were there more than one?—and let her into the room.

She entered, her dark gaze sweeping around the apartment and cataloging everything in sight. "Sorry, took a minute or two longer than I'd intended."

"A minute or two is inexcusable." He smiled at her.

Her brows wrinkled for a moment before she registered his sarcasm and let out a quick sigh as she turned and relocked the door. "In a lot of cases, it is."

So serious. He searched her expression. Her lips were pressed together and her eyes weren't focused on him anymore. Instead, there was the barest moment in which she was lost in memory.

"In this case, I think the worst consequence might be cold coffee." He regretted having brought up unfortunate recollections. Everyone had them. He made it a practice not to delve into his if at all possible so bringing them up for someone else wasn't something he did purposely.

"The cups are decently insulated." She moved to the small table and set down the cup carrier.

He followed, stepping into her personal space by a couple of inches to see if she got standoffish. She didn't back away but she turned immediately to face him and glare. He prudently held up his hands and stepped to the side to give her room, but he wasn't about to back away from the cups she'd brought.

Enticing scents rose up to tease him. Decadent chocolate and rich cream were cut and complimented by the bittersweet, slightly nutty aroma of coffee. Wherever she'd picked these up, these drinks were worth their fluid weight in gold if the taste was as good as the smell.

She lifted a regular twelve-ounce cup. "Coffee. Dark roast. Sweetened with raw sugar. The store included a few extra packets in case it isn't sweet enough, I guess."

The packets were laid flat in the well of the cup holder. Good eye. He hadn't even noticed them.

"I'm assuming at least one of those is your hot chocolate." He took the coffee from her before he managed to rile her up enough to toss it at him. He'd made that mistake in the past with another woman.

"Mmm." But she didn't lift the smaller cup to her lips. Instead she held it out to him, as well. "Drinking chocolate, also known as sipping chocolate. Not hot chocolate. I'm a firm believer in everyone trying it from this place."

He raised an eyebrow but took the cup from her. It was about the size of an espresso cup. To go. "Thank you."

"Don't mention it, Mr. Yeun." She took the last, espresso-sized cup and headed to the armchair in the corner. Then she breathed deeply of the aroma wafting from her prize.

"Kyle, please. No reason we can't be on familiar terms even in strained circumstances." It would actually help put him more at ease.

She nodded in acknowledgment but her attention seemed to remain on her precious cup, taking tiny sips and savoring.

Curious, he followed suit. Chocolate. Cream. More complex subtlety than he'd expected though with undertones of sweetness and bitterness. "What's the difference between drinking chocolate and hot chocolate?"

Her eyes were half-hooded as she sipped. For a second, it didn't seem as if she'd answer him, but then she did. "Different ratio of chocolate to milk, for one thing. And drinking chocolate doesn't have cocoa powder at all, I don't think. Some hot chocolate mixes are nothing but or a mix of cocoa powder and shaved chocolate."

Amusement bubbled through him. He couldn't remember the last time he'd competed against food for a woman's attention and lost. Here, with Isabelle Scott, there wasn't even a competition. And he was not coming out the winner.

"No packets of instant hot chocolate for you, I'm guessing." He grinned when her eyes opened all the way so she could glare at him. "I'll take that as a no."

She checked her smartphone and glanced around the room as if ticking off a mental checklist. Then she took another sip of her drinking chocolate, obviously enjoying it. And ignoring him.

Well, that wouldn't do.

"Did you want to make yourself a sandwich or shall I put all this back in the refrigerator?" He tipped his head to indicate the table full of sandwich fixings since he was apparently double fisting beverages.

Nonalcoholic beverages.

It might be another first. Actually, he was fairly certain it was.

"Leave it, please." She unzipped her duffel bag, letting it sit open enough to reach inside and pull things out quickly. "I'll make myself a sandwich after I've finished this."

"No rush." He chuckled. Placing his two beverages on the table, he took a seat in front of his sandwich and began his meal. "So what's the ratio for drinking chocolate as compared to hot chocolate?"

He only partially cared. What was more fascinating was that she knew. And apparently, was discerning when it came to her chocolate intake.

"Hot chocolate is one part chocolate to two parts milk. Drinking chocolate is one part chocolate to one part milk." She hesitated. Sipped. "The shop I stopped in makes other special drinks. Today's was a salted caramel hot chocolate or drinking chocolate. But I decided to get the classic for starters."

He found himself grinning again. It seemed to happen often with her and he'd only encountered her less than twenty-four hours ago. "So you plan to visit the shop again."

"Maybe. It's one of the places where I can see something being made from start to end. Harder to slip anything into what we order." She pressed her lips together. "Or I'll have one of our colleagues make a run tomorrow. It wouldn't be good to develop an observable pattern to tip anyone off. I don't think you've been observed with me yet, but it's possible."

He frowned then. "How so?"

She'd been careful to keep her hair tucked under a hat and wear nondescript clothing as they'd left the Safeguard offices. They'd driven away in separate cars out to some ridiculous distance away from the city before changing vehicles to return together. It was far greater lengths than he'd anticipated and even Officers Weaver and Austin had been disgruntled about all the driving.

"Hotel lobby last night had security cameras." She shrugged. "Puts us in the same place at the same time. Plus you made inquiries about me. Safeguard won't answer any queries about whether you contracted with us but a smart person could make logical connections. Then they'd just have to look for me to find you."

Her reasoning was sound. In fact, she delivered it so simply, he kicked himself for not thinking of it himself.

He needed to be smarter if he was going to be responsible not only for his safety, but for that of others in the future.

"I'm changing up appearances each time I leave but I'm going to keep it to a minimum if possible." She nudged her duffel with her toe. "I've got enough changes of clothes to head out about once a day to pick up whatever we need to supplement the supplies but if we absolutely had to, we've got enough here to make it through the next couple of days without actually going outside."

"I see." He sighed. "I suppose I'm not to go out at all."

"You are not to even look out the window." She sat up straighter in the chair. "Actually, don't go within three feet of any window. Stay far enough back not to throw a shadow when it gets dark enough to have to turn the lights on."

"Do you get attacked through windows very often?" He tossed the question out there in a flippant tone.

Her expression went blank. She rubbed the toe of one boot along the back of her opposite calf. "Shot. Sniper took aim at shadows in an apartment through a glass window. Caught the team by surprise."

Not what he'd been expecting. The deputy marshal and police officers had given him example scenarios. They'd lectured him on what to do in the eventuality of certain situations. All of it had been theoretical.

Here sat a woman warning him from personal experience. And she hadn't insisted on showing the scars she had to prove it. Both sank in and made an impression.

He tried his drinking chocolate. The chocolate flowed over his tongue with a sweet start easing into an almost red wine sort of fullness before finishing smooth. "You were ri—"

Car tires screeched somewhere outside and metal crunched with some sort of heavy impact.

Isabelle was out of her chair and at his side in an instant, pressing down on his shoulders with one hand. "Get down. Now. Into the other room, get into the bathroom. Stay low."

She herded him, a gun in hand. He'd never seen her retrieve it. She was just suddenly armed. In a rush, she had him in the bathroom crouching in the bathtub as she remained low at the doorway. A bundle hit him in the chest and he barely caught it before it fell to the ground. As he unfolded it he realized it was a vest.

"Get that on and put your shirt back on over it."

He rushed to comply, his fingers suddenly clumsy with his shirt buttons. His own breath sounded harsh in his ears.

Isabelle wasn't watching him. From her position, she was calm and seemingly motionless. Waiting with an air of readiness. Her demeanor helped him regain his own balance and he steadied.

"Scott here." She spoke softly, almost inaudibly. "Decker, spot report."

"What's going on? What's happening?" Kyle kept his voice low, his questions short. The urgency came across as demands for answers but she heard the tension, the fear there.

Couldn't blame the man. He was used to getting immediate responses from the people around him. Being in control. Most people didn't want to die and he was pretty damned sure someone was trying to kill him. Depending on what Decker had to say, Kyle might be right too.

"Shots fired." Decker's voice was low, grim. "Austin and Weaver are injured. Ambulance is on the way. Vehicle traffic is at a standstill. Local authorities are making their way here."

Not good. Obviously. But Decker could've provided more detail. She needed to know more to determine the next course of action. "Are we compromised?"

"Negative." Decker paused. "Not confirmed."

She was not waiting for a confirmation. By then, it'd be too late. She motioned for Kyle to come to her side. He'd gone silent but carefully climbed out of the tub and joined her, staying inside the bathroom until she led him back across the bedroom.

"Exactly how were Austin and Weaver injured? Was the shooter on the ground?" She continued her questions in the same tone as previously as they moved. As she spoke, she motioned for Kyle to grab his travel bag. Once she had him tucked against the wall to one side of the door into the apartment, she moved to retrieve her own backpack and duffel bag.

"Shots were fired through their windshield multiple times. Both of them were hit. Nonfatal." Decker's response could've won prizes for calm amid calamity. "Location of the shooter is unknown."

"Are you pursuing?" She tugged Kyle close by her side and tapped her shoulder. Once he placed a hand on the spot she indicated, she opened the door. Quick glances up and down the hallway confirmed it was clear. She led them down the hallway to the stairwell.

"Negative. I will not leave my post with our mobile

unit down. Keeping an eye on the street." Decker was following procedure to the letter. "Stand by. Will report when the street is clear."

"Copy." She tugged her comm from her ear and tucked the earbud with attached wire into the neckline of her shirt.

Problem was, the street was choked up with vehicle traffic and she was willing to bet the sidewalks were full of people rubbernecking to try to get a look at the accident. There was no way Decker had a clear line of sight to the entrance to the apartment building. If someone took shots at Weaver and Austin, they'd identified the mobile team as security. It was a distraction. And Decker, even if he wasn't watching to see what happened to their police colleagues, wasn't going to be able to visually clear every person on the street.

The situation was too unstable to remain where they were or follow standard procedure.

"Stay with me, be ready to get down," she whispered over her shoulder without looking back at Kyle. She was busy making sure the stairwell remained clear.

There were a couple of possibilities. Their attackers might know exactly where Kyle was being hidden. So she was absolutely going to move him. Even if their mystery pursuers didn't know Kyle's specific location, they'd obviously made the mobile unit and, from their route, could identify which city block Weaver and Austin were circling. Smart assailants probably had a position high on top of one of the nearby buildings or in one of the apartments overlooking the street. Which meant they were far above the street and in good position to see Kyle if they managed to flush him out into the open.

She didn't know if his attackers knew about her.

As she and Kyle reached the ground floor, she rummaged in her duffel bag. She came out with a wild red wig and handed it to him along with her baseball cap. He took it without arguing. She was going to have to gamble that they wouldn't be able to visually identify Kyle if they caught sight of him.

Smart man.

As he pulled them on, she carefully looked out the window of the heavy fire door onto the street. It was only around the corner but it was on a different street from the main entrance. Up and down the street seemed clear and she couldn't see any sign of a shooter in the windows of the apartments facing the street on this side. No telltale silhouettes or irregular lines along the tops of the buildings within view.

She took a deep breath, glanced at Kyle and bit the inside of her cheek to keep a straight face. The man looked ridiculous. But unless someone looked closely at his face, he wasn't easily recognizable with the shock of red coming out from under the baseball cap. "Slouch. Drag your feet when we walk. Stay on my left as much as you can."

It was a gamble to step out on the street. But their chances were worse staying in the building. And her gut instinct was screaming at her about all the things that hadn't gone right in the space of a few hours. Time to be less predictable.

"Here we go."

Chapter Seven

"Here, go into the bathroom and take off the wig. Swap the cap for this one. Change your shirt too but keep the undershirt. Toss all of the discards into the backpack. We might use them in different combinations later."

Despite the strain of walking, not running, the past several blocks, Kyle smiled as he accepted the offered trilby. Isabelle was being absolutely serious. Perhaps she didn't realize how ridiculous her demand sounded out of context, but he had to admire her focus. And he'd be more than happy to hand over the impromptu wig.

To her credit, she'd gotten him out of the building and quietly murmured instructions as she directed him into the crowded chaos of Pike Place Market. He thought she'd wanted him dead when she'd insisted he walk. They'd become lost in the press of people and come out on the other end of the market. Without her, he'd have bolted most likely.

"Why didn't we run?" He'd been wondering the entire nerve-racking journey. Hadn't asked because they were out in the open and the look in her eyes had threatened dire consequences if he stopped to ask questions.

They'd just entered a coffee shop tucked just below

street level on First Street and she'd herded him toward the restroom. It seemed to be a recurring theme today.

"Quickest way to draw attention on a crowded street is to move at speed in the opposite direction of everyone else." Isabelle answered him in a matter-of-fact tone, pitched low for only his ears. "So we walked. We went with the flow for a half block before breaking away in our own direction. Now change before anyone checks you out long enough to remember you the way you look now."

The café was only half-full. The other patrons were lingering unhurriedly over cups of coffee or espresso, reading or chatting quietly with a companion. No one was near enough to overhear them and none had given them a second glance.

Of course, Seattle was full of unusual personalities. He rather doubted anyone would find him interesting enough to remember. But she was the expert.

"Are we staying here long?"

She glowered at him, clearly irritated. He only waited. He'd followed her directions to the letter earlier, without question. This was a lull in their movement and he needed a break from unquestioning obedience. Otherwise, he'd be too tempted to make a bad decision later when it might matter more.

Or at least, that was the way he rationalized it to himself. Isabelle very likely had her own opinion on his current dallying. He struggled for a moment, on the edge of apologizing and going to do as she'd said. She was keeping him alive, for God's sake.

And she acted like she wanted him to remain that way. There was no resentment, no dirty look, no grimace at anything they'd had to do so far. She hadn't treated him like a job or a paycheck. She'd acted with immediate urgency, like she valued his life. Outside his actual family, she might be a first.

Before he could apologize, she ground out an answer to his question. "Awhile. I want to log on via a private proxy server and decide on our next move. They'll be searching the streets in a wider search pattern by now and it'd be better to be out of easy sight until we know exactly where we're headed."

He breathed a sigh of relief. He could use the time to regain his balance. Then maybe he could get his more ridiculous impulses under control and quit giving her a hard time. "The coffee flight, then."

"What?" If possible her glower grew deeper and a spark of temper flared up in her gaze.

She was too much fun to tease.

He lifted a chin to indicate the menu behind the coffee bar. "I'll take the coffee flight while we wait. It'll calm my nerves."

Okay, maybe not quit entirely. But he'd try to keep his teasing in reasonable parameters if he had something else to occupy his attention.

"Take your time in the restroom. I'll keep an eye on anyone coming in from here." She was already turning away from him, her gaze sweeping the café.

The men's restroom was clean and compact. He opted to head into a stall to make the changes she'd requested rather than have an awkward moment if someone walked in to see him changing his outfit. It took only a few minutes but he paused to wash his hands and splash his face with water. Now that they weren't on the move, his hands had begun to shake with delayed reaction.

There'd been shots fired on part of his security detail.

That was all he'd learned so far. And it'd been Isabelle who'd acted quickly, calmly, and gotten him out of the area. He'd been right to hire her.

What if he hadn't?

Any number of possibilities blossomed in his mind but the recurring image in every scenario had him dead. Shot full of holes. There were no second chances unless a person managed to stay alive.

He needed a second chance, not for himself but for people who would be depending on him. Soon.

He stared at himself in the mirror. A part of his brain still narcissistic enough to care noted he was looking somewhat haggard. Dark circles were forming under his eyes. Coffee would help. A full night's sleep would help more. But he hadn't had one since he'd cut his deal and gone into protective custody.

The events of today only served to convince him there was something completely irregular about this trial. Perhaps Isabelle Scott would have insight he hadn't considered yet. She'd certainly exceeded anything anyone else had accomplished so far when it came to his situation.

He found her physicality extremely attractive and he was about to see if she proved to be equally remarkable in terms of intelligence. The anticipation was enough to gain control of his earlier panic for the moment.

When he exited the restroom, he found Isabelle seated in a booth tucked far away from the front windows of the café. She sat with her back to a wall in a position to see anyone entering the establishment or approaching the booth in specific. As he walked to meet her, keeping in mind her earlier warning about staying away from the windows, she stood and had him slide into the booth beside her.

Not the seat he'd have chosen for himself but when he
spotted his requested coffee flight sitting on the table,
he decided to meet her halfway.

As he sat, Isabelle reached across him to stick Post-
it notes on each of the French presses. "The guy behind
the counter offered to come over. If you really wanted
the super detailed description of your coffees you'll have
to be disappointed. We don't want him over here making a show out of it."

He chuckled at her dry tone. Perhaps he might've
been irritated if someone else had been making decisions for him but he suspected she preferred to avoid
being the center of attention in any place, regardless of
the situation. Besides, her reasoning made sense. "I'm
happy knowing what each coffee is, thank you."

Isabelle grunted and turned her gaze to her laptop.

Her brow furrowed with her concentration and a stray
strand of hair fell forward. It was entirely possible the
server had offered to come back simply because she
was a beautiful customer. She didn't seem to consider
the possibility and he found it entertaining.

Kyle poured a small cup of his first coffee—a variety
of bean from Jamaica—and savored it sip by sip, set-
tling in to enjoy this simple thing. It helped him com-
partmentalize, gain distance from the fright of fleeing
the apartment that was supposed to have been his safe
house. In a way, it helped him organize the jumble of
questions in his head. He'd give her a minute or two to
accomplish her tasks, then he'd ask her what their next
steps would be. In the meantime, he could enjoy the view
too. Her look of concentration was very appealing, especially the way her lips pursed as she read the screen.

Isabelle, he'd found, tended to be more forthcoming

than Austin or Weaver, most definitely more communicative across the board than Decker. She seemed to be of the opinion the more he knew, the more likely he would be to take action when she needed him to.

He was most definitely inclined to agree.

The laptop only had a portion of Isabelle's attention though. She was still glancing up every few seconds to assess who was coming and going from the room. What each person was doing. Her eyes even took on the far-off look of someone staring out beyond the windows to anything outside.

Doing his best to maintain his calm, he went for what he hoped would come out as a light tone. "Are we expecting company?"

"Mmm." She continued to type away at her laptop. "Always expect the worst company. That way, if they don't show up, you're pleasantly surprised."

It occurred to him then, she might be prepared for a fight. Here, in a public place. She'd placed her backpack on the seat between them and the main compartment remained open. Her duffel bag was on the other side, also open. She had easy access to any weapon she'd brought with her. If he recalled, she had at least one impressively large firearm.

The legalities of it all boggled his mind.

"What about our friends?" The idea of saying their names out loud twisted his gut. There'd been a reason they'd run in the first place. He'd only heard Isabelle's side of the terse exchange but none of it had sounded good.

Her fingers paused on the keyboard and she lifted her head, pinning him with the full focus of her attention. "From what I could learn, they are not in the best shape but they'll be okay. In fact, they weren't absolutely sure we needed to move at all."

Indirect. But at least she was giving him answers. If he wanted more he'd have to be every bit as circumspect. "Will we be chatting again with them soon?"

Isabelle's lips curved in an approving smile. That mouth of hers was ever so enticing. "Not yet. But things are up in the air. I'm sure we'll catch up with them once everyone has had a chance to rest for the afternoon."

Kyle raised an eyebrow at her. "So it's just the two of us."

And not a private place in sight to take advantage of the situation. Yet.

"For a bit." She lifted one shoulder in a shrug. "Consider it an opportunity to spend a few hours being people we usually aren't."

Her message was clear. He grinned. Because it was the perfect opening to take her hint well past the intent and he absolutely wasn't going to pass it by.

"Well then," he drawled as he stretched his long legs under the table and lifted his arms to rest along the back of the booth bench. "I think that's a great idea."

She harrumphed and returned her attention to her computer screen yet again.

Oh no, he had his equilibrium back now and he was more than ready to prick her temper a bit.

"Tell me, who would you be if you weren't you for an afternoon?" He leaned toward her and brushed the stray lock of wavy dark hair from her cheek.

She batted his hand away and turned toward him, mouth open to deliver some retort.

He darted in, capturing her mouth and whatever heated words she'd planned to give him. He guessed he was risking physical injury but he hadn't died yet and she was supposed to be his bodyguard so she couldn't kill him for daring.

Anger surged and battled with her short-circuited libido. He'd caught her by surprise but that was no excuse for letting him inside her guard.

No. She was pissed at herself because she'd been imagining exactly what kissing him would be like.

And now she was.

And melting into his arms wasn't in the plan.

But his lips on hers felt damned good. It'd been a long time since chemistry with a man sizzled this way. So maybe a little melting was called for.

His lips brushed over hers and his tongue flicked out, teasing her lower lip.

Hell, she wasn't going to think about this. At least she wouldn't for the next few seconds. She opened for him.

He deepened the kiss at her invitation, his tongue sweeping in to explore. She met him halfway and tasted him in return. The man was a very, very good kisser.

When they parted, it was slow and reluctant. She drew in air through her nose and let it out slowly through her mouth, struggling to pull her scattered thoughts together. Warily, she scanned the room. The habitual check gave her a chance to get back to intelligent thoughts without looking him in the eyes. No new people had entered. None had left either. Not a single person seemed to have noticed the public display. Thank God.

Her cheeks burned and she cleared her throat. "That—"

"Was nice." Kyle's voice had deepened a note or two to a husky tenor.

Yes. "Not the point." She probably sounded like a bitch but she needed to be firm. "It shouldn't happen again. It's too distracting."

There was a beat of silence. "May I take that as a positive reaction to the kiss in general?"

She scowled at him, trying to cover her discomfiture. He kept knocking her off balance. Other men would've been more butt-hurt over her assertion. It made it easier for her to do her job.

A tiny part of her warmed though.

"What would you do next?" She tossed the question out in an effort to move the topic along to something else, pulling up a list of her private notes on her laptop.

He shifted in his seat and leaned toward her again. "After a kiss?"

"No." She lifted her hand and tapped his chest with her fingertips without taking her gaze away from her screen. "After leaving a place in a hurry."

"Why?" He sounded genuinely puzzled. "I honestly haven't rushed out of a place in quite that way."

She snorted. "You've never had to make a break for it? Ever?"

A pause. "It's been a long time."

An image of a much younger version of him running popped into her mind. There might have been amusement there, but she thought she heard an underlying bitterness. Layers. The man had too many of them and she couldn't understand why she had the urge to explore.

"I'm guessing whoever is after you has studied you and had time to observe your protective detail too. At least enough to recognize the pattern of their circuit." She might've been identified already as well and she'd include it in her planning. Chances were good they didn't have enough information on her yet to predict her moves. Especially since they were currently in the wind. "I'd like to have an idea of what you'd do on your own so I can take a guess at where they'd be looking for you."

"Ah." He sat back. The air in the sudden space he'd left was still warm with his presence. "I'd find temporary accommodations, probably with a passing acquaintance. It'd seem unwise to go to my own flat."

She thought about the brief hesitation before he mentioned an acquaintance. Uh-huh. "You mean 'lady friend'?"

Even that was indirect. Unusual for her but no need to make assumptions or get judge-y.

Fabric rustled as he shrugged. "Some are actual friends, others are more temporary associates with a practical price tag attached to the pleasure of their company."

She nodded. The weight of his stare increased as he studied her but she wasn't going to give him any of the expected reactions.

"Most women seem to react less than favorably when I admit to seeking out company." There was a question underlying Kyle's statement. Not too probing.

Because he wasn't interrogating her or making stupid assumptions based on whatever his idea of what most women would think, Isabelle continued running her searches and responded to him. "I've heard some people refer to my line of work in the same general context as prostitution. People can be capable of committing some incredibly awful things to each other. In comparison? A few hours of sexual gratification seems closer to the positive side of ways to earn a living."

She'd had people tell her what she'd done was worse

than exchanging sex for money. Considering how many times she'd been deployed, how often she'd had to do things no one talked about when they returned Stateside, she'd be inclined to think so too.

"Agreed." Kyle sounded impressed.

It startled her, the way his comment came on the tail end of her line of thought. The idea of him having such a negative opinion of her unsettled her too, twisting her gut uncomfortably. She shouldn't care. She'd made a habit of not.

Something about the discussion niggled at her and she gladly followed that line of thought as a distraction. "You're circumspect. I can understand referring to it delicately in a larger group. But it's just me and you here and you're not paying me for polite company. There're people out there who'd call a prostitute a lot of other things besides 'passing acquaintance'."

He was silent long enough for her to look over at him. When she did, his expression was uncharacteristically serious.

"Words like *whore*. *Slut*. They're powerful." There was sadness in his eyes until he closed them and shook his head. "They don't just hurt when one person throws them at another. They can be labels. Other labels—like call girl, escort, courtesan—might be kinder but they carry as much judgment with them. They can haunt a person and follow them from day to day, place to place. If enough people throw them at a person, those words become a part of perceived identity. Even if money exchanges hands in return for sexual favors, I don't assume it has anything to do with who the woman actually is."

She considered him for a moment. He'd known someone or maybe more than one person in such a position. It was personal for him somehow.

"A lot of ways to hurt a person." She found herself turning her body to face him, opening up her posture as he bared a part of himself to her. Somehow this discussion had gone dark and she got the impression he presented the lighter persona to avoid this part of his personality. Hell, if she was any good at being funny, she'd do it too.

He nodded, still caught up in his mood. "Indeed. In any case, you have your answer."

She pushed her laptop over to him. The screen displayed a map of downtown Seattle. "Any of those locations shown here?"

He raised an eyebrow. "Is this to determine where to go or where not to go?"

She tipped her head to one side. "It's sort of a balance. The trick is to not be quite where they expect you to be but close enough that they'll overlook you as they try the next likely spot."

"And you have a way to manage this?" There was definitely amusement in his voice now.

"I made several reservations at varying types of hotels under pseudonyms." She tapped the map on the screen. "Once you answer my question, I'm going to pick one. I'll check back in with the rest of the protective detail just before we leave. Once I do, we move and don't stop until we're established securely in the new location."

Whether she'd share their exact location was something she'd decide later. A lot of it depended on the details of the shooting on Weaver and Austin and any theories they had on how they'd been targeted.

Chapter Eight

As they entered the lobby, Kyle paused to watch a family and their dog waiting on the nearby sofas. The dog was well enough behaved, sitting patiently near the adults, and it was on a leash. The family was all dressed in identical T-shirts and obviously visiting on vacation.

Most definitely a family-friendly atmosphere but he was pleased to see the decor remained elegant and sophisticated. Often, family-friendly places attempted to create an almost cartoon-style atmosphere to entertain the younger demographic.

He turned his attention back to the dog. It had an endlessly patient expression for a canine. Considering the bounding energy of the children running laps around the sofa, the pooch probably needed quite a lot of that particular virtue.

Isabelle paused to follow his gaze. "Not a big fan of dogs? Seattle is a fairly dog-friendly city."

Kyle shook his head. "I've spent most of my life here in the United States but it still catches me by surprise to see pets out and about with their owners in public spaces."

"Yeah?" Isabelle nudged him with a shoulder to continue forward to the front desk. "Some cities are more pet-friendly than others."

"Where I spent my childhood, dogs were not commonplace pets in the household." His childhood wasn't filled with fond memories either but it had never occurred to him to want a dog the way some of his classmates had when he'd entered school in the United States.

His mother had been afraid of any pet larger than a hamster, really.

"Ah. We do make way for a lot of lifestyles here." Isabelle kept him close to her side as the desk clerk turned his attention to her. "Hi. Checking in?"

The man gave her a friendly smile. "Of course. Name?"

Isabelle didn't hesitate. "Reyes. Two guests."

Kyle kept his expression bland, his gaze wandering to fish in the bowl behind the front desk and reading the sign next to it. Isabelle turned, her dark gaze scanning the lobby and the area beyond the front doors while the clerk found their reservation and prepared their room keys. While she was scanning the room, he caught the eye of a young lady behind the desk.

The pretty employee smiled as she turned toward him and he pointed at the fishbowl. Then glanced significantly at Isabelle and winked, placing his finger over his lips. The young woman's eyes widened with comprehension and she smiled, nodding.

Kyle grinned as the woman stepped over to the clerk's side, whispering discreetly.

Once they received their keys and headed to the elevator, Kyle waited for the elevator doors to close before he asked his questions. "What happened to the reservations at the other hotels?"

"Standard operating procedure. Safeguard will monitor and adjust the other reservations under the naming convention I use for a delayed check-in each night until I check in and confirm we don't need them. It sounds excessive but we've negotiated corporate rates so it isn't as expensive as it sounds." Isabelle explained, watching the elevator floor indicator light up each number in turn.

"All as a matter of practice, no unnecessary communication." He leaned back against the wall. "You must have amazing administrative support. Or is there a different title for that position in your organization?"

She shrugged. "Our operational support personnel are very good at what they do. Most of the time, I make the initial reservations but they manage it from there. They do a pretty good job of adapting to the way each of the resources in the field does things. Sometimes what we do requires us to go dark for undefined amounts of time. Keeping tabs on the reservations gives Gabe an idea of where we are without us having to report in but outside groups would have more trouble tracking the information."

"And yet you share this procedural detail with me." Kyle wondered about the increase in information sharing. "You were not as forthcoming with Decker right before we left the café."

Kyle hadn't overheard Decker's side of the conversation and the exchange had been terse. She'd basically let Decker know they were alive and headed for a more secure location. Nothing else to give them away.

"He didn't need to know. You're more likely to cooperate with me if you understand my logic." She made the statement and he didn't refute it. It was an accurate assessment of his temperament and he rather appreciated her acknowledgment. "In any case we're fairly familiar with all of the hotels in the downtown area. This one is more of a boutique, not too mainstream. I've never stayed here personally but I also figured you're more likely to stay put in accommodations you like."

He smiled. "True. And if it helps, I've never stayed here either. It seems to be one of the better choices for families."

"Yes." Isabelle tensed as the elevator doors opened, pushing him back against the wall and out of view until she was satisfied the hallway was empty. "Let's get you into the room and take next steps."

"Under other circumstances, I'd be very happy to be pushed up against an elevator wall by a woman and rushed to our hotel room as soon as we arrived to our floor." Kyle paused. "I can't say I'm not happy, but I imagine I won't enjoy it as much as I have in the past."

She might have rolled her eyes if she hadn't been maintaining vigilance. "Room. Now. Smart mouth, after we've got you secure again. Maybe never."

He grinned. She'd been maintaining a distance from him the entire circuitous route down to the waterfront and back up the streets to arrive at this hotel. Every instance of contact had been deliberate, as if she'd thought carefully about whether she wanted to make it.

Perhaps he shouldn't have kissed her back at the first coffee shop. But he wouldn't regret it. Her lips had been soft and the kiss had been hot. Both qualities he enjoyed in a first encounter. He'd pursue further if she gave him any sign of it being welcome.

Yet Isabelle Scott was an interesting combination of contrasting personality traits. She moved with confidence, a certain arrogant swagger in the way she stepped out into the world. She made a violent encounter seem like a graceful dance. She was a person of action, decisive and devastatingly effective.

But she hadn't killed him for his infringement on her personal space. He'd considered it a good sign. Now she was maintaining an invisible bubble around herself and he wasn't sure if it was a result of their having gone back out into the open to travel or if she didn't want further personal interaction with him.

He wanted to know. Very much.

As she entered the room, she paused then pulled him into the entryway closing the door behind him. "Stay."

His gut reaction was to refuse. Experience over the past twenty-four hours squelched the habitual urge to be contrary and he remained where she put him.

For her part, Isabelle proceeded farther into the room with a handgun held up and ready to respond. She approached the bathroom door in a wide arc as she peered inside. Apparently satisfied, she checked the closet and pulled the heavier drapes closed across the windows at the far end of the room.

As the drapes closed out the outside world, a tension eased in Kyle. Apparently, Isabelle had instilled a very healthy wariness of windows in him. He hadn't realized how tense he'd been until she'd effectively hidden them from searching eyes.

Irritated with the level of fear he'd been maintaining through all of this, he deliberately strode to the bed and laid down on it, shoes on and all.

Isabelle stared at him, her expression blank. After a moment, she murmured, "Sit tight. I'm going to head out to secure a few more things. You'll be okay here. If anything suspicious happens, head down the hall to the stairs and go down to the ground floor. I'll meet you there."

She opened her mouth as if she would say more, hesitated and shut her mouth. Turning on her heel, she left.

Kyle sat up on the bed. The woman was irritatingly hard to read.

"What is this?" She peered into the glass bowl full of water and caught sight of a fairly active, chubby fish.

"He is Frederick." Kyle made himself comfortable on the sofa, the long-limbed length of him draped over the entirety of it in catlike fashion. "He's a goldfish."

She continued to study the fish in question swimming busily in the simple bowl with a bit of gravel in the bottom. In the reflection on the side of the glass bowl, she also considered her client. "I can see he's a goldfish. Why is he here and how do you know he is a he?"

Kyle stretched and placed his hands behind his head, leaning all the way back. "This hotel is particularly known for being pet-friendly and family-friendly—a place no one would consider a possibility when looking for me, by the way, I've been well-known to love a bachelor's life—and a goldfish is provided compliments of the hotel for the length of your stay upon request. Families love having a vacation friend. The hotel staff also thoughtfully provides a fish to keep lone business travelers company."

"Huh." It still didn't explain why they'd ended up with one.

Kyle glanced at her sideways without actually turning his head to face her. "Since you seem…uncomfortable alone with me, I thought Frederick's company might improve your mood." Kyle paused. "I honestly don't know for sure if he is a he but his name seems indicative of gender."

She snorted. Then she paused to wonder whether Kyle had stayed in some hotel alone before with only a goldfish for company despite his commentary. Actually, the alone on business part seemed likely. Question was, how many times? Or more sobering, how often had he stayed elsewhere alone and wished for the company of even a goldfish?

"Thank you." It came out quieter than she intended but she didn't repeat it louder.

Kyle was silent for a moment and she thought maybe he hadn't heard her but after a minute he did speak. "You're holding up your end of the contract. I'm not the easiest person to be around but I can at least make an effort to make this less of an ordeal. I…have a lot of things to live for."

She could've made light of his statement but he hadn't delivered it in his usual bantering tone. He'd sounded serious. And unusually introspective. Curiosity tweaked again, she fished for a little more information. And hell, she'd admit she was doing it too. "Most people do value their lives and what they planned to do with them."

"True." Kyle's tone didn't perk up. If anything, he became even more serious. "Months ago, I'd have said I have things to do. Period. For me."

She turned to lean against the table, careful not to jostle Frederick's bowl. "What changed?"

"My life wasn't just about me being responsible for me anymore." He kept his gaze on the ceiling. "I have a sister and she wanted to come here to the United States from Korea with her son to live with me."

"Ah." Instant family. She tipped her head to one side as she regarded him. "That's a big life change."

"I could've said no." Kyle made it sound matter-of-fact. "I did not. Considering why she made the request—what they'd both been through—I couldn't say no."

She waited. No pushing or coaxing. She got the sense that if she did, he'd drop back behind his carefree bachelor facade.

"I decided I needed to live a…cleaner lifestyle if they were going to come stay with me." He sighed. "I have the skill set to land another good job with comparable salary after this trial is over. What I needed to be sure of was that I wouldn't end up incarcerated for white-collar crimes when my family needs me."

Made sense. The court documentation she'd seen had been redacted thoroughly. This wasn't a simple trial. Didn't make what he'd done in the past right, but his reasoning had a certain logic to it. She'd done enough in her own past to consider herself the last person to judge someone else's right to a fresh start.

"Most of what I've done wrong was limited to keeping quiet when I had knowledge of illegal activities. Other people actually committed the insurance fraud or the illegal dumping." Kyle pushed himself up to a sitting position, swinging his legs down off the sofa and resting his elbows on his knees. "My silence was tacit support."

"So you're not testifying just because you cut a deal." If so, she thought better of him for it. She touched the side of the glass fishbowl gently and Frederick swam over to investigate.

He shook his head. "Not just because, no. I'm testifying because it's time to share what I know."

She folded her arms across her chest, considering

him. "Insurance fraud and illegal dumping, even bio-hazard material, don't seem to be enough to go through all the trouble we've seen over the past twenty-four hours."

He huffed out a laugh. "I did not expect the level of spite my company has gone to."

"But you were sure your life was in danger." And neither she nor Gabriel Diaz had disagreed with his assessment. Those men sent after Kyle the night before had been too happy to draw their weapons to be planning to just intimidate him into not testifying.

Kyle finally raised his gaze to meet hers and the look in his eyes was bleak. "I was certain. And I am still afraid."

She pressed her lips together. "It's not just about getting to you at this point. Something about your testimony was worth firing on two police officers. They're going to up their game coming after you and there has to be a better reason than what you've told me so far."

Kyle surged to his feet and began to pace. "Take valuable chemical reagents intended for laboratory research and realize they've expired or gone past effective use date. Recoup the loss by having those supplies dropped overboard en route from Korea to the US and then file insurance claims for the purportedly valuable lab supplies 'lost at sea.' It's repeated illegal dumping of biohazardous waste in ocean waters followed by insurance fraud. Those are incredibly serious criminal and civil charges with enough instances on record to bankrupt Phoenix Biotech. I have knowledge of each instance, the time they occurred and the resources assigned to those transport ships. I even have records on the shipping container numbers to identify them if they are recovered. All this, I knew about and tracked as an effective project manager, but I didn't stop to think about whether it was ethical. Not until I realized I needed to look beyond my comfortable lifestyle and provide for someone else."

It would be cheaper to eliminate the one witness providing testimony than pay the fines associated with each instance of the civil case. Plus, multiple instances meant executives involved could be facing enough back-to-back sentences in jail to miss the majority of their lives.

No wonder people wanted Kyle dead.

"Once those containers are recovered, I believe— even if I can't prove—authorities will discover they were smuggling other goods." Kyle dragged his hand through his hair. "I'm not sure what though, so there are further investigations going on. I don't even know if this is the only trial I need to get through."

There were a lot of red flags as far as she was concerned, enough to make her restless.

"Not knowing what you don't know is dangerous. It could be key to keeping you alive." She slipped past Kyle and headed for her duffel. Pulling out her slim tablet, she set it on the coffee table along with a small wireless router.

Kyle paused in his pacing. "For a person in what I considered to be a very physically focused job, you spend a large amount of time on technology. What are you doing now?"

"I'm firing up my personal mobile hot spot and logging in to Safeguard's virtual private network." It didn't take long to get everything up and running. "I don't like waiting around to see if someone is going to take a poke at me. I'm going to do some digging into your friends Tall, Slow and Grumpy from last night. Could be they were hired by the same interested party or could be there's multiple contracts out on you. It'd be good to know who is active in the area and likely to be looking for you."

He resumed his pacing. "I don't suppose your research will be instantaneous."

"Nope." Though she was already sending an update to Diaz to let him know what she was doing and reaching out to a contact or two who might be able to run some queries in parallel with her own line of research. "I like to keep busy at times like this."

"And here I thought you'd spend most of your time watching the door or the window." There was no edge to Kyle's words but he did have a hefty dose of sarcasm in there. "I really am not the type to watch movies."

She paused. "Do you have experience in this kind of research? Background checks? Organizational contacts?"

It would actually put a new perspective on things. She'd start wondering what sorts of resources he managed when he was overseeing the projects he managed for Phoenix Biotech.

But Kyle shook his head. "All of the projects I oversaw had to do with chemical formulation and manufacturing process development, production scale-up and quality oversight before the chemicals we sell are shipped to various biotech companies worldwide. I was responsible for project management and financial accountability on those projects. The chemical engineers and raw material vendors in my networks were in support of those areas of concentration. Not a one of them would employ Tall, Slow or Grumpy."

He smiled as he used her labels for the thugs. And

she let herself smile in return. Actually, a part of her was relieved. It helped her believe he truly hadn't been knowingly part of the uglier side of whatever Phoenix Biotech was up to.

"I hate the comparison, but they're likely to have more in common with me professionally than you in terms of network connections." And didn't that just burn to admit.

Kyle raised an eyebrow. "I imagine the scope of what they can do is extremely limited as compared to your range of skills."

"You'd be right." She continued to bring up search windows, fingers flying over the ultralight wireless keyboard. "But that doesn't make dealing with them more enjoyable in any way."

"You're not pleased at all in working around large, heavily muscled men of action?" His tone had gone back to teasing.

She fired off one more query and slowly raised her gaze to meet his. "I respect people who are good at what they do. Not a one of those men was above average in strength, dexterity or intelligence. They weren't exactly charismatic either."

Kyle held her gaze for a long moment. "Someday, I hope to have the opportunity to demonstrate for you how very good I am at the various things I do."

Chapter Nine

Kyle studied Isabelle a few moments longer. She was studiously ignoring him at this point but there was a telltale hint of dusky rose showing through her bronze complexion. His commentary wasn't entirely unwelcome.

Grinning, he decided to give her some space. Or as much as was possible in a shared hotel room. Even a junior suite layout with a sitting area. His longer stride made pacing the room less than a valid option for keeping himself busy.

Instead his gaze landed on the bags she'd brought up from the front desk. She'd specifically said they wouldn't be ordering room service either. If she'd gone and gotten takeout, it had to be something nearby and ready in record time.

Resigned to fast food, he strode over to the bags to investigate what was for dinner. He'd only had a few bites of the excellent sandwich he'd put together and he suffered a pang of regret for having had to leave those supplies behind.

What he found instead was a series of small containers, carefully labeled, and he froze. "Where did you go for food?"

Isabelle didn't even look up from her laptop. "Safeguard has connections to an excellent catering company in downtown Seattle. I had them deliver directly to me a couple of blocks away. That way, we don't need to worry about room service or who made the food we're about to eat. Standard practice for me and other Safeguard operatives on longer engagements. The shorter ones, we just don't eat or drink anything we didn't bring with us on the job. There should be a note in there telling us what everything is."

Kyle wasn't sure whether to be irritated or complimented. The contents of these bags were enough for more than one meal. "You told them my ethnic background?"

Isabelle shrugged. "I didn't. But the owner of the catering company experiments with a lot of ethnic cuisine. She knows I'll eat anything she sends me. No questions asked."

Interesting. "I'm concerned about this woman having access to my personal information."

"Not likely." Isabelle waved a hand. "It's not our procedure to share those. What probably happened was when she received the order from me via secure email, she contacted Gabriel Diaz to see what happened to the previous order for food that was supposed to last us several days and asked a couple pointed questions to see what else she could send. Was there anything we didn't like? Do we have access to a microwave? Questions like that."

"And Gabriel Diaz would've let her know about my ethnic background. The coincidence is a little too unlikely." He didn't give a shit if Isabelle was starting to get irritated at his line of questioning. They were supposed to be ensuring his safety. Obviously, there'd been issues ever since he'd gone into protective custody. This sharing of information, however benign, came across as unprofessional to him.

Isabelle sighed and stood to face him. "Most likely, she asked what type of food would be appreciated. Most likely Diaz would've taken a guess. I can confirm at my next communication checkpoint if necessary. But think on this—last time I headed out on a mission I got some great Brazilian dishes. The first time I met her, she packed us muffuletta sandwiches. She starts with something interesting and branches out from there. What did Maylin send this time?"

His temper cooled as he realized Isabelle still didn't know what had been sent to them for dinner. From her exasperation, and the slight edge to her voice, she was also ready to push back on him for the insinuation that she or her superior at Safeguard might have been anything less than professional.

Reaching out, he flipped the switch to the lights on the wall and ignored her glare. If he was going to eat, he was going to do so in comfort without feeling like he was under observation. The light behind her was more than enough to see by without being too much.

He approached the lower coffee table—they'd need the space to spread out properly—and motioned for her to move her laptop. Her jaw tightened but she did without comment. He started to take out the various dishes.

"Korean food, prepared in a traditional style." He glanced at Isabelle.

She shrugged. "I haven't had much Korean food. Not many of my coworkers have historically been as adventurous about food as the Safeguard people are."

A shame. He was more curious as to whether she simply didn't care what she ate or she was open to trying a variety of cuisines. He was betting the latter considering her earlier enjoyment of the chocolate beverages. She had a palate, a refined one.

He grunted. "These smaller containers are called *banchan* and are side dishes to accompany a main meal with rice and a soup. There's a variety, always, and they're meant to be shared. If we don't finish them in one sitting, they're to be put away to be brought out again at the next meal."

Isabelle's eyes widened. "There's a ton of them."

"Nine here. There's always many served with a meal." He pulled out Korean-style chopsticks and a long-handled spoon for each of them and set them out. "She sent *haemul-sundubu-jjigae* as our soup. It's a sort of spicy soft tofu stew with seafood."

Isabelle took up a small container of rice and extended her spoon to the *sundubu*, catching up a small amount of broth and sipping experimentally. "It's good."

"There are restaurants that serve just the *sundubu* or with a bowl of rice and a plate of fried whole fish. But not with a full accompaniment of *banchan* like this." He tried one of the *banchan* nearest him. "These *kkwarigochujjim* are very tasty. They're steamed, seasoned *shishito* peppers."

Isabelle extended her chopsticks and snagged one. "I've had them grilled before in other dishes, not Korean."

He nodded. "They're used in other cooking. Not too spicy. Good flavor."

"What are these? Are they supposed to be cold?" She used her chopsticks to tap the side of a container.

"*Eomuk-bokkeum*. Spicy stir-fried fish cakes." He

raised an eyebrow. "Some people prefer not to know what they are eating before they try it."

Isabelle seemed unfazed. "I'll give them a try either way but I'm generally interested in what I'm eating so I can try to remember what to call it if I like it and want to find it again."

Fair. His anger was slowly leeching away and he had to admit it'd been a long time since he'd enjoyed a meal with someone. Here, in this moment, with the dim lighting and sophisticated decor, he could imagine they were dining in privacy by choice rather than necessity. The sofa was small and as either of them reached for food, shoulders bumped and knees touched.

Every chance contact zinged through the fabric of his clothing to his skin, heightened his awareness of her.

He'd been out to dinner on dates frequently enough, to be sure. But there hadn't been this element of exploration and discovery in the dinner.

It was pleasant. Something he found himself enjoying despite his continued concern.

"You're going to confirm that your supervisor did not share my private information with this chef and I appreciate that." He decided to return to his initial concern and put it to rest so they could enjoy the rest of the meal. "Do you really believe your supervisor simply told her we might enjoy Korean food?"

Isabelle nibbled at a piece of napa cabbage kimchi before answering. "Maylin would've felt bad about the earlier food being left behind. She'd have wanted a challenge to make up for us not being able to enjoy it. He probably told her to go for Korean to stretch her skills and give her something she could roll up her sleeves and dive into. He cares about the people around him that way."

"A good leader does those things." Kyle could acknowledge the consideration. And it was obvious Isabelle was very loyal to the other man. Considering her fiery personality and independence, Gabriel Diaz must be a man worth following. The kind of person Kyle hoped to be if he survived all of this.

"Yeah." She paused in her eating, setting her chopsticks down.

Studying her, Kyle deliberately placed a piece of food in her rice bowl. An offering of sorts.

She huffed out a quiet laugh and picked her chopsticks back up. "He is a good leader. Let's just say leadership is not one of my strong points."

"I find that hard to believe." Kyle helped himself to more food. If he was eating, she might be inclined to share more. And he wanted to hear it.

Isabelle shrugged. "When you work with a new team, there's a key time frame in which you establish yourself, earn their respect, so they will follow your orders. Otherwise, they question, hesitate. And in combat, none of us can afford that split second. Not everyone who meets me gets the best impression."

And people may have died because of it. It went unsaid, weighing down the silence.

"Anyway, depending on the nature of my assignments in the foreseeable future, proving myself to the people around me continues to be a work in progress." She deliberately popped a piece of food into her mouth and chewed.

Kyle considered her words. It explained a lot about the way she confronted the men in the elevator lobby. He'd been intrigued but others might have found her attitude grating, intimidating. He wasn't sure if she altered her approach based on the people she met but perhaps it was as she said, a progression.

"What you're eating is called *tongbaechu-kimchi*, by the way." He paused to taste it himself. "Please pass on a message to the chef that her cooking is quite good."

"Yeah? On par with the restaurant quality you prefer?" Isabelle reached for a dish of soybean sprouts.

"Better." He used his chopsticks to separate the fillet from the fish and place a portion on his rice. She hadn't tried for the larger main dish yet. Perhaps she wasn't familiar with how it was served. "Her food has a home-cooked quality to the dishes that is sometimes lost in restaurants when they substitute for more easily obtainable ingredients here in the United States."

Isabelle had been watching him. Carefully, she placed her rice container back on the table and copied his motions to acquire her own helping of fish. She didn't lift her rice back off the table again.

Different cultures ate with different table manners. He appreciated the way she respected his and followed his example. Not many people in his life ever had.

"I'll let Maylin know." Isabelle continued to eat.

"The soybean sprouts you tried earlier are *kongnamul-muchim* and these are seasoned dried anchovies or *myeolchi-muchim*." He indicated a container next to the soybean sprouts. Really, this was an enjoyable meal.

"Crazy range of texture between dishes. Won't get bored." She was trying a little bit of everything and she'd gone back to the grilled fish a few times. "Aren't these the same kind of little fish?"

"Dried anchovies, yes. Those are stir-fried. *Myeolchi-*

bokkeum." He was also amused to note she had no trouble with fish served whole. The larger grilled fish entrée had the fish head and tail intact. The tiny dried anchovies were to be eaten whole. Isabelle had met both without hesitation.

There were a lot of people who'd have balked at any of those.

Isabelle let out a happy sigh. "I'm never going to remember all of these but they are good. Really good. What are these?"

He studied each in turn. "*Kkaennip-jangajji*. Perilla leaf pickles. And those are *ojingeo-bokkeum*. Stir-fried squid. The last one there is *sukjunamul*. Mung bean sprouts."

"And this is the way every meal is served? Seriously?" She surveyed the table covered in dishes. Even though they'd sampled everything and finished their rice, there was plenty for another meal or two.

"Traditionally, yes." Kyle eyed the table. "The *banchan* can vary greatly depending on the cook and the region, the local vegetables and the season. Many restaurants I've visited here specialize in serving just the entrées or dishes ordered à la carte instead of providing all of this."

"Hmm." Isabelle spent time savoring a spoonful of the *sundubu*. It was fairly spicy but she showed all signs of enjoying it. "Maylin's going to ask so is there anything you wished would've been included? And this is probably one style of meal, right? What other meals do you like? Because I'm seriously game to try more Korean food based on this."

He grinned. "Well, Korean fried chicken and beer are a fantastic meal. The fried chicken is very good quality, with very crispy breading and not nearly as greasy as the fast food I've seen in the United States. There's at least one restaurant chain that I know of in this country that does it well. The flavors can come in soy garlic or spicy here. Very flavorful. And in Korea, you can get several other flavors."

She blinked. "Fried chicken. That's a Korean thing?"

"Very Korean." He smiled. "It's well-seasoned and tender, never dry. And the chicken is served with pickled radishes. Makes for a great palate cleanser so you can eat more and more."

"That sounds deliciously dangerous." Isabelle sat up straight, placing a hand over her belly.

"You don't look like the type to diet." He wasn't against eating healthy but he'd had countless dates where his companion decided to forego the specialty of whatever fine restaurant they'd been eager to try for a generic salad in the name of being on a diet.

Isabelle shrugged. "I'm more a believer in portion control. I want to eat all the things, but my metabolism isn't magical. I stay active and I try not to overindulge. When you talk about that fried chicken, for example, I'm thinking I'd go for more fried chicken and just a little bit of beer. It's important caloric intake decision making."

He chuckled. "Wise."

"Anything else come to mind?"

He glanced over the dishes again and sighed. "It would have been difficult to manage these two dishes. Both are served in heavy stone or earthenware pots but they are very comforting."

Isabelle stared. "Stone."

He nodded. "*Bibimbap* is served in a hot stone bowl. It's white rice topped with *namul*—sautéed and seasoned vegetables—and various sauces. Like chili pepper paste, or *gochujang*, and *doenjang*, a salty soybean paste. There's also thin-sliced beef or other meat, marinated, and a raw egg. The stone bowl is so hot, it is literally cooking the rice. The trick to it is that the stone bowl is brushed with sesame oil or similar. When it's served, you stir the rice to mix up the various things piled on top without scraping the final layer of rice directly against the sides of the bowl. Given a few minutes, you get a crispy crust of fried rice for added texture to your *bibimbap*. Very filling."

"Huh." Isabelle's eyebrows had risen during his description. "I have no idea how Maylin would've managed to put that together for us to enjoy easily under these circumstances. Might have to go to an actual restaurant to find it."

"Agreed." He had a sudden urge to offer to take her to one or two restaurants he knew of, but didn't. It seemed…awkward.

Under other circumstances, he'd want to pursue her and enjoy further conversation over good meals. Here, like this, it was both more intimate and limiting at the same time. He had no idea whether they'd be in contact after this was resolved.

"What was the other dish?" Isabelle started putting covers back on the dishes and stacking them.

"A true comfort food." He shook his head. "It's a very simple sort of egg dish. Steamed in the stone or earthenware dish."

"Yeah, I can see how that'd be hard to serve this way." She reached for the grilled fish and started to flip it over, presumably because they'd finished taking all the meat from one side.

He reached out and touched the back of her hand. "Don't turn over the fish."

Isabelle looked up at him but didn't withdraw her hand from his touch. "Why?"

"It's a Chinese superstition. Your chef friend is Chinese, right? To turn over the fish is to symbolize the capsizing of a boat." As he shared the etiquette consideration, a chill ran down his spine. Disturbed, he withdrew his hand.

Still watching him, Isabelle finished covering the dishes but she didn't flip the fish.

"In any case, thank you for pausing in your research to join me for this meal break." He stacked the dishes and took them to the mini refrigerator.

Silence stretched out over several moments before Isabelle broke it. "What do we feed Frederick?"

Chapter Ten

Lizzy woke out of her light doze to a familiar sound, which shouldn't have been in the room. She opened her eyes, drawing in air as she did to wake herself up completely.

No lights. The curtains were still drawn and there was little to no daylight peeking in around the sides of the windows. Just a hint from the indirect lighting fixture installed underneath the counter in the bathroom to make sure guests didn't break their necks getting up to go to the bathroom at night. Kyle must've left the bathroom door open to give him something to see by.

Meaning it was still early morning.

It was the breathing pattern that woke her, Kyle's. It'd changed to a slow intake through the nose and sharp "oosh" through the mouth. Controlled. Conscious.

She found him in the darkness, on the floor between the bed and the sitting area, doing push-ups. Shirtless.

"What are you doing?" She whispered the words into the dark.

Kyle continued for a few more repetitions before halting in a plank position and quietly chuckling. "I'm guessing you know what a push-up is. This is part of my morning routine."

Lizzy sat up straighter and stretched. "Hmm."

Her vision in darkness was good. So was the view. The man had a solid physique with incredible muscle definition. He kept in very good, very attractive shape.

Have mercy.

He went through another set of fifteen push-ups, pausing again in the plank position. "Am I disturbing you?"

A plank was core work all on its own so using it as the resting position between sets of push-ups had to be a challenge. She considered giving it a try herself. "Nah. As morning habits go, there are worse things than physical activity. Go for it. You can even turn on more lights if you like."

She wasn't too worried about shadows. The drapes in front of the windows were heavy and completely opaque. No chance someone was going to see anything through them.

"Well, there are workouts and then there are other, more interesting, forms of physical activity in the morning." He left his bait out there as he rose smoothly to a standing position and started doing squats.

"Uh-huh." She stood then, unable to just sit there and keep watching. Instead, she checked her laptop to see if any of the searches she'd set up had resulted in any hits. Some data there but not a lot yet. Her queries might require more time before they turned up something useful. "Question is, do you still go through your exercises whether you indulge in other forms of physical activity or not?"

He laughed. "Would you?"

"Maybe after I've got some time to myself, yeah. A partner doesn't generally react well when cuddle time is cut short so I can get my workout routine in for the morning." Although she had used it as an excuse to leave when she hadn't wanted to linger. She wasn't going to bring it up if he wasn't though. When it came to casual encounters, there was a certain understanding among participants that outstaying a welcome was awkward. She tried to avoid the feeling as much as possible.

"I...used to travel a fair amount for business." He paused for a moment. She didn't blame him since he was going to be testifying against his former employer. He currently didn't have a job. And one never knew what the next position in a given career was going to bring. It probably took some getting used to. Maybe it was only just starting to really sink in. "In any case, the gyms in hotels are usually mediocre at best and I don't enjoy adjusting my routine based on equipment available so I tend to design my workout for limited hotel room space."

She nodded. "I can see that. I do the same for basic stretching and some strength training, but access to a gym and free weights can provide a lot of variety."

"True." He moved from squats to burpees, stretching his arms far up to the ceiling then bending to touch his toes. He placed his hands on the ground and jumped his feet out behind him to plank position. He executed a push-up and jumped his feet back to his hands before returning to a standing position. "And I make sure to do strength training at least three times a week at an actual gym."

He did another burpee.

Burpees were an exercise she loved to hate.

Everyone added their own little zing to it. Some lifted their hands and jumped at the end of each burpee. Others did various kinds of push-ups as part of the exercise.

Still others did things with their footing as they went through it.

Kyle kept to the simple form with just the added vertical jump at the end. What she had to appreciate was how smoothly he was going through the exercise. And silently. Sometimes people would do these at the gym and just two or three people could sound like a stampeding herd of grunting, groaning wildlife.

It took a lot of strength, balance and agility to make this exercise look that easy.

And he had the reserves to continue conversation. "I've memberships to one or two chains so there's always a decent gym reasonably close to my hotel when I'm traveling in the US."

Lizzy rolled her shoulders. Watching him make burpees look easy made her want to join him in working out. "Any particular reason a businessman like you maintains this level of fitness?"

He was as fit or better than most servicemen, even on active duty. His level of cardio looked to be very good based on the way he was able to maintain a conversation with her through each exercise. And any of those exercises might be simple but they weren't as easy as he was making them look. She appreciated the dedication it took to keep up a routine alone, with no one around to keep him accountable. Hard to persist in pushing oneself without a workout partner or personal trainer. It took a driven sort of mind-set.

Damn it, he was doing more burpees than she usually did and she wasn't sure if she was more irritated by the realization or that she was keeping count.

"There are a lot of reasons." He snorted. "None of them are particularly witty or clever when I think about them. There's a decent amount of conceit behind it, perhaps. Some past friends have called it narcissism. I prefer to look in the mirror and appreciate what I see. I want to be proud of myself, both in appearance and in performance."

On the surface, his statement was flippant and she thought it was deliberately intended to allow a person to think of him as shallow. But there were a lot of kinds of performance, and she didn't think he was only referring to the obvious innuendo.

"You're very good at the things you set out to do, huh?" She tossed it out there experimentally.

"Of course." The man was finally starting to sound short of breath.

With the light from her laptop screen supplementing visibility in the room, a fine sheen of sweat shone on his skin. Candlelight would be a fantastic idea at the moment. She loved the way a flickering flame could show off the human form and it'd been a long time since she'd had a partner patient enough to set up small details like that in a room.

Nope. Kyle was not a partner and this was not headed in the direction her thoughts seemed to be going on their own. There would be no fantasizing.

"If something is worth doing," Kyle huffed, "it is worth doing well. I'm not satisfied if I haven't done my personal best. In anything."

Oh, but he was very good at inspiring all the naughty fantasies.

Turning back to her laptop, she attempted to focus on something else, anything else. "Maybe tomorrow morning I'll go through my routine at the same time. We can draw the curtain between the sleeping and sitting areas."

She disliked doing it because she preferred to have line of sight on the person she was protecting as much as possible, but so far he'd been careful to honor her instructions on staying away from the windows. He hadn't once asked to leave the room.

He paused and faced her, his hands on his hips as he stood there with a relaxed posture. "You prefer your workouts without an audience?"

"Correct." She bit the inside of her cheek. She'd just watched him go through his and hadn't even thought about whether it'd be rude or not. She shouldn't have made the assumption that he'd want an audience. Maybe she should've at least asked if he minded.

He shrugged. "Okay. I can take my time in the shower if you'd like time to work out now."

"I'm not sure the hotel's hot water heaters can handle it." She gave him a small smile though. He really was surprisingly considerate.

"Ah well." He lifted his hands, palms up. "I've always showered with a lady sharing my room. To conserve water, of course."

She narrowed her eyes and glared at him. "Pass."

He grinned at her. "Consider it a standing offer, with global conservation in mind."

Irritation warred with a tiny spark of interest. She immediately squashed any and all thoughts resembling fantasies of the man. She'd let him lure her in some but he was a player and a womanizer and she was having none of it.

Standing, she stalked toward him. To his credit, his grin didn't fade and he didn't give ground, but the look in his eyes turned wary. At least he wasn't idiotic enough to think her approach was some sort of triumph for him.

Without a word, she reached for the curtain and pulled

it across most of the room, leaving a small space for a person to slip through if necessary. Not completely blocking him out, but still a definitive shutdown.

Argh. She was as irritated with herself as with him. He had a knack for getting under her skin. One minute his charm seemed sincere and genuinely engaged her. She found herself drawn to him, liking him even. Which she would not be letting him know anytime soon. Then he'd switch gears, turning vapid and transparent. Shallow.

It was infuriating.

And it shouldn't be.

Normally, she had no fucks to give about what a man did with his time. If he was a player, well, there was a certain accountability to the women who fell into his bed willingly and she tended to figure it took two to make the decision. As far as she could tell, Kyle was up front about his intentions. No strings attached. He wasn't the type to lead a girl into thinking there was a committed relationship of any kind. It wasn't like he was a bad person, just not relationship material. So there wasn't any of the duplicity there to set off her anger.

No. That wasn't quite right. He was being dishonest in a way. Not in what he said but in what he wasn't saying. She got the sense there was more to him. He wasn't shallow. He wasn't an asshole. But he was far too good at letting people think he was.

Maybe what was pissing her off was that he might've been pretending so long, he was starting to believe his own bullshit.

He needed to stop being an asshole.

Hot water ran down his back as Kyle let the shower wash away the sweat of last night's nightmare along with what he'd worked up doing his morning exercises. It had been less of a concern with his police escort or with the bland deputy marshal. None of them had been kind to him, or considerate, or thought much of him. And so, it was easy and even amusing to encourage the string of little judgments they would make about his character based on his jokes and innuendos.

They hadn't considered him as a person from the outset and he felt no compulsion to prove himself in their minds.

Isabelle Scott was proving herself to be even more unique than he'd first thought. It was refreshing, intriguing and uncomfortable. She'd met him and given him a blank slate as far as he could tell.

Oh, every person made judgments based on their impressions. It happened within seconds of first meeting. There was a certain wisdom in learning to assess people within moments of an encounter. He considered it a survival skill, whether out on the city streets at night or in a high-powered business meeting.

Perhaps what was different about Isabelle Scott, or Lizzy as her commander called her, was her attitude. She hadn't dismissed him out of hand when they first met. She'd been fairly brusque to all of them in turn. There had been no singling him out. Each one of them had been met with the same level of professionalism, impersonal and efficient.

Perhaps Austin and Weaver were put off by her lack of deference but she also didn't give respect before it had been earned. A sentiment he shared.

Wetting his hair, he grimaced at the idea of using the hotel shampoo but was slightly mollified to find it was a reasonable brand at least. Working up a lather in his hair, he dug his fingertips into his scalp in an attempt to massage away the headache he'd woken up with this morning.

He'd dreamed of gunfire. He'd fallen to the street with Austin and Weaver standing over him, looking down as he bled out onto the pavement. Decker had been nearby, making an impersonal report of his death. Isabelle Scott had been nowhere to be seen until he'd looked up and beyond them. She'd been up on the roof of a building, shooting at someone else.

All he'd been able to think was that he had others to keep safe. Lizzy would care about his family, protect them, if only he could ask her to.

But he hadn't had a chance to tell her how to find them.

He ducked his head under the hot spray, rinsing away the shampoo.

It wasn't necessary and there was no reason to mention it now. In any case, there'd be no need to remain in protective custody once he'd completed his testimony in the trial. Only a few days and this would be behind him. At least he hoped it would. Follow-up trials would take much longer and there'd been no mention of him remaining under witness protection. Perhaps if she continued to prove as effective a bodyguard as she already had, he would look into keeping her on retainer.

Even though he couldn't imagine a reason for needing personal security, it never hurt to keep good resources in easy contact if unforeseen circumstances arose. He maintained a record of any number of services for the same reason. You never knew when you were going to need something, anything. And it was best to have an idea of who to call.

The heat of the shower had eased tight muscles in his neck and across his shoulders. He rolled his head to stretch, hearing a few pops as his cervical vertebrae adjusted on their own. Standing with the shower spray directly on the back of his neck, he rolled his shoulders to encourage circulation in the area.

He was carrying an immense amount of tension in his neck and shoulders, as well as his back. He doubted Lizzy would allow him to order a massage, even in the privacy of the hotel room. He was absolutely certain she would react in a definitively negative way to his asking her to give him one.

He grinned. Perhaps he would ask just to see the anger flare in her eyes. She was incredibly attractive when angry. Moved to action, she was magnificent. He could hardly be blamed for wanting to see it more often.

Finishing up his shower, he stepped out and toweled off. He studied himself in the portion of the mirror that had been treated to remain unobscured by steam. Usually, he was amused to see it because it tended to surprise any feminine company he might have with him. And it proved interesting if he did take a shower with a lady. Hot, steaming showers, plus the perspective a mirror could provide, made for added fun.

But today he was alone and he looked haggard, gaunt even. It wasn't only because of the fear from yesterday. It was the result of weeks, months, of having to allow events around him to govern his decisions and actions. There'd been no one to work with and no way for him to take constructive steps.

All he'd been able to do was hide and swallow a hundred not-so-subtle indignities handed to him by police and the district attorney.

Well. He'd changed the game. And the person with him was a different kind of protector. Perhaps she could be convinced to become an ally. Otherwise, the next few days were going to be very, very long.

Wrapping a towel around his waist, he stepped out into the bedroom area. Lizzy was on the small sofa in the sitting area tapping away at her laptop. But there was a change in her appearance. Same clothes, but her hair was slightly mussed. A few more strands of dark hair had escaped from the knot at the back of her head. The skin of her neck glistened slightly with sweat.

She actually had taken the opportunity to exercise while he'd been in the shower.

He was disappointed he'd missed it. Then again, it was entirely possible and probably likely she wouldn't have exercised if he hadn't given her the relative privacy of going into the bathroom. Perhaps he should develop a longer morning routine in the bathroom to give her more time. It wouldn't hurt him for a day or two.

Lizzy stood then. "I'm going to head out to check on a lead and grab some food. It won't be long. Are you going to want restaurant takeout or would you be okay with fast food?"

She didn't even blink at his state of dress. Or lack thereof. There hadn't been a hitch in her voice or any sign of discomfiture, definitely no sign of interest. If nothing else, she was a lesson to his pride. He was used to women drooling, or stuttering at the very least.

"I'm going with you." He reached for his clothes.

"No, you're not." Her tone was matter-of-fact.

He turned to face her, clothes in hand. "The last time you left, there was an issue shortly after you returned.

Before you joined my protective detail, I was attacked while my police escort had left me in the hotel room."

Her lips pressed together. "You were attacked in the elevator lobby, not where you were supposed to be."

"And I doubt it would have gone as well if they'd found me in my hotel, as I've mentioned to many. Those men knew where to find me. It was only luck I encountered them in a public area." He kept his voice reasonable, no added sarcasm. He got the impression she'd shut him down if he went his usual route. Besides, her own tone had remained reasonable thus far. "While staying here might be the usual policy, I respectfully disagree with the plan because it's what seems to be the standard. I strongly feel I would be safer directly at your side at all times. I will follow your instructions when we are outside, you have my word, but I most definitely will not if you leave me here to my own devices."

Perhaps ending with an implied threat hadn't been the best way to finish out his statement, but he was at the end of his patience with cooperating.

He struggled to maintain a respectful, rational tone. "I make much better decisions when I'm not going insane hiding in a tiny, dark place, hoping the bad guys don't find me. At least let me remain in the loop with your line of investigation."

Lizzy stood motionless and silent for so long, he was starting to feel the chill of the air-conditioning against his skin. Finally, she sighed. "I'll show you what I plan to go check out. That doesn't mean you're going with me. But first, get your damn clothes on."

He grinned. She *had* noticed.

Chapter Eleven

Kyle leaned over to study the building. He wasn't touching her but he was inside her personal space. Hell, she wasn't sure if his body heat was actually warming her skin through her shirt or if her mind was doing bad, bad things to her at the thought of his proximity.

"You think the shooter you're hunting down was in this building?" Kyle didn't seem to notice her issues.

Good. He really shouldn't ever know how much her body was trying to convince her that chemistry was a good thing.

She tightened her jaw and tapped the screen. "It's an old neighborhood and just about every other building in the area is fully developed with either office space or tenants living on every floor. This one has several of the top floors not only vacant but under renovation."

"The top floors." Kyle chuckled. "There's at least one well-established business on the third floor and several others on the first and second."

She craned her neck to look at him and had to lean back to avoid accidental contact. He'd been leaning in very close. Ostensibly to see the laptop screen. Which was fair. Sure. "And you know this how?"

He straightened, giving her space. "I've done business

with them. They're a third-party vendor we've used in the past to build databases for us or customize content management systems we've used to store and manage documentation related to contracts."

She didn't respond immediately, her mind processing several things in parallel. First, he was up to something. The corner of his mouth was pulled back ever so slightly in the barest hint of a smirk. Second, she was more aware of the space between them than she'd been before he'd leaned over her.

This definitely wasn't the line of thought she wanted to pursue. Back to the smirk. She could be irritated with the smirk. "So you've been inside the building."

He tilted his head just a bit as he nodded. "There's security in the front lobby. Anyone without a badge must have a visitor pass and an escort from someone who works in the building. All of the emergency exits have alarms, so there's no slipping in a back entrance without setting one of those off. Any employees wanting to go out for a smoke have to go out the front door."

Not the toughest security she'd ever gotten past but she wanted to be in and out without leaving any evidence of her visit. "Maybe it'd be better to wait until tonight then."

He shrugged. "I was out to drink with a couple of the resources from that vendor. One of them told me a story about the time he'd been working so late, the security system came on. Apparently, badges stop working throughout the building after eight. There's also motion sensor lights."

She scowled. "Your friend just happened to tell you this?"

He lifted his hands, palms up. "What can I say? We

work late hours on some projects in my line of business. There are times when you're sitting at your desk and your hands at the keyboard aren't enough movement. The lights go out and you have to wave your hands above your head to trigger the sensors to turn them back on again. When that happens, the roving security guard stops by to ensure all is well."

Ah. However he came by the information, it was handy to have. While stealth was a requirement to her specialization to a certain extent, her experience as a sniper had rarely included bypassing security systems to get to her chosen perch. It'd take much more time than what was available to gain access to the building on a hunch.

After a few more moments of silence, she came out of her own head to the sight of Kyle watching her intensely. The look in his eyes was unreadable. Not the usual glint of humor or the expression of interest as if she was a kitten that'd done something hella funny.

Uncomfortable with his scrutiny she frowned up at him. "You have an issue?"

His expression didn't change but he shifted his weight forward a fraction, intent on her. "You are certain this building is where this sniper was hiding to take a shot at me?"

She considered his question, not because she didn't know her answer but because trying to anticipate where he was going with a line of questioning was a challenge. "My gut says a person took a shot at our police partners. It could've been lucky, or it could've been skill. The person could've been a trained sniper, or they could've been a contract operator taking a long shot. I'll be able to tell a lot more once I find where they were hiding."

"This building is on the same side of the street and same block as the apartment building we emerged from after the incident. How would he have been able to see us?" His voice had dropped a few notches in volume and gone rough.

He'd done a good job of handling fear so far. His observations were valid too. "I don't have sure answers for you. There could've been another team out there looking for us. Or they could've thought we were in a different building. Maybe the one our deputy marshal was parked in front of at the time of the shooting."

There were still too many variables, too many different ways things could've been planned. She needed to know more.

A pause. "And you won't have confirmation or more information until you have a chance to investigate this building."

She nodded. "Either I'll find what I'm looking for or I'll rule it out as a theory."

He snorted. "How many theories do you have?"

It was her turn to study him. She got the impression he wasn't the sort of man to stay with all that many things long-term. "If I run out, I'll come up with new ones until I have my definitive answer."

And her response seemed to satisfy him. "Well then, it appears we will be going to investigate this building tomorrow."

No.

"You stay here." Not a request.

"You need answers and we both need them fast. There's only a couple of days to the trial." He raised an eyebrow. "I would like to stay alive both to testify and to walk away afterward. My best chances seem to be remaining with you, at all times. I mentioned that a few minutes ago and will keep doing so until it sinks in. Besides which, helping you find the person or persons trying to kill me seems as if it would increase my probability for survival. I don't want to walk out of the courthouse only to be shot from a distance."

She gritted her teeth. "That could happen before the trial if you try to tag along with me."

"You've already shown me how to navigate the streets, blending and changing my appearance as we go." He tapped the tip of his index finger to his temple. "While I didn't enjoy the wig, I found the endless change of hats and shirts you seem to have in your backpack wildly entertaining. A couple walking the streets of downtown doing a bit of afternoon shopping is much less likely to draw attention than a lone woman circling a corporate building looking for a way inside."

He had a point. Worse, she was inclined to agree with him.

"The point behind you being under my protection is to keep you safe and hidden." She sighed. "You seem to have a serious problem with hiding."

He gave her a sharp smile, one that made her the slightest bit uneasy. Oh, he wasn't threatening. But it wasn't a soft civilian smile either. He was his own kind of dangerous. "I don't take well to cages, even gilded and especially when I can't order room service. I am also safest when you are with me or I am with you." He rolled his shoulders and slipped his hand into his pocket, the overall effect managed to look both relaxed and incredibly sexy at the same time. The man should be on the cover of a freaking magazine. "Besides, I've been in the building before and I can get us both in again with minimal effort. It gets you your answers faster and keeps me from sitting here wasting away from boredom."

Interesting proposal. "Won't they know you're not working for your old company anymore?" Worse, wouldn't they report having sighted him? "It isn't exactly keeping a low profile walking up to a security desk and handing over your ID."

He tipped his head to one side, considering. "Perhaps but unlikely. Phoenix Biotech is notorious about keeping communication with our vendors to an absolute minimum need to know. I can recall several projects where the vendors weren't aware our internal resources had moved off a particular project or left the company. They weren't involved in my most recent projects so there's no reason for them to have found out I'm no longer there."

It was convenient, which made her suspicious. Maybe she was leery of Phoenix Biotech after having been blown up leaving one of their facilities not too long ago. And perhaps the current line of conversation was blurring the line between Kyle Yeun as a client versus Kyle as a partner.

There were too many questions. She needed to start finding the answers. And considering who his previous employer was, she felt more inclined to keep him close.

From a practicality perspective, she was out of contact with Safeguard and her team members. Solo. Their police detail and US Marshal counterparts were also probably not fond of her at the moment or likely to suddenly coordinate in her choice of investigation. His suggestion would save time and in this scenario, the faster she could enter, investigate and exit, the better.

"Okay, we'll head out about lunchtime." There'd be more foot traffic with businessmen out to lunch. "Your idea was good, but you'll need to be dressed for work to make your visit look good. We'll do a change or two en route, but you'll walk into the building in your own suit."

Risky. But if they kept moving, it should still work well.

He nodded. "I presume we'll be working out the details for the next few hours to lunch?"

She nodded.

"Well then, I'll heat up some of the leftovers for us to snack on as we chat." He stepped toward the refrigerator.

"I know I skipped breakfast, but aren't you eating kind of often?" Not that she minded. She could eat, right about now.

"It is very healthy to eat small portions throughout the day. I prefer to eat five or six times, every two to three hours, if possible." With one large box in the microwave, he was taking out the various boxes and stacking them in some sort of order. It reminded her of when Victoria lined up her guns for cleaning. Meticulous and precise. Orderly.

"You're enjoying this." She couldn't see his face but he straightened and ran a hand through his thick black hair.

"This is constructive. I enjoy planning, preparing and ultimately executing a well-laid-out project." He turned to face her, leaning back against the table with his hands braced on the table edge on either side of him. "This is much better than sitting still, watching streaming videos, waiting for people to come kill me."

"They will try." She didn't know why she needed to add the qualifier. There was a flat, resigned look in his eyes. He was selling himself short.

On some missions, mentality meant the difference

between being trapped or getting out alive. If you believed you were going to die, you generally did.

For his part, Kyle seemed to warm at her correction. "People will *try* to kill me. At least in this, I am living before we find out if they succeed."

"What exactly are you looking for out here? I thought you had a specific place in mind for lunch." Insisting on coming with her had seemed a good idea at the time. He wouldn't take it back. But he hadn't anticipated how exposed he'd feel out in the open again.

A reminder the danger was very real and they had no true guarantee that he was safe.

At all.

"I'm not looking for anything specific, just keeping my eyes open for interesting things along the way." Lizzy continued to hold his hand casually as they walked, for all the world like a tourist enjoying downtown with her boyfriend.

Come to think of it, he'd never explored downtown on a date. Relationships weren't a priority so he'd rarely dated a woman more than a few times before she figured out he put work before pleasure.

She'd taken him on a winding route to this street, stopping in two different cafés for a quick change. It was amazing how little people noticed of the comings and goings of other customers in those places. Had circumstances been different, he'd have never given credence to the precautions. Surely, someone would notice the ridiculous behavior.

But no. People moved about their day on the streets and didn't look twice at either Lizzy or him. Like ants, rushing along their paths, not even acknowledging his existence unless he stepped directly into their path. What Lizzy had taught him was to look, see and blend into the rush so that those searching for him wouldn't find him amid the sea of faces.

There was comfort in the anonymity of crowded places. A new perspective for him.

"Okay." The smile spread across his lips without effort, really. Tense as he was, the idea of Lizzy enjoying a simple pleasure like running around a city sightseeing appealed to him. He kept his volume to a murmur so it'd be hard for anyone not walking directly with them to overhear. "So what amorphous something would convince you to take a detour from our current plans?"

She shot him an irritated glance and he returned it with a raised eyebrow. Neither of them was trying to make a scene and the banter probably looked very normal to anyone not actually listening to the content of their conversation.

She huffed out a breath. "I'm looking for the hiding spot, the vantage point the shooter chose when he, or she, took a shot at our friends."

"Ah." Well, it explained why she was spending so much time looking up. "I assume we would end up on a roof somewhere?"

Lizzy shook her head. "Not likely. Possible. But if that was where our shooter decided to set up, it'll tell me a lot about them."

He narrowed his eyes at her. "And if your original lunch spot is still the best choice?"

"The location will tell me a lot regardless, but if they were careless enough to choose an exposed position like those rooftops on either side of this street, they were likely sloppy enough to leave a few presents behind too." She paused and glanced in a shop window or two.

He noted she didn't look into the chocolate store, which was across the street, but she did peer into the glass window directly across from it. Tricky girl using the reflection. Still, she really did love her drinking chocolate. He wouldn't mind trying more.

It was a sensual pleasure. Perhaps Lizzy didn't think of it that way, but it was an easy progression from imagining sharing a hot cup with her to tasting the chocolate directly from her lips.

She might not appreciate his imagination at the moment.

"Talk to me about vantage points, then. I'm in the mood to learn."

Her head whipped around and she pressed her lips together. "Do you actually want to know? Or are you just chatting with me to keep me distracted?"

He considered for a moment. "I'm actually curious. Though, I will admit, I enjoy the absentminded tone your voice takes on when you're sharing information with me. It becomes rather husky, very sexy. So please, do share."

Maybe too much. It'd been truth though and he rarely held back on such candor. Few women believed it anyway so there was little sacrificed in being honest. It made it easier to avoid discussing other things he preferred not to.

Still, Lizzy didn't like it when he laid it on too thick, so to speak. And that last had been a bit heavy-handed in the delivery.

After a moment, she stepped forward and tugged him to get him to move with her. As he did, she released his hand and slid her own higher up his arm in a loose hold.

She was warm against his arm and the semiembrace—just his arm—sent chills through him, exciting him. He surreptitiously adjusted his belt and the fit of his briefs.

"A good vantage point is crucial." She muttered as they walked. Her volume had dropped even lower and her gaze swept across the street and up the buildings. "The choice isn't just about effectively eliminating your target."

"No?" He took the opportunity to lean his head close as they walked. His lips brushed her hair but she didn't seem to notice. Or if she did, she was allowing it to pass. He'd prefer the latter rather than the former even if the former was more of a challenge. For some reason, being close to her was a heady thing, irresistible.

"It's not like on television or in the movies where the barrel of the gun is right up against the edge of a roof or windowsill. We're looking for cover when we choose a position, with enough depth for us to shoot from. Preferably one with a broad view of the area we're targeting." She leaned her head against his upper arm then and it struck him how petite she was.

Oh, he'd been around her for over twenty-four hours by this point but her sheer presence was larger than life.

"So a rooftop isn't the first choice. Understood."

"Well, not here, in any case." She used her free hand to point out a few buildings with particularly interesting architecture as they walked. Just another pair of tourists. "There are too many taller buildings around them. We like areas with a lot of potential spots to choose from because it makes it harder to figure out which one we're actually shooting from, but we don't like to choose anything where there are other nearby points from higher ground."

"Too exposed?" It seemed like a reasonable guess.

She paused, fixing her hair as she used her reflection in another storefront window as a mirror. "If there's another shooter nearby, the one with the higher ground tends to come out of the situation alive."

No need to guess about the fate of the other.

After a moment, she took his hand again and they continued to the corner. As they crossed the street, she remained silent, tense. They walked at the same steady pace but there was a vibrating sort of excitement to her touch now.

"Here we go." He bent his arm so that her hand rested in the crook on the inside of his elbow.

Her fingers squeezed his arm lightly in response.

As they entered the building, Kyle let his expression settle into a lazy, mildly friendly smile. It was generally a good idea to be on good terms with security. It made getting to business meetings smoother.

A disgruntled security person could make the visitor badge and check-in process draw out until there was no hope of reaching a meeting on time.

"Mr. Yeun, it's been a while." An older man stood up from his seat behind the small security desk.

"Too long. I'm glad to be working on a new project." Kyle widened his smile and reached for his wallet, pulling out his driver's license.

"Oh, no need, Mr. Yeun. I've got you in the system. Will you be here all day?" The man busily snagged a label from the miniature printer and assembled a temporary badge.

"No, this is just a quick visit before we have an official project kickoff. I was in the area on other business and decided to stop in."

The security guard's gaze took in Lizzy and returned to Kyle. The older man gave him a wink. "Ah, well then, why don't I put together a visitor badge for the lady as long as you promise to be her escort."

Kyle solemnly placed his right hand over his chest. "You have my word."

The guard laughed. "I trust you, but, miss, you should watch out for this guy. He's a tough catch."

Kyle raised an eyebrow. He didn't refute the commentary. It was a familiar type of bantering. Minutes later, they were through the security gate and headed for the elevator.

"I'm guessing I'm not the first lady you've had with you when you've ducked in for a quick meeting?" Lizzy's tone was teasing, in line with her role as his date.

For the day.

It was who he was and not anything he'd ever hidden. He had many companions and never committed to one. A day, an evening, mutually enjoyed but with no strings attached. It was how he preferred his liaisons and he had no regrets. And yet, her question was one he was loath to respond to, even as a joke.

Finally, he murmured quietly, "Work always takes priority. If someone wants to spend time with me, it is a required understanding that occasionally these things happen. However, this is distinctly different and I am following your lead. You are a completely new experience for me in any number of ways."

He cocked his head at an angle and watched for her reaction. For her part, she glanced away before he could spot the telltale blush he was coming to hope for.

As they approached the elevator, Lizzy recovered and applied slight pressure to his arm as she spoke at normal conversation volume, "If you don't mind, I'm trying to hit my step goal on my fitness tracker. Could we take the stairs? Please?"

Chapter Twelve

It didn't take long to climb the flight of stairs up to the fourth floor, but Lizzy took them farther up to the top of the building. By the time they'd finished the quiet climb, Kyle's thighs were burning and he resolved to add stairs at least once a week to his workouts.

The contrast between the developed third floor and this one hit him first when air rushed past as they opened the heavy fire door from the stairwell.

"Promising," Lizzy murmured.

He wasn't sure if it had been to herself or him but he rather thought it was the latter since she didn't seem prone to unnecessary dialogue. He rather liked that she was communicating with him unprompted. "How so?"

"Windows. There are some missing. That would be key." Lizzy touched his chest. "Let me clear the floor first.

And so he waited as she did a sweep of the mostly open expanse of space. The building developer was remodeling this floor but apparently progress was halted for the time being. Supplies had been dropped off on pallets toward the center of the room and covered with clear construction plastic but there were no signs of workers.

Lizzy lifted her arm in a beckoning motion and then

proceeded on another tour of the floor while he caught up with her.

He glanced around. "It doesn't seem as if anyone has been up here."

"Mmm." Her gaze swept across the floor slowly, her head turning as she studied every corner. "Not necessarily."

"No?" He watched her as she cast back and forth, admiring the intensity of her concentration.

"Did either of us leave any footprints on the way in?" She tossed the question to him over her shoulder as she crouched to take a closer look at the stacked pallets and a nearby shop vacuum.

He glanced back. "Actually, no."

It seemed like an easy thing to check for and a detail he should've been able to take note of earlier. It simply wasn't something one looked for in day-to-day life.

Lizzy stood, the light from the windows framing her hair in a halo effect.

Well, not his life. Hers, he was coming to learn, involved different details. Her awareness of the world around her existed on multiple levels from the inconspicuous minutia to the broad perspective.

"There should be dust all over the floor, but it's blown to the edges of the room." Lizzy pointed to the places where the walls met the floor all around them. "It could've been the gusts of air coming in from the open window frames, but it's too thorough and too even. This floor was cleared on purpose."

"I see." And he did, now that she'd pointed it out.

She pulled gloves out of her backpack and put them on. "Perhaps I shouldn't be surprised but do you often carry gloves with you in that bag of yours?" He bit the inside of his cheek to suppress a chuckle.

Her expression was so severe at the moment, dark brows drawn together as she chewed her plump lower lip in concentration. The temptation to poke fun at her, just a little, was too much to resist.

"Latex gloves come in handy when you don't want to leave behind any sort of calling card." The comment was matter-of-fact. "Also good if you need to administer first aid. There's a couple of other situations where they'd be useful."

"And a few unorthodox uses in moments of more adventurous play, if one was so inclined." He took a prudent step back.

Lizzy shot him a sharp glance, then bent and grasped the edge of construction plastic. "I haven't used them that way and I'll pass on hearing details."

"But I'd be happy to share—"

"Don't."

He grinned. "If you ever change your mind about either the information or—"

"Nope." Lizzy didn't sound mad, but the last word had been definite. Instead, she dragged the construction plastic off the pallets and across the floor until it was closer to one of the windows. Then she stood there, staring at it.

This time, he wanted to see something before she pointed it out so he joined her where she was standing.

"Not too close to the windows." She bumped him with his shoulder and he obliged by moving a few feet but not far.

"What are those impressions on the plastic?" He pointed. The way the plastic had been spread over the pallets, there shouldn't have been those sorts of marks in it but this sheet had the sort of marks he'd seen left in carpet when heavy furniture had been sitting on top of it for too long. "Are there pallets missing? Maybe they were stacked on top of the pile over there."

Lizzy shook her head. "Close, but no. And good spot. The shooter dragged this plastic over here to the open window frames. Not too close. Just far enough inside to make sure he or she wouldn't be seen from the street or nearby buildings during the day. None of the lighting works yet in here and the sun was behind the building at the time of the shooting. Decent amount of shadow."

He looked out the window. "I can see the street from here, but not well."

"Uh-huh." Lizzy moved to stand even with one of the indentations. "Shift those pallets of supplies over here and they become a makeshift table or platform. Shooter probably laid on top of it for stability to set up the shot."

Apparently satisfied, she returned the plastic back to where it had been.

"There's nothing else." He had hoped to find something. Perhaps a bullet casing or piece of clothing, or even a small pile of sand. He seemed to remember something about it in one of those police procedural shows constantly on television.

"No, there isn't. And that tells us a few things too." Lizzy pulled him farther away from the windows, then paused. "Do you smell something?"

Come to think of it, something had been setting him on edge and started the beginnings of a headache. "Yes. Something sweet. Candy sweet. I don't prefer sugary things because they give me a headache."

"Huh." Lizzy drew in a deep breath through her nose and exhaled through her mouth. "Bubblegum."

"Someone was chewing bubblegum?" He couldn't keep the incredulity from his tone. The shooting had been yesterday. He seriously doubted any human's olfactory senses were that good.

"No." Lizzy returned to the plastic and took another sniff. "It's the plastic. I didn't notice the smell until I pulled it off. Vapor must've been caught under it with the pallets. Our shooter uses an e-cig."

"Those are supposed to be very unobtrusive." He still wasn't sure he believed it could have lingered so long and fear was starting to twist his guts. Perhaps the person they were looking for had been here much more recently. Or they were coming back.

"Compared to cigarettes, e-cigs are a huge improvement." She wrinkled her nose. "But the vapor scent can hang around longer than the marketing says it does, especially the sweeter flavored scents. Under the plastic, it's not like it had any place to go anyway."

Well, it was an explanation for the smell of bubble gum, however long a stretch it was for Kyle to have considered. "Is there anything else?"

Lizzy cast one more glance around the room. "Not here. No. I'd like to check the other floors just to be sure, but then we can leave."

Relieved, he waited until she returned to him and walked with her back to the door to the stairwell. "Is there a chance the shooter will return?"

"Not likely." She paused, pushing him to the side as she opened the door, still being careful. "Another thing snipers like to be sure to have when they choose a perch is a quick escape route. This one took the time to clean up after he or she left, so I'm guessing they didn't plan to come back. Actually, the chances are very slim."

She hesitated. Looked at him.

That didn't mean they might not stumble across the person on a different floor. He wanted to raise the argument but perhaps it would be stating the obvious.

It was the first time he saw indecision in her expression as her lips pressed together and her eyes darted around the room and down the stairwell. Kyle pressed back, away from the door, as he waited for her to think her options through. They'd been quiet on the way up but not perfectly silent. Their conversation here had also been in low tones, not likely to be heard from more than a few feet away, but there was still a chance someone waiting could have heard something.

"Shit." She muttered under her breath. "It's still extremely unlikely. But we'll clear each floor as we go down to be sure. Stay close, right behind me. If Murphy's Law kicks in, we don't want someone coming out from above us while we're still going down the stairwell."

"The elevator?" Security would notice but right now it would be so much faster than stairs, less exposed.

"Those can turn into death in a box." She gave him a hard look and there were ghosts, memories in her dark brown eyes. "If he or she was here long enough to set up their perch and break it back down again this way, they'd have had the chance to set something up in the elevator to buy them time in case of pursuit closing in. It'd be a contingency plan."

He considered that. "You would do it."

"Yes."

* * *

"All set, Mr. Yeun?" The security guard stood and smiled as they walked out into the empty lobby.

From this angle, Lizzy spotted three small monitors giving the old man a view of the lobby behind him and the emergency exits in the two stairwells. He hadn't even been monitoring who was on each of the floors once he'd issued them badges.

Obviously the businesses in this building required some security, but not incredibly tight. It would be a long shot to try acquiring the footage from the day before to try to spot their shooter. Possibly worth it though. If she could get her hands on it.

Doing so meant bringing official scrutiny here. She couldn't do that without also giving away their location. For at least the past twenty-four hours, she'd been in blackout with no communication to either the police or the federal marshals. Safeguard could probably guess she was alive and her whereabouts because she'd checked into the hotel but they'd wait for her to report in first.

This was one of those times when she wouldn't feel a drop of shame in being paranoid. She wanted to get Kyle safely back to the hotel and maybe even moving to a different spot before contacting each of her contacts.

Doing all of that would delay getting the right people here to conduct further investigation and forensics.

"Everything all right, darling?" Kyle's question prompted her to make a quick decision.

It was unorthodox, but hell, it'd answer another one of the dozens of questions she had about this entire situation.

She smiled at the security guard apologetically. "I

know I took the stairs, but I was wondering, does this building have a fourth floor?"

The guard gave her a quizzical look. "Well, there are a bunch of floors above the floor you went to and that was the third floor. Four comes after three so I'd say yes, there's a fourth floor."

Duh. She popped out a giggle and pitched her voice for embarrassment. "Oh! I didn't explain my question very well. I was reading up on Asian cultures, see. And you know how a lot of buildings don't have a thirteenth floor? Well, some buildings don't have a fourth floor either because it's bad luck or something. It's a superstition thing and those kinds of things are so interesting. So I check as often as I can to see if I spot a building like that. I totally forgot when I asked that we take the stairs up."

"Huh. To be honest, I never noticed." The security guard scratched his head and waved a hand toward the elevator. "Why don't you go ahead and take a look?"

Lizzy looked up at Kyle with wide eyes and blinked a couple of times. "Do you mind, sweetie?"

Amusement twinkled in his eyes as he looked down at her. "Of course not."

She gave them both the brightest smile she could flash and skipped over to the elevator.

It took a long minute or two to arrive. Slow elevator. All for the better, they'd be leaving quickly. When the elevator opened, she leaned in to get a look at the button panel and pressed the button for the top floor using the top of her knuckle.

"This one has a fourth floor." She returned to them in a rush, letting out a breathless laugh.

"You might want to check out a few of the corporate buildings in Chinatown, miss." The security guard smiled. "Might have a better chance of finding a building like that there."

"Thank you." Lizzy hooked her hand in the crook of Kyle's arm and the two of them waved as they left.

"What was that about?" Kyle asked.

"Walk first. We'll need to get a little distance." She set the pace to match several other tourists heading toward Pike Place Market. "And did you put your hand on my ass as we were leaving? Seriously?"

Kyle shrugged, completely unrepentant. "It's a habit. It would have appeared odd if I didn't do it as we left. Our friend at the security desk would've been disappointed."

"If you want to keep using that hand, don't do it again without permission." She closed her mouth with a click of her teeth, instantly regretting the phrasing.

Both his eyebrows went up. "Really? Well then, I promise not to do it again until you give me permission."

"Not what I meant."

"Perhaps not, but I will enjoy reminding you of the promise in any case." He chuckled.

Fantastic.

"However, I do want to know what you did in the elevator. I thought you said it would be dangerous to go inside." Kyle hadn't forgotten his question.

And he'd be getting his answer in a minute or so. It was a damned slow elevator.

At that moment, there was a muffled boom. She let them both turn to look back the way they'd come like everyone else on the street. Then she tugged at Kyle to get him moving.

"I sent it up to the top floor." She pulled them into a

café and started to reach into her bag for pieces of cloth-ing to change.

"Was that an explosion?" Kyle's hand covered hers on the bag and he leaned in to whisper intensely. "Wait. You said it could be a trap of some kind. What if some-one is hurt?"

Here was where she hoped her gut never led her wrong. "As a contingency, it wouldn't be set to blow up and take the whole building down and it didn't, as you saw. The sniper would just want enough of a delay to buy him or her time to escape. Most likely the elevator would be disabled, even fall back down to the ground floor with the intent to injure whoever was inside but not cause damage to any of the other floors or the people on them. The elevator was empty when I sent it up. No one should be hurt."

Kyle was silent for a moment. "But why do it at all?"

"To disable it before someone goes up there to do real work." Which was true but not her main motive. "And to bring some attention to that building. Here. Out of the suit. We'll put you in jeans with a T-shirt and vest. Keep the other vest on."

Kyle took the items without argument but he looked unsettled.

She didn't blame him. Of course there were doubts. Especially in a heavily populated area like a city, she figured an operative good enough to hide the evidence of their presence the way they did would also be sure to limit collateral damage unless absolutely necessary. It was a gamble, but it was almost certain she was right.

And she needed the police to investigate that build-ing. And the fact that it'd been an explosion and not just a broken elevator added to her suspicions.

Safeguard had crossed paths with another skilled sniper not too long ago, one with an added joy for setting up explosives. The presence of explosives right here in combination with the connection to Phoenix Biotech was starting to point to Edict.

And Jewel.

Which meant Lizzy needed to take steps to confirm or rule out the possibility. Gabe would need to know for certain if this was more of Jewel's work. This was a lead, but it wasn't irrefutable. Lizzy liked to dig until she had the clear picture.

She needed more pieces to the puzzle.

It took her just a minute to change, clip a few dyed hair extensions into her hair, then twist it into a bun. With a cute cap on and just the hair extensions falling in loose curls, her look was sufficiently changed. She also pulled on jeans over the tight dress she'd been wearing and threw on a jacket.

Done, she exited the bathroom and tapped on the men's room door. Kyle emerged a few seconds later.

"I don't think I want coffee after all. Let's go. We'll pick up a late lunch on the way back." She took his hand in hers and they proceeded to stroll out onto the street.

Sirens announced the arrival of police cars and they stopped to stare along with everyone else before heading toward Pike Place Market.

"What's next?" Kyle adjusted his hand in hers until their fingers were linked.

A funny butterflies-in-the-belly feeling tickled her and she immediately decided to ignore it. "Lunch. Like I said. And some thinking."

He released her hand and a pang of disappointment hit her just as quickly as the butterflies had happened.

Then he wrapped his arm around her waist and pulled her close, whispering in her ear. "There was a bomb in the elevator I wanted to get into a few minutes ago. That doesn't bother you at all?"

It was a fair question. Normal people would probably be very unsettled. Some of the people who worked in the building would probably be seriously freaked out.

"We weren't in it. It's been set off before someone else triggered it." She turned her face toward his and pressed a kiss against his jaw, playfully. "I call it a win-win situation."

Chapter Thirteen

There were few greater challenges than to put a project manager in the midst of events he could not control. For Kyle, it was torture, and he was back in the hotel room.

Alone.

Lizzy had stepped out soon after they'd returned and no amount of argument could convince her to take him with her this time. In fact, she'd seemed very much prepared to restrain him if necessary. Not something he generally found exciting but the threat, coming from her, had given him a few lightning quick fantasies as distraction.

Ah, the woman was delightfully uncommon. He was oddly grateful he'd met her now, in the midst of change, as opposed to prior to this insanity when he might have wasted the opportunity to get to her know her on a one-night stand.

That was, of course, assuming she'd have accepted his offer.

She was too sensual, too full of vitality to be the type to abstain. No. He was certain she did entertain propositions on occasion. But he was also equally sure she chose her trysts with more care than he had in the past.

Restless, Kyle rose from the bed and walked across

the room, stopping in front of the fishbowl. Frederick swam in lazy circles, stopping only here and there to pick at the colorful gravel in the bottom of the bowl.

There had been conference rooms at Phoenix Biotech casually referred to as fishbowls. All four walls had been made entirely of glass with minimal or no frosted section to provide any sort of privacy for groups utilizing them. The fishbowl conference rooms had normally been on the executive levels, ostensibly to allow natural light farther into the interior of the floor. But it was more obvious that the company had taken transparency very literally and the executives kept an eye on everything.

Some people were like Frederick, content with their existence.

Kyle might have been too, but in the past several months, things had changed. As self-centered as he'd grown to be in his adulthood, and perhaps even a bit narcissistic if certain disenchanted ladies were to be believed, he had compelling reasons to adjust his lifestyle. There were more important things in the world than his bachelor life.

Speaking of which…

He headed over to the sofa and sat facing the laptop Lizzy had left behind. Using login information she'd given him for the guest profile, he accessed the desktop and brought up a browser. He typed in a URL by memory and a site loaded.

It was a live streaming video platform with a forum community for gamers. Normally, the broadcaster he was looking for was online at this time, even though it was late at night in South Korea. But at the moment, the boy was off-line. Odd.

Personally, Kyle had no interest in games. It was the broadcaster he was looking for.

Ji Sung was diligent, both in his studies and in his game play. Kyle's sister had written him many emails about his nephew. In fact, the boy's abilities were professional level and there had been more than one team to offer Ji Sung a place. Ji Sung's father had refused though.

At first, Kyle had thought the man had been irritating, unsupportive of his son's talents. But after some time and research into the actual career a player of Ji Sung's talents could build, Kyle realized the father was standing in the way of a huge opportunity. The gaming industry was booming. South Korean players at the professional level could bring in substantial earnings via tournaments.

In fact, when one took a look at developing markets for the gaming industry globally, South Korea was arguably the leader in many ways. Several players had actually been awarded special visas to the United States usually reserved for baseball players or other athletes. It was a chance for Ji Sung to pursue an incredible career.

Frustrated, Kyle pushed to his feet and began to pace. In his fishbowl, Frederick seemed to keep pace.

Without access to any of his personal accounts or email, Kyle had no way of communicating with his sister. There could be no video calls or texts, no emails or other messages. He'd warned her he would be out of communication for a time.

But the streaming video broadcast would've been a way for Kyle to see his nephew and be reassured that both Ji Sung and his mother, Eun-bi, were well. With the boy off-line, Kyle was left to wonder…and worry.

For the first time since coming under Lizzy's protection, Kyle chafed at his restrictions.

He did not take well to sitting and waiting for things to happen. He preferred to be proactive, shape events based on his planning. This entire situation had left him powerless and vulnerable until he was able to testify. It left his pride bruised in countless ways.

Needing something to do, he moved back to the bedroom area and gathered the few clothes Lizzy had obtained for him besides the suit she'd saved and the clothes he'd had on his back when they'd bolted from the initial hiding place. He shook each article of clothing out and folded it carefully. After a moment's thought, he also retrieved the toiletries in the bathroom and tucked them into the bag.

If they had to run again, at least he'd be ready to grab the bag and leave quickly. Besides, it kept his hands busy.

He was alone with too many thoughts. It'd happened too, over the weeks he'd been in protective custody and the other night when he'd met Lizzy. His frustration had driven him to leave the room to move, to walk, to do anything but remain in one place while he waited for events to happen around him. How anyone could come under witness protection and not lose their sanity was a mystery to him.

But he'd promised Lizzy he would stay in this room, within the safety she'd established for him. A promise to her held weight where he hadn't cared about the police officers.

Perhaps she was his only chance to get through all of this. Or it could be something about her as a person. She was certainly a woman of action and determination. Her ability to assess situations and make definitive choices quickly had impressed him. He respected her.

And so a promise to her meant something to him.

She was worth admiring, a reminder that he was striving to be a better person himself. And the more she inspired him to evolve and improve, the more he wondered what past had shaped who she was today.

"When I invited you to contact me directly, Miss Scott, I had hoped it would be more immediately following any issue requiring my attention." Nguyen stood this time by the chocolate bar.

Lizzy sat perched on a stool with her back to the wall so she could see both the front and back of the store. "I reached out once my client was secure again and I had something to report."

Nguyen stared at her for a long moment. There was no temper in his eyes, no telltale reddening of his face. The only sign of his anger was a tiny muscle jumping as he tightened his jaw. "I see. Will you be sharing the location of your client so I can have Decker join you in surveillance?"

Not yet.

"How are Austin and Weaver?" Lizzy wasn't ready for Nguyen to lead this discussion.

His nostrils flared. "Alive. It was touch and go for a few hours but they will both make it through and be able to return to their jobs if they want to after a recovery period and some physical therapy."

Good. She hadn't particularly liked them but she hadn't disliked them either. In general, she respected police officers and wouldn't wish them harm.

"I'd like to get a copy of the ballistics report for any

bullets found in them or their car. Both if possible."
Maybe she should have made it a request. Her temper
was short and her patience was running low.

Kyle had not been happy when she'd left him and she
wanted to get back before he got antsy. If the man got it
into his head to go wandering again, she was going to
have to resort to freaking tying him up.

On the other hand, the shooting and the subsequent
retreat to a new safe location had seemed to put a healthy
dose of fear into him. And that was a good thing. But
their little outing earlier in the afternoon had left him
cocky. Could be bad, sure, but he wasn't the type to remain cowed by fear for any length of time.

As risks went, she'd rather the risk be with her nearby.

She grabbed her drink and took a sip to hide her
ghost of a smile. It was a dark Valrhona hot chocolate
this time. Rich, complex, with just a hint of bittersweet.
Dealing with Kyle required fortification of the chocolate kind even if she did reluctantly respect his desire
to take action.

He wasn't the type to sit around and wait for things
to fall into place. A preference she shared.

Nguyen placed his hand on the counter beside them
and drummed his fingers on the surface. "I thought you
said you had something to report to me."

"I do. But I think the ballistics report will let me know
if I have even more to share." She lifted one shoulder
briefly.

Nguyen snorted. "All right. We'll trade. I'll have the
report sent to the email account you provided."

Lizzy shook her head. "I'm in blackout. Whoever
took out our colleagues might know I took this contract.

I don't plan to leave a virtual bread crumb trail. Leave a USB here for me."

After a moment, Nguyen nodded.

Interesting.

"How much confidence do you have in Decker?" She tossed the question out there because she didn't have the time to be circumspect. Besides, she preferred the direct approach.

Nguyen scowled. "Absolute. He is dedicated and trustworthy. No doubts."

"But you made sure I knew how to contact you directly." She considered her own statement. "He's too dedicated. Does everything by the book."

"He never misses a step in any procedure. Meticulous. Thorough." Nguyen pressed his lips together. "Sometimes it takes him longer to get to the right conclusion because he does everything step-by-step."

A person could do worse. Decker probably rarely made a mistake with his approach.

"There are situations when there's no time to think through a situation." Her ability to take action, the right action, in those instances had kept her team alive in the past. "He'd probably argue."

"Oh, he's jotted down notes to make sure he doesn't forget any points he wants to make when he comes face-to-face with you again." Nguyen actually smiled with that statement. "He's incensed you broke protocol and just disappeared."

"We passed through his line of sight." Sort of. They'd been in a heavy crowd and there'd been a slim chance the deputy marshal would've been able to identify them in his line of sight. She hadn't been sure he hadn't been a part of the attack meant to take out a portion of their security and flush Kyle out into the open.

"I'll let him know." Funny how Nguyen didn't seem concerned.

She stayed silent and waited.

Nguyen sighed. "I'm aware of the possibility of a leak internal to either my organization or the police. I don't think they'd set up their own to be shot and I can tell you I haven't found any sign of a leak in my organization. Can't blame you for being wary but I'm telling you it's not a leak."

Could be true. But then again he could be wrong.

"There's the possibility the shooter was canvasing the area and spotted Austin and Weaver based on their driving pattern. It'd explain why Decker wasn't shot but he was probably observed when he didn't react the way any normal person would witnessing the incident." Another reason she didn't want him reengaged. Having the deputy marshal sitting a short way from their new location, establishing his line of sight, would be like placing a big neon sign indicating their location. "If that's the case, they're good. And they know Decker's face."

"I almost prefer there be a leak." Nguyen shook his head.

"No you don't." An internal breach in security was any organization's worst nightmare. Suddenly, one of the people you rely on to watch your back could literally be the one to shoot you. Gabe had found that out the hard way.

Speaking of which.

"Ballistics report is still something I want, but quick question." She finished off her drinking chocolate. "Did they identify what kind of rifle fired those shots?"

"An AK-101." Nguyen stared at her, intent on catching whatever tells her expression would give him.

Not the best news she'd heard all day. But it wasn't definitive. For one thing, Jewel didn't smoke. Not even e-cigs. A sniper who also set small explosives didn't necessarily mean it had been the former Centurion.

Jewel preferred to be unpredictable. Too much about what had been in the building she and Kyle had visited that day had been predictable. Boring.

No one who'd ever worked in the Centurion Corporation could be described that way.

"Were you all called in for the explosion in the elevator earlier today?" She'd figured he would be. It'd been too close to their initial location to ignore.

"If that was you, we can't ignore it." A warning note entered Nguyen's voice.

She shook her head. "I was there and I took a look at the top floor. I did not place any explosives."

Silence greeted her.

"Forensics should take a close look around that top floor." Pressing on seemed like a good idea.

She and the Safeguard team had managed to operate within the letter of the law within city limits thus far. But eventually, any job could push a person into questionable circumstances. This was one of those days where she had to choose her words carefully.

She hadn't placed the explosives, but she had triggered them.

"Anyone hurt?"

It was another few long seconds before Nguyen answered her. "No. A few very frightened people and one seriously confused security guard, but no one physically harmed. Forensics teams found a lot to occupy them on the top floor."

She nodded. Good.

During the time they'd been there, Kyle hadn't touched anything. Something she'd noted and been grateful for. She hadn't wanted to have to wipe down after him, potentially obliterating other evidence. Their predecessor had handily blown all the dust away from the floor making it very unlikely either she or Kyle had left footprints either.

Forensics might get lucky and if they did, her job would be easier. But she was guessing the sniper was too professional to have left enough to identify himself or herself.

She was more interested in the police reaction to the finding.

"I'll look forward to the findings along with the rest of the information I requested." She slid off the stool and stood.

Nguyen offered his hand. "Working solo isn't easy. You have to sleep sometime. What do you do with him when you do?"

A few choices images popped into her head.

"I've considered several options to keep him secure." It was all she would admit to Nguyen.

"If you change your mind about backup, let me know." A wry smile spread across the federal marshal's face. "But I hear from Safeguard that you do well on your own."

She shrugged. "I'm alive."

Nguyen's smile broadened. "Exactly."

He might be complimenting her. It wasn't something she was proud of.

Chapter Fourteen

"What are you doing?" Lizzy's voice was a hissed whisper.

Kyle hadn't heard her return at all. A feat, considering the way most hotel room doors eased close with a rather loud click. Then again, exercise was his form of meditation in many ways so maybe it wasn't so much of a surprise that he'd stopped paying attention to his surroundings. He completed his set with two more push-ups and stood to face her. "Exercising. Again. What else is there to do in this room?"

A pause. There were several possible answers to his question and the sight of her expressions as she obviously thought through some of them made him grin. He was standing in nothing but his boxer briefs, after all. The rose flush rising up on her cheeks was incredibly intriguing.

The open vulnerability lasted only a moment, then she recovered and scowled at him. "Pants."

Not a response he'd anticipated. But then, it was part of why he enjoyed her company. He raised an eyebrow at her. "Excuse me?"

"From here on out, you need to be wearing at least pants." She stayed rooted where she was, back to the door with her arms now crossed.

Other women did it with calculated intent to enhance what assets they had. When Lizzy took on the posture, it indicated a completely different attitude and seemed generally the time to cede with prudent haste.

The pants he had on the bed were his suit pants. They'd do for the time being but he'd probably wear sweatpants the next time he chose to work out.

He picked up the pants then turned to her, holding them loosely in one hand. She might make the decisions when it came to his safety, but in this, he was going to point out the ridiculous. "I have limited clothing and I doubt you'd want to allow me to make use of the hotel's dry cleaning service. I thought it best to minimize the need for laundering by working out in my boxer briefs. At least these, I can rinse in the sink as a minimal effort to keep my clothing somewhat less soiled."

An exasperated sigh let loose and she dropped her arms to her side. "Point taken. It would still be a lot better if you had pants on."

A momentary pang hit him, right where his pride should be. Normally would be. But he found with Lizzy, all sorts of things were amusing he'd never noticed before and other quirks of hers were endearing where he would normally be grinding his teeth and posturing for control of a situation. She spun his perspective around and set it off-kilter.

And here he was, sure he was considered an attractive male to most women of the interested orientation, hurt because Lizzy wanted him to put his pants on.

Or…

Want and prefer could be two very different things. In fact, one tended to be more honest than the other.

While Lizzy had been quite brutally candid and

straightforward with him from the very beginning, he was getting the impression she tended to avoid it with herself.

"We are two grown adults, to the best of my knowledge." He watched her carefully as her eyes strayed back to her laptop. It wasn't just that she was dedicated to her work, he thought, it was a refuge for her. Especially from things she didn't want to pay attention to. Like him. "Is it really that much of a distraction for me to be walking around in my boxer briefs? Surely your teammates and you have done the same in certain times of rest."

Her lips pressed together, pursed, as her gaze remained on the laptop.

"Dare I ask whether most of the men you work with wear boxers or briefs?" His amusement was leaking into his voice now and he didn't bother to hold it back. She wasn't angry with him. If anything she was giving way little by little, her shoulders relaxing almost imperceptibly. "Or do they go...commando?"

He might even see the corner of her mouth lifting. Maybe. A tiny bit.

This was not the time to be jealous. He had no reason to be. Wasn't sure if he wanted one. But pondering whether her teammates wore underwear or not wasn't having the intended outcome in his own damned brain.

He'd really prefer to consider what she tended to wear. Or not. "Do you go commando?"

Temper sparked in those chocolate-brown eyes and she glared at him. "Seriously?"

Inordinately pleased with having succeeded in baiting her, he took a step toward her. "Hard to know what a person prefers under their clothing."

She might be counting to ten under her breath. "Not a

good idea to go without under a combat uniform. Foundation garments are key."

"For comfort or for practicality as well?" He hadn't expected her to play along with this line of conversation but he was delighted. Discussion with her never seemed to go where he thought it would.

Her eyes narrowed. "Both. Especially for women. A good bra helps in a lot of ways on an active day."

He could imagine too much, and the way she was staring at him just about dared him to make an ill-advised comment regarding her mention of a bra. No. The both of them could take unexpected turns in conversation. Keep things lively.

"When you're not on assignment protecting people, what do you do to keep up your level of fitness?" He'd honestly been curious in any case.

"I work out every day," she admitted, her tone wry. "Even on this assignment I did a modified workout while you were showering."

He was sorry he'd missed it.

"Why?" He could guess, but knowing her, he had a fifty-fifty chance of being incorrect.

She rolled her shoulders, possibly to ease strain across her back. "I prefer to work out alone unless I'm doing hand-to-hand drills."

If she'd been one of the normal type of companions he spent time with, he'd have offered a massage. The suggestion was not likely to be received well in this case.

"When you mention drills, do you mean sparring?" Now, there was something very interesting. Better than doing all too familiar exercises over and over again.

Her gaze fastened on him. "Serious sparring would be a bad idea. No pads, no mats."

Kind of her, to not mention her potential level of skill as compared to his.

He gave her a nod, partially in thanks and partially in acknowledgment. "You are the professional bodyguard. More than that, you have more experience in danger-ous situations. I was more curious about lighter timing drills. A more good-natured way of learning about the skills each of us might have."

A hint of a smile played around her lips, much more than previously. "Generally, I don't practice with any-one outside of Centurion Corporation."

"It would seem a limited practice." He tossed his suit pants back onto the bed behind him. The topic had been dropped and he didn't want to put them back on until he'd had a shower.

"You'd have a point there, but I also prefer to let a po-tential opponent guess about what I can and can't do." She paused. "I was itching for a fight the night we met. I'll admit it. It'd been a long workday and it's frustrat-ing to be irritated at people all day. The men hounding you gave me the perfect excuse to let off some steam."

"You have my sympathies." And he meant it. "Let-ting off steam is exactly what I was trying to do when you returned."

Too much thought. Too much worry. Too far out of the structure of the comfortable life he'd decided to leave behind.

After a moment, she eased her backpack off her back and set it on the floor against the wall. "You asked about sparring. What experience do you have with martial arts?"

He grinned, tension inside him giving way to anticipation. Yes. This was good. "I practice *Gongkwon Yusul*, a sort of Korean hybrid martial arts form."

Her right eyebrow rose as she regarded him with more interest than he'd seen yet. "Unusual."

"It's a more modern martial arts system," he admitted. "Comparisons could be drawn to Western mixed martial arts in the way it combines traditional techniques. My instructors have repeatedly stated that it emphasizes the application of striking, locking and throwing. A practical, free-flowing response in unexpected fighting situations. Good for self-defense."

Practical as it was, it also maintained traditional philosophies such as respect for others and personal development. It'd given him a constructive outlet for the rage he'd nursed in his younger days.

He hadn't appreciated tradition as much as the variety when he'd first started. "I started in my youth and continued practicing the drills when I came to the US. No instructors were available as I was completing high school and college. Besides which, my uncle couldn't have afforded paying for it. Practice alone was all I could do. I find it to be a learning opportunity when I can spar with someone else."

Lizzy pushed away from the door and took a step toward him. "I haven't studied this Korean martial art."

"You, I imagine, have mastered many arts though." He held his hands out, away from his sides, palms up. "I could learn all sorts of things from you."

She snorted. "Timing drills. Fine. Not full-contact sparring. We don't have protective gear and it's too easy to do too much damage."

He raised his eyebrows but nodded. Timing drills took better control in any case. It was more about speed, precision and, of course, how well timed a move could be. Besides, you could learn quite a bit about a person working with them in this way, like dancing. And he was finding with every minute spent in Lizzy's company, he wanted to learn more about her.

"First, *pants*."

How did the man make baggy sweatpants look sexy?

It was both better and worse than the sight of him in snug-fitting boxer briefs. She'd always been a fan of boxer briefs in general. Much better than tighty-whities. Occasionally she'd enjoyed the sight of a man in loose boxers but too often, the freedom of boxers let way too much hang loose to peek out at the world at inappropriate times.

Kyle stood before her now, with pants on, his posture loose and relaxed. She put her hands up to guard. "We'll start slow, see where this takes us."

He gave her a nod and a sign of respect, then got his guard up.

A big part of timing drills or sparring was to know your partner well enough and eventually trust them to be able to block the strike or kick you were putting out there. Otherwise they ended up hurt and you ended up with too short a workout.

So she started out easy. Light jab, slow cross. Soft hook to the body, followed by another slow cross. He blocked each with ease and responded to the combination in kind.

Nice. Maybe one of the easiest ways to start out a drill. He moved smoothly and echoed her combination with the confidence of someone who recognized it for what it was.

She added in some footwork, leading them in a dance within the confined space of the hotel room as they traded light strikes back and forth. Her blood started flowing and her muscles warmed up. It felt good.

As she threw another cross, Kyle changed up the game by trapping her wrist in a move she hadn't seen before.

"Not bad." She recovered and caught his own follow-up strike in a move of her own, twisting as she did to throw him off balance.

Warm-ups were over and it looked like they were both ready to have some fun.

"You have been going easy on me." Kyle's words came smoothly, with no sign of overexertion.

She wasn't surprised though. He'd been keeping himself in good shape. Conversation during a workout was one way to monitor your partner's status. If they were breathing too hard, overheating and out of breath, then it was time to slow down and cool off.

But Kyle's breathing was good. Even though a healthy, fine sheen of sweat was starting to show across his brow, he was most definitely ready to up the intensity.

So she did, adding in a low kick to force him out to medium range and following up with an outside slanted kick to the thigh. She was careful to make it a tap and not a real kick.

He ended up taking the second kick rather than dodging, but he'd zoned to his right to reduce the force of the impact and threw a punch to force her to block instead of going for what would've been his momentarily weakened leg in a real fight.

"Nice," she admitted. Only a few minutes in and he was showing better sense than most.

They picked up the tempo, exchanging hand strikes interspersed with kicks as they circled each other in the small space of the room. They kept contact light but increased the intensity and speed as they went.

He was good, clean, keeping his guard up and his movement efficient.

"You tend toward defense." She jabbed to force him to guard his handsome face then drove a knee toward his belly.

He only managed a partial block and grunted as her knee contacted with his abs but otherwise shook it off without a problem, driving an elbow toward her throat.

"My training is mostly for self-defense." He huffed. She was making him work for it now. "And I find I get too hotheaded when I go on the offense. I make mistakes."

"Fighting safe can be wise." Sometimes. She'd give him that. Not always though. There'd been places, times, when speed and decisiveness meant she and her team survived. "And it's fine for stuff like this. But let it go on too long and you're more likely to lose."

He shot a low kick at her and closed the distance faster than he'd done so far, lashing out with a right cross. His longer reach gave him an advantage and it would've been a great move if she hadn't been expecting it.

As it was, she slipped to the side just enough for his punch to whisper past her face. Then she raised her shoulder, pushing her cheekbone to her shoulder to capture and tuck his fist against the curve of her neck.

Kyle started to pull back in surprise.

Perfect.

She stepped forward inside his guard and put her left

foot behind his right. Seeing her coming forward, he instinctively tried to step back and get his guard back up.

Nope.

She caught his ankle in an *ashi harai*, driving him backward and down toward where he expected his foot to be bracing his back-step. Tall as he was, he relied on his solid stance to keep his footing too much.

Instead, she threw her right arm up between the two of them and quickly swung it around in an exterior loop to place his still-retracting arm into an under armpit lock. He lost his balance and toppled, taking her with him. Which was fine.

She landed heavily on top of him, forcing grunts out of the both of them. Somehow, she wasn't even going to mind the bruises. This was more fun than she'd had in a while.

"Minx." He was breathless now and still a little stunned.

The clothes around her throat tightened as his left hand took hold, and he pivoted his hips under her. Throwing his left leg up, she found herself in the beginning of a triangle hold.

Really?

She got her feet under her and heaved herself—and him—up until she was half-standing and slammed him back on the ground. He loosened his hold. Pivoting to her right, she released his right arm so she could get into position to secure an arm bar on his left.

Before she could manage it, he rotated on top of her. "No you don't."

She half snarled, half giggled. "Yes, I do."

And she blocked his right knee with her leg, raising her hips, placing the ball of her right foot on the ground near his other knee and pushing with her right. As he came off the floor, she pulled him to the left to continue the momentum of the roll...

...and landed on top of him.

He chuckled and repeated the move right back on her, rolling them even farther until they both hit the wall, laughing.

She buried her fingers into his hair and his hands gripped the back of her neck.

They met in a kiss, hard and hot and so incredibly good. If she'd been breathing hard before, she lost everything in that kiss.

Suddenly, she didn't care about anything but his body against hers. He wasn't her client anymore and she wasn't on contract. This was between them, person to person. They were safe enough for an indulgence, here and now, later they might not be. They twisted and rolled, and he was under her again as she straddled him. His hands roamed over her as she had her way with his mouth.

She let him up for air for a second as she decided whether she wanted to lick his pulse or nip at his collarbone.

Kyle's voice rolled over her, husky and dark, sending delicious shivers down her spine. "Let's get rid of the pants."

Chapter Fifteen

She agreed with him about the pants, she did. But strad-
dling him the way she was, she couldn't resist rocking
her hips against him and enjoying the hard ridge of his
cock pressed against her through the layers of clothing.

Kyle sat up, his hands on her hips, encouraging her
to grind into him again.

So she did. And then she groaned because it felt really good. Or maybe they both groaned.

He slid one hand up her arm in a skilled caress, running his fingertips up the line of her neck before cradling
her head and drawing her in for another kiss. She drank
him in, reveling in the sensuality he awakened in her.
This was good, really good, and she wanted to enjoy it.

His hand tightened in her hair as he broke away to
trail kisses down her jaw and neck.

Damn, it had been a long dry spell.

She gasped for breath, clutched his chest, loved the
play of muscles under his skin. When he set his teeth
against her shoulder, not enough to break skin but definitely enough to mark her, she nipped at his ear.

He caught her mouth for a kiss again and sucked on
her lower lip briefly. Then kissed the small hurt he'd left.
She liked this, the mix of gentle and sharp. His whisper-

soft, featherlight touches alternating with the strong grip of his fingers in just the right places.

She tightened her legs, her thighs pressing hard against either side of his, encouraging him. He cupped the curve of her ass, pulled her in close as he pressed kiss after kiss against her collarbone. His fingers tightened on her, alternating between gripping and caressing.

Barely a minute or two of play and she was all ready to have him inside her.

She let her head fall back, closing her eyes and enjoying the sensations. She arched her back, lifting her chest to meet him, her breasts heavy and aching for his touch. When he found the nipple of her right breast, he sucked at it through her shirt and bra, the heat of his mouth burning through the layers of fabric as she tightened for him. He squeezed and kneaded her ass as he turned his attention to her other breast, nipping this time until she cried out and jerked her head up.

"Come here, Isabelle." His voice had deepened, dark and intimate. Liquid heat built between her legs.

She looked down into his face, her sight too unfocused to really see him, her hair falling around them in a curtain. He'd undone her ponytail and she hadn't even realized. Didn't mind either. He chuckled, a sound full of masculine pleasure and arrogance, and captured her mouth again. He kissed her deeper this time, his tongue darting deep into her mouth in sure strokes. His hands wandered over the curve of her back, one arm supporting her while he slid the other hand around to her front, grasping the swell of her breast.

He groaned then, against her lips. "I want to taste more of you."

When he coaxed her arms above her head, she let

him take off her shirt and toss it to the side. He passed one hand across her back and her bra fell loose around her shoulders.

She laughed. "Got a lot of practice?"

"Saves time and frustration," he murmured, completely unashamed.

Her thoughts scattered as his mouth closed over one nipple and he cupped her other breast in his hand. He sucked first, brushing the pad of his thumb over the opposite nipple as he did. The dual sensations, contrast between the scalding suction of his mouth and the slightly rough texture of his thumb shot through her and scrambled her brain.

She'd have fallen backward if it hadn't been for his other arm curved around her waist, holding her in place for him. As it was, she grasped at his shoulders for balance as he licked at her nipple as if it was his favorite lollipop, circling and tasting.

But she wanted to taste too.

She changed her grip on his shoulders, pushing him back with her palms. "My turn."

He ceded control to her, letting her press him down onto his back. His gaze burned into her as he watched her undo the drawstring at his waist, even as he lifted his hips to help her ease his pants down and off. He was at attention in every way, his erection hard and impressive.

Oh and she wanted him in her mouth.

But she didn't take him right away. The man was a tease and good at it. The least she could do was give him a little of his own back.

She ran her tongue along the length of him, keeping her gaze locked with his as she did. If anything, he grew harder and his eyes started to glaze.

Good.

Swirling her tongue around his tip, she caught the tiniest taste of salt before she opened wider and took him into her mouth. He groaned then and his eyes rolled up and back. She smiled.

It was a pleasure to make a man lose himself in what she could do to him. Too many men tried to control this and she tended to get irritated. But Kyle was letting her do as she pleased, and letting her know exactly what worked for him in the process. This was the way she liked it.

Besides, she enjoyed the texture of his soft skin in contrast to the hardness of his erection. And there were his balls.

Easing back, she flicked the tip of her tongue along the ridge around the head of his penis. Propping herself up on one elbow, she used her free hand to caress his balls. The delicate skin of his scrotum tightened at her touch and her fingertips found the super soft spot just behind his balls, lightly brushing him until he lifted his hips.

She took him into her mouth then, as much as she could fit, until his head bumped the back of her throat.

He let out a cross between a moan and a groan. His hands reached out to her, gathered up her hair and held it clear of her face. He didn't try to grab her head and force it toward his hips, didn't try to control her at all. So she withdrew in a slow, steady suck as she met his gaze again.

His eyes were wild, lips parted, and he watched her with an intense hunger as he held her hair back. He was enjoying watching her, she realized. The eye contact was intimate, electrifying.

She laved the length of him with her tongue, getting her taste of him and taking her time doing it before lowering her mouth over his tip and sucking on him again. Starting light, she sucked and licked and sucked increasingly harder, watching him enjoy more and more until it was a little too hard and the muscle at his jaw tightened.

Wrapping the fingers of her free hand around the base of his penis, she eased back to the suction she'd found he liked best. His eyes shuttered closed and his head tilted back as those delicious, well-defined abs tightened.

"Isabelle," he gasped. "This. Incredible. Won't last long."

His hands coaxed her back and she let him, smiling. He was honest too and she appreciated it.

"Condom. In my toiletry kit."

She raised an eyebrow but hey, she tended to pack for any situation too and a toiletry bag was something she kept assembled and ready to toss into whatever bag she was packing. She imagined he did the same.

Rather than make him get up to get it, she gave him another teasing suck over the tip to leave him gasping and went to retrieve the condom.

He opened his eyes as she straddled him again, watched her roll the condom over his length. His hands took her hips and helped her settle over him. When the tip of his penis found her entrance, he caught her gaze and asked quietly, sincerely, "May I?"

She bit her lip then. His consideration undid her. Lost for words, she nodded, bracing her hands against his chest as she lowered herself down on him and he lifted his hips to meet her.

He entered her in a slow, delicious slide.

She shuddered as he filled her, stretched her just

enough to make her core clench around him. Oh, he was magnificent, no lie. He buried himself to the hilt inside her and they were a perfect fit.

After savoring the feel of him for a moment, she started to rock her hips. He watched her with a lazy smile, his hands lightly playing over her hips and the curve of her ass as she moved, then his hips started to move to match her.

The change in motion made her clit rub against the very lowest part of his abs, the light brush of skin against her a fantastic tease. She leaned forward, trying to increase the friction, and let her nipples rub against his chest.

He lifted his head to her lips and kissed her then, deep and long until she was drowning.

When the kiss ended, he gently placed a hand against her shoulder and pressed her back into an upright position. His hips still lifted into her, picking up speed. Her breath caught as his hand slid from her shoulder to her breast, kneading and toying with her nipple. His other hand coasted over her thigh and reached between her legs until his thumb pressed against her clit.

His hips surged up then, his cock driving into her as his thumb rubbed tiny circles around her clit.

She cried out and held on to him.

He froze. "Hurt?"

"Oh my God," she gasped, "If you stop, I swear I'll kill you."

He laughed then and did it again. And again.

It felt so incredibly good. She rocked her hips to meet him, encourage him, as the pleasure of it took over. She threw her head back as the muscles deep inside her tightened.

"I'm coming." She gasped out the warning.

His hands settled on her hips as he drove upward into her one more time and she went over the edge, crying out as she did.

He sat up as the orgasm shook her, wrapping his arms around her and holding her to his chest. He buried his face in the side of her neck and came with her.

Kyle came to awareness slowly, noting with appreciation that the carpet beneath his back was reasonably easy on the skin. No rug burns, though he'd have considered them a small price to pay for the amazingly enjoyable time they'd both just had.

Lizzy had lowered herself to lay tucked against his side, her legs entwined with his and her head pillowed on his biceps. "Welcome back to the world."

He chuckled, supremely satisfied for the moment. "Was I gone long?"

She shifted next to him, propping herself up on one elbow and leaning over him to trail a fingertip over his chest. "Only a few minutes. Long enough to catch your breath."

She sounded smug. He smiled and reached up to play with a few loose strands of her dark hair. She had every right to be.

He let his eyes close again, relaxing under her fingertips and curving his arm around her so he could enjoy the softness of her skin under his own hand. He stroked her back gently, amazed at the supple softness of a woman so strong. He couldn't get enough of touching her.

"Mmm. We're going to end up falling asleep here." Her warning was half-hearted.

He opened his eyes and looked up into her playful

gaze. "You look wide-awake. But if you are so inclined, I have no qualms with pulling the blankets down off the bed and making a nest right here."

He'd dispose of the used condom and perhaps move a few others to a more readily accessible location. Just in case.

She chuckled. "It wouldn't be the first time I've slept on the floor."

"I can imagine your line of work has taken you to some uncomfortable places." He found himself curious. He'd never been much for pillow talk but she fascinated him.

"Sure." She rose though, sitting back on her heels, and gathered her hair into a tidy ponytail. "Deploy enough times and you learn to catch sleep however it comes to you. Mostly, I catnap but I don't sleep in often and I don't crash on the floor unless the bed is too soft."

"Ah." He paused. Her background was mostly a mystery to him, he realized, but he could make some guesses about the kind of danger soldiers lived through. "It must be hard to sleep in the presence of a stranger."

"I generally don't, if I can help it." She definitely wasn't sleepy. He propped himself up on his elbows as she stood and walked into the sitting room. Naked.

"I'd think you'd like the comfort of a good mattress." It seemed wiser to retreat to a more harmless path for their conversation. He was enjoying the view as she checked the door and then her laptop. She was continually vigilant, even in the midst of an unexpected tryst. He should be grateful even if his pride did end up somewhat bruised to be so easily set aside for work.

She shrugged as she returned and stepped into the bathroom, only partially closing the door as she ran water and freshened up. "Some hotel beds are too soft, like trying to sleep on a marshmallow. Pillow tops aren't my favorite and I definitely don't like memory foam."

There he agreed with her. "It's hard to move on memory foam mattresses and I wake up with a sore back."

"Yeah." She emerged and sat on the edge of the bed, holding out a washcloth. "This hotel has promise though. The bed doesn't seem too squishy."

"It's quite firm, actually." He rose and stood in front of her, other parts of him waking up in response to her continued relaxed exposure. Every inch of her was sleekly beautiful and he appreciated how comfortable she was in just her skin.

Instead of handing the cloth to him, she proceeded to gently wash him. "I can see that."

He'd become erect under her gaze and he was getting harder as she continued her ministrations. He enjoyed her consideration too. Usually he was the one to take care of such practicalities. Cleanliness was important to him. He'd set the earlier used condom aside discretely and he was happy to see she'd brought a handful with her along with the washcloth.

"Perhaps I could convince you to give the bed a try tonight." He pressed her back, pausing to nuzzle her breasts as she lay down for him.

As interested as he was in conversation, he was also ready to explore other means of getting to know her better.

Lizzy rose and stretched, completely naked and utterly satisfied. No doubt about it, good sex was the best kind of therapy, especially when her partner was up for several rounds through the course of a night. They'd gone from the floor to the bed to the sofa and back to the bed again with only enough rest in between for her to assure herself that their room was still secure. And she was seriously hoping they'd have time to consider the bathroom counter.

Kyle sat in the bed, looking rumpled and equally as satisfied. His eyelids heavy over his dark eyes. "Don't tell me you're getting back to work already?"

His tone was light but there was an underlying hesitation there. Maybe she imagined it but she knew better. It was a worry she'd experienced herself.

She turned to him, smiling. "I'm hungry. And I figure this might be a long day, so I was going to get us something to eat."

He returned her smile. "I see. Do you already have our next meal planned, then? Or are you willing to entertain orders?"

"I was thinking room service." She retrieved the hotel's menu from the dresser and tossed it onto the bed before bending to sort through the random articles of clothing to grab hers.

"I thought your rules stated there would be no room service." His voice took on an edge.

Temper, temper.

Though to be fair, she hadn't explained that particular rule fully. "No room service to this room, no. And you shouldn't order it at all. But I think I mentioned I have more than one room booked in this hotel."

Bundling her clothes and tucking them under her arm, she grabbed her laptop from the sitting area and brought it all to the bed. This was new for her, but she'd been working with Kyle rather than near him and she didn't want to put the distance between them at the moment.

Bringing up her surveillance, she selected the room located in the same hotel as them and made the streaming video full screen.

"No one's been in there and no one's knocked on the door." She tapped the screen. "I'd put the do not disturb sign on the door and every time I've left the hotel, I've made sure to stop in and move a few things around. No maid service, same as what we've been doing in here. But I can head down there and call for room service, then bring the meal back up here for us."

He studied the screen. "And there's more than one room on your surveillance."

Wariness made her respond slowly. "Yes."

She'd been checking the other security feeds throughout the night, even though they'd been indulging in each other.

He held up his hands. "I admire the thought you'd put into all of this. There was every possibility we could have stayed in that original apartment, if I am correct?"

She nodded.

"But you had all of this in place. Alternatives. Backup plan after backup plan." He shook his head. "And you had less than twenty-four hours to set it all up."

When he put it that way, it sounded like a lot more than it was. Her cheeks heated and she busied herself getting her pants back on. "I like options. You can't be sure there will always be choices so leaving yourself with as many as possible makes sense."

"It does," he agreed. After a moment, he tapped the menu. "Rather standard fare here. A few specialties by the restaurant attached to the hotel. I think the lamb burger looks the most interesting with the whipped feta cheese and olive tapenade."

Yum. "Actually, that sounds really good."

He grinned. "Would you like to share and get an appetizer too? I find I prefer to order several things so I don't get bored halfway through my meal."

Considering the traditional Korean meal Maylin had taken the time to send them before, she wondered if it was a cultural thing. Could be, though there were other cuisines that encouraged a broad variety of tastes and textures in a meal. She loved tapas and small plates, for example. Whether it was a preference born of his background or not, it suited her very well.

Sharing small bites of food with Kyle on the bed had its own range of tempting possibilities.

"They've got the usual starters, don't they?" She slipped her bra straps over her shoulders and leaned forward to peer at the menu as she settled herself into the bra cups and hooked the back. Actually, the restaurant menu was fairly eclectic. She paused to take in the choices and really consider the options.

When she glanced up, his gaze was on her cleavage and filled with heat. As soon as he noticed her watching him, he met her eye to eye. Her heart rate kicked up and a low heat grew in her lower belly with a hunger of a different kind. She licked her lips.

It was Kyle who eased them back from the brink of jumping all over each other. He tapped the menu again. "I think we'd enjoy each other better if we have fuel to sustain us."

True. And she had more work to do, ensuring they were still safe here. She was hungry enough to gnaw at random things at this point and while she did plan to have her mouth on various parts of him again later, she didn't have any desire to do him damage while she did it. Exactly the opposite.

"How about the truffle fries? There's a little store in Pike Place Market that had samples out with some of their white-truffle-infused salt and I've been thinking about it ever since. The fries sound fantastic." Her mouth was watering just thinking about it.

"The burger does come with fries already so I imagine we could request a substitution." He was seriously considering the menu.

This was an odd situation. Sure, she'd tumbled with her share of partners. And she'd lingered with them if she could deal with their company past the pillow talk stage. But this comfortable chatter was different. The chemistry between them was still going strong like whoa but it was unhurried, simmering. As if Kyle had every intention to enjoy her over the course of many hours.

Her chest tightened and expanded at the same time, if that was possible. It was a warm, fluttering tickle. She liked it.

"Agreed. We'll get them to substitute the truffle fries for the regular fries with the lamb burger." She sighed. "Oh, they have poutine."

His eyes held a twinkle of amusement as he glanced at the appetizer and back to her. "Duck confit poutine, no less. Sounds delicious. You do have quite the palate."

"I'm going to take that as a compliment." She straightened. Maybe he didn't notice, or maybe it was habit, but his tone had taken a teasing edge. It was still warm, inviting her to smile with him, but she'd heard him add dry sarcasm to a compliment before. Sweet words could quickly turn cutting.

Gah. She just had to go looking for things to be cautious about, didn't she?

"It's meant to be a compliment." That came quietly, earnest and with sincerity.

He was back to watching her again. Intense without pressure. Open desire tempered by patience.

The man definitely knew how to make a girl feel wanted.

It wasn't that she didn't appreciate it. But while falling into bed with him was a reasonable risk, falling for him wasn't. A breather would do her good. She could get her head right, then come back and enjoy him the way he was probably hoping to enjoy her.

Uncomplicated. No expectations. No strings attached. None of this overthinking shit. Suddenly she was caring too much about something that wouldn't matter in a few days' time.

If she kept this up, she'd ruin the good the deliciously sweaty exertion had done her and just be stressed again.

She shoved her feet into her boots. "I'll be back in a few minutes. Did you want to pull up something to watch on the laptop while we eat?"

He chuckled. "Do you think we'll be paying attention to a movie if we play it?"

She grinned at him. "It could be background noise."

"I'll take a look."

Chapter Sixteen

Lizzy returned to the room, balancing the room service tray laden with stacked plates on one hand, her backpack slung over her back to keep one hand free. She scanned the room as she entered and closed the door behind her.

The atmosphere had changed.

Kyle sat on the bed staring at her laptop, his face twisted with anger.

No, he'd gone past that and well into cold rage. It was the kind of thing she'd seen before, when men were pushed to a point where they were willing to do anything—kill—because of whatever caused it.

"Hey." She set the covered plates on the side table. Better to have free hands. If he was about to go out on a rampage, she'd need to stop him. Based on their light match earlier, it was doable but not as easy as stopping most people. She'd have to be careful or they could both end up seriously hurt in the process.

But Kyle's voice when he spoke was calm, neutral, quiet. "Would you please come watch this?"

Warning bells clanged inside her head. The quiet ones were always the ones to watch.

She crossed the sitting room to the bedside cautiously,

giving herself time to react if he decided to try to surprise her. "I'm guessing I'm not going to like what I see."

His lips pressed together in a grim line. "Watch. Tell me what you perceive and I hope I am simply paranoid."

Maybe. But paranoid wasn't necessarily wrong. In her experience, it was about a fifty-fifty chance as to whether there was a legit reason to be. Trick was knowing which side of the fifty you landed on in a given situation.

She stood patiently, still just outside of easy reach, while he tapped the touch pad to start the streaming video.

It was a news interview, streamed live early this morning, based on the logo and time stamp displayed at the corner of the feed. "We're here live with Jaime Douglas, Vice President of Research and Development, biochemical division, at Phoenix Biotech as he welcomes the latest sponsored family. Phoenix Biotech, and Mr. Douglas's department in particular, has begun an initiative to support charities this year."

The pretty news correspondent beamed at the silver-haired man in the expensive suit as he tugged self-consciously at his jacket hem. Not a man comfortable in front of a camera.

"Yes." He cleared his throat and tried for a stronger start. "We at Phoenix Biotech believe in making an impact not only in life sciences, but with humankind. And so we polled our employees to determine what charities mattered to them, taking a vested interest in their cares, their hopes for their families."

Grand words but they dripped with honey. Lizzy narrowed her eyes. Not all sweet things were actually good for you. Antifreeze, for example.

The man continued with his goodwill-toward-all-men speech until the news correspondent asked him directly about the slender Asian woman and teen standing to one side. "Ah yes, this is the first family of several we've extended the hand of sponsorship to. The young man has key talents and will be attending a university here in the US on scholarship. His mother has accompanied him. We're hoping to reunite them both with his uncle, her brother, once we're able to locate him. They're wonderful people. I'm sure it would just kill them if we're not able to find him. "

Uh-huh. Cue dramatic music. Three guesses on who they were looking for, considering the way Kyle surged to his feet and started to stalk around the bed. Since he stayed in the bedroom area and didn't seem to be heading to the door, she didn't stop him. But she did stand up and move into the sitting area to give him room, and give her time to respond if he did decide to go charging out of here.

"So are you the kid's real uncle?" Could be his son. There was family resemblance in the lines of the kid's face, his bone structure.

"Yes." Kyle was apparently still struggling with his responses because he'd gone terse. She sort of missed his lengthier conversational habits. It wasn't often she got to be around a man who could converse with more than four-letter words and the occasional grunt.

Not fair. The Centurion Corporation, her fire team in particular, tended toward the more intelligent. But they'd all developed a habit of short sentences.

"Did you know they were in the States?" Keeping him talking was the best idea for now. She needed to know what he wanted to do, whether she was going to have to subdue him to keep him safe, and what could be done about them. If there should be something done.

Even family could betray a person.

"No." He stopped and dragged his fingers through his hair. "Not yet. I knew they were requesting visas. I was helping them prepare to come here. They were supposed to wait until after all of this was resolved and I could make permanent arrangements for us all to live together."

Part of her melted a little. The battle-ready part of her tensed. All the more reason for him to go rushing out there to attempt a save he wasn't equipped to manage.

And damn but Phoenix Biotech had some serious reach if they could find and pluck his family out of a different country to use them as bait.

"This is a trap. You understand that, right?" She was sure he did, but best to get it out in the open. Sometimes forcing a person to speak the words out loud helped them think more rationally. He wasn't doing badly so far.

He only nodded at first. "Douglas worded his message to be incredibly obvious. I imagine he's expecting me to call the office, contact him via his direct line. I have it."

Tempting. "Let's wait until we talk through the options first."

"We?" Hope made his voice crack. "I had expected to have to argue with you, find some way to get past you to help them."

Not a bad guess. "I haven't said I'm letting you go anywhere. But we can talk about what options there are too because I'm not the sort to leave the situation as it is. First, do you really think they'd kill your family?"

He stood perfectly still.

"Think. Rationally. As public as this interview was, nothing could happen immediately. Someone would notice somewhere that the two of them disappeared." Most likely.

"Not so." He resumed pacing. "It might be a national news channel, but this was broadcasted for the local feed. Hard to say what level of exposure the cast had gotten outside the Seattle area. Truly, fairly few people will remember this beyond the brief feel-good moment any other charity news spot would engender. Even fewer would think to inquire or research what happened after the moment in the spotlight."

He had a point. A reasonable one. This wasn't reality television and there wasn't a follow-up episode to see how the people were doing a few months later. Some news stories had follow-ups but plenty didn't.

"This is the type of short public relations clip to fade into obscurity." He waved a hand at the laptop. "What actually happens to my sister and her son will matter very much to me, but isn't going to be noticed by anyone else."

"All right. Then we need to know more." These situations sucked. Hostage, kidnappings, these had a nasty chance of going badly. And the last time they'd had to deal with one, there'd been a lot of explosions and gunfire involved.

"What else can I tell you?" Agitated. And rightly so.

She needed him to calm down. "Walking out there to trade yourself for them is relatively stupid. Thank you for not doing that while I was gone."

Actually, the relief she felt about that was something she should probably think about later. It was almost dizzying.

Kyle blew out a breath and sat on the edge of the bed. "What can I tell you that will help?"

She opened her mouth, but he held up a hand.

"These are people, good people, better than me. I want you to think of them as such." His gaze bore into hers with his determination to make her believe his words. "They deserve a safe and happy life far more than I do."

"You said they were applying for visas. I'm not going to make assumptions or guess." She didn't relax but she did give him a small nod to acknowledge his message. "Where were they and why did they want to come here?"

A small smile flashed across his lips. "I am slightly surprised you ask why. Many would simply assume that of course people would want to come here. In truth, my older sister was very happy in Korea. She chose to stay with her husband when my family moved here."

"Okay." Well, Korea was not one of the countries she'd ever been to. Being able to recognize people from different parts of the world was one thing, and a useful skill, but actually having traveled there was a completely different life goal.

Kyle continued, "My sister's marriage was *seon*—a type of arranged marriage in Korean customs."

"They still do that kind of thing?" Normally, Lizzy bit her tongue about things like this. Different cultures had different customs. With Kyle, she tended to let herself go a little unfiltered. For good or bad, it was what it was for the time being.

He held up his hands. "In South Korea, marriage is considered to be a merging of two whole bloodlines. Such a decision involves the families of both the bride and the groom. Often, parents encourage and arrange a meeting for the two intended in the hopes of a match but the decision is ultimately theirs. For my sister, there were several *seon* with different suitors before she actually married."

"Ah." Lizzy didn't know what to say. It seemed less arranged and more like parental involvement. Which, if she thought about it, could be a different kind of pressure but just as tough to live with.

"Our parents were, of course, eager for her to choose her husband. He and his family were a good match for ours. He, in particular, seemed a good balance for her in personality, achievements and appearance."

"Of course." Okay, maybe her tone had gone dry, deadpan, whatever.

Kyle's gaze found hers again and he smiled, but there was sadness in his eyes. "When any dating can start, here or there or anywhere, what can anyone go on but such things? And of those three characteristics, only two are actually quantifiable. Parents do their best, but there's no way to know for sure. They can only hope. It is not unusual to hope our loved ones can be happy, I think."

She could give him that. But she wasn't going to say anything for the moment. Family interference in her choices hadn't ever been something she'd been willing to accept—not in childhood or as an adult.

"In any case, my sister dated her husband for a year before they married. It's not so different from the way it works here in the US." Kyle shrugged. "If anything, in such arranged marriages, there's less chance of strain during the actual marriage. Since parents are involved in the choosing, there is significantly less chance of family opposition to the union."

Familiarity. Culture. What a person grows up with

and considers normal. It'd be an interesting conversation to explore under other circumstances.

"I can imagine." She rolled her shoulders, trying to ease the tension out of them and stay loose. "I'm not sure I'm good with the tradition itself. It's something to think on when there's more time to consider the context, but I'm to going to go with it for now. If she was happily married, then why are she and her son here now, on their own?"

The sadness spread across his whole face now. His shoulders slumped. "I'm not sure. I only know her husband decided on a divorce a year ago. She was going to tell me why when she and her son arrived here."

"Was his family in agreement with the divorce? Was yours?"

He tipped his head. "You were listening."

She resisted the urge to tap her foot. For a man in a rush, he was telling a long story. Or maybe he didn't know how to tell it when he was still trying to unravel it himself. "Yes. I was listening. I'll process my own opinions on it later. Right now I'm taking mental notes on what might matter to help you with your current problem."

He nodded. After a moment, he started up again. "Our family came here to establish a presence in the US while her husband's family saw to the combined family business interests back in Korea. My father did well enough starting a software company to support life sciences. I learned some of what I know of the industry from him. But the stress of it, of living in a place so different from where you grew up, of trying to make a name. It overwhelmed him. He died of a heart attack. And with him, the US presence of the family business was gone, as well. My mother got sick and passed away not long after. So for my sister, there is only me left here. Our extended family fell out of touch with me when I didn't try to resurrect the family business here."

His recounting had become flat, his voice distant. He'd compartmentalized his feelings about those times and he wasn't willing to feel right now.

She didn't blame him. While the background information was necessary, the confusion brought on by old angst wasn't useful. "And his family?"

"I would guess they were eager for him to make a connection with a new wife, most likely with a family to provide more valuable networking for the business in Korea." Still delivered with a flat tone, sparks of anger were showing up in his gaze now. "Either way, once the divorce was final, he saw to it they had some funding but there was little to hold them in Korea. My nephew has a potential for a bright future here, doing something he loves."

And Kyle was reinventing himself and his lifestyle to provide for it.

She didn't know this woman or her son. But the man who was her brother, the kid's uncle, she was starting to see some incredible things about him.

"All this means no one to come looking for them if something happens to them. I get it now." Thus his agitation when she'd returned. The danger to them was very real if Phoenix Biotech could easily make them disappear.

"There is only me." Kyle was quiet, his pride completely set aside. What was left sitting in front of her was a man determined to do what it took to make his family safe. "Please, Isabelle, let me go get them."

"No." She'd have given the same answer even before she'd known the nature of the leverage Phoenix Biotech had on him. "Whatever it is you're going to testify is enough to be worth not just your life, but theirs too. So no, you are not going to run straight to them."

If he hated her for it, so be it. They had chemistry. Respect for each other. And while the first had been freaking amazing, losing the second would hurt more.

Neither he nor she was going to have any sort of respect left if he did what Phoenix Biotech wanted him to do and prove he was too stupid to live.

Kyle stood but didn't take a step toward her or the door behind her. Instead, he copied her stance. "What will we do instead?"

"Gather more information, for one thing." It was her turn to pace, keeping him in her peripheral field of view as she did. He was smart enough to be sneaky and she was not about to let him surprise her now that she was absorbed in the problem at hand. "I need to head out to get a report I was waiting on anyway. While I'm out, away from here, I'll put in a call to our friend in the streaming video. We'll find out what they wanted you to do."

"I'm going with you." He tensed, ready for an argument. Even if his fists weren't up, his guard was in every other way.

"Yes. You are." She smiled, ridiculously amused for no good reason. But they were about to go out and make some things happen. A challenge. So much better than hiding, even if it was crazy. It didn't make sense. But that was the beauty of it. It was unpredictable. "They're expecting you to either come rushing out into the open or stay hidden. They're expecting you to have to fight with your protection personnel either way. It's time better applied to finding a solution. Something they don't think you can pull off."

"But you and I together can?" Humor was softening the hard line of his lips pressed together. "Whimsical. How much can the two of us really do to make my sister and her son safe?"

No room for whimsy here if they were going to be goddamned heroes.

She took the cover off one of the plates of food and snagged a barely warm truffle fry. "We can do recon, then plan. Then we can do something they won't expect."

Unfortunately, since their opponent seemed to have a solid idea of how Kyle and the regular authorities tended to think, she was going to have to do some improvisation without his involvement in the decision-making process.

"I'll tell you what we're doing, when I can." She held out a truffle fry to him. After a moment, he crossed the room to where she was standing and took the offering. "And for when there's not time to tell you, make sure you understand and then get your agreement, you're going to have to have some faith and follow my lead. No questions. No hesitation. Deal?"

"Do I have a choice?" His voice was wry now, but his anger had been tucked away. Controlled.

"Not really. You hired me to protect you. To get you to the trial alive and in one piece, that's going to mean saving you from your own too-stupid-to-live moments." She wanted to reach out, touch him, give him the reassurance actual tactile contact could give in ways words couldn't. But this thing between them was so new, she didn't know if it would be welcome. "If that means I need to figure out a way to help your sister and your nephew too, then I will. But we're still going to do this my way."

She thought he might balk. His stubborn streak wouldn't be a surprise here. It was in his nature to be the leader and expect others to follow. Hell, she was fairly sure it was why Austin and Weaver had had so much trouble with him.

Instead, Kyle took her hand in his and lifted it to press a kiss against the back of her hand. Then he turned her hand over and touched his lips to the pulse point on the inside of her wrist. "You're in the lead. For now."

Chapter Seventeen

It always seemed to be different with Lizzy.

Kyle hid a smile as the two of them left the hotel together. Previously she'd made them leave separately, one after the other at varying time intervals. This time, they left as a couple and bid each other goodbye at the street corner while he got in a cab and she walked.

She'd scowled about it, considering it a risk to be separated from him for long but his cab ride took him up to Pike Place Market uneventfully, where he waited by the tourist-filled area watching parents take pictures of their children climbing over the metal pig. Cognizant of her warnings, he stayed under the cover of the market's permanent roof.

In minutes, she was there, in a different outfit and wearing sunglasses. Her hair was up and tucked under another of her endless supply of cute hats.

Studying her, once she joined him, he couldn't help but grin. "You enjoy this."

"What?" Behind her sunglasses, she must be scanning the area. She didn't simply look out over the streets at the people, he'd learned. She looked up over the balconies and rooftops, into windows if possible, and shadowy areas between buildings.

Places he'd never thought to look for watchers—or shooters—until he'd met her.

"You enjoy the different hats and sunglasses. Even the wigs." Of course, it made sense to change looks as they were remaining in the city. "It's amazing how accessories can completely change the way a person looks, but it isn't just about the practicality. You relish trying new ones."

She turned her face toward him slowly. Telltale flags of color had risen up on her cheeks. She didn't say anything.

He grinned even more, delighted, actually. Her lack of commentary meant he was right. She seemed to prefer silence to lying. A preference he appreciated.

"Hats, sunglasses, scarves." The gift possibilities were endless. "You have excellent taste, in every style I've seen so far. How many variations do you have packed away in your backpack?"

She sighed and tugged at his elbow, taking them into the crowded market. In a tucked-away corner between stalls, she handed him a hat and sunglasses while she swapped her own.

Actually, it was very clever. Such items packed small, compact, and required little effort to shake out and wear. It allowed for effective, quick changing. At first, he'd felt ridiculous but now it was a precaution with an element of fun to it.

"Mix and match helps with variety." Lizzy didn't look at him as she spoke, letting her hand trail along the edge of a vendor table as they wound through the market. "I started with just a couple, but one of my teammates got me hooked on picking up a little something wherever we went."

"A good idea." Even though she was going through the motions of browsing, he'd noticed she never bought anything. "But you haven't done that with me. Too familiar with the items here?"

She lived in the Seattle area, after all. Or at least he presumed she did. She hadn't actually shared much information about herself.

Picking up a trinket, she paused to give the vendor a quick smile. As she set it down and continued to browse, he almost missed her answer. "We're in the middle of a live contract right now. Even if I don't mean to, something I pick up is a memory. For me, and for anyone watching me. It's better not to."

"No souvenirs, then?" A heavy weight dropped into his stomach, surprising him. "You prefer not to remember this time?"

Well, it was a good thing to know. He'd enjoyed their tryst. It was always good to have the correct expectations when interacting with a person. Refreshing, actually, the way she was breaking it to him. He'd usually had to let his companions down gently.

"Slow down whatever thought process is going on inside your head. I prefer to do as little as possible to tie me to the person I'm keeping safe when I'm in the middle of a contract." Her words had an edge to them, and tinged with real anger, not irritation. "Would you prefer I remembered you as my client or as a person?"

Her question rocked him back on his heels. Without a doubt, he wanted her to remember him as the latter, not the former. He didn't know when he'd stopped considering whether he'd extend her contract as a personal bodyguard but now, he was wondering whether he even had a chance of convincing her to let him see her again.

Sometime in the past day or two—had it really only been that long?—he'd started looking forward to starting his life over. It wasn't because he should, or to provide a life his sister and his nephew deserved, but because Lizzy had made it fun. The first two had been good reasons, the last made him happy.

Lizzy had added a spark to life, expanded his world and threw him off balance. They were all very interesting things.

For example, being completely wrong in his perception of a situation was new for him. She had a knack for getting through his guard, coming from an unexpected angle and knocking the breath out of him. And all with simple verbal sparring.

He very much hoped to have the chance to tangle with her more over the next couple of days, physically and verbally. Intimately, as well.

For the time being, he lengthened his stride to cover the step or two lead she had on him. "Perhaps one day we'll have the opportunity to acquire a few keepsakes after the trial."

"We need to get you to it first." She led him across the street and up into a small shop at the corner of Post Alley. "I like the white peach ginger beer here."

It took a few minutes to acquire their drinks. He'd chosen a different flavor, not because hers didn't sound interesting but because the idea of trading tastes appealed to him. She was a generous soul, whether she was conscious of it or not. There was no hesitation in her when it came to sharing and he was enjoying it.

After a moment, she led them back out of the store. "Too many windows there, no place to sit without being exposed. I'd risk it without you but having you out here with me is enough without adding to it."

He didn't argue. Wearing the Kevlar vest she'd given him gave him a sense of security but it was only a vest. They headed up the open street, blending in with a walking tour group led by a man in a utility kilt.

Kyle narrowed his eyes. "A chocolate-tasting tour. Did you time our walk to be here as they passed?"

She shrugged, keeping her voice low to match his. The tour mostly had personal headsets attached to small receivers so they could hear their tour guide. None of them was listening. "They're a regular tour and I knew the schedule. I figured we might be able to stop in at a store or two with them before the tour guide tells us to move along or sign up for our own tour."

He shook his head, then took a risk and wrapped his arm around her waist. Her body stiffened for a split second, then relaxed against him as she matched his stride for three steps. Then she pulled away, ostensibly to check her shoe, before straightening and slipping her hand into the bend of his arm. "Better for me to hold on to you so I can let go if necessary. If I need to react fast, I can't afford the time it'd take me to untangle from you."

A practical reason. Of course. He wondered if she knew how warm a balm to his ego her touch was. The momentary pang of rejection he'd experienced when she'd pulled away stabbed surprisingly deep considering the brevity of their involvement. He'd been overly sensitive not once, but twice now.

It was disturbing. And fascinating. In the middle of the most precarious time of his life, he was as bad as an adolescent boy trying to navigate his way through his first dating experience. The thought made him chuckle.

"Don't get too relaxed." Lizzy gave his arm a squeeze. "We're out here doing this because I didn't trust you to stay where you were supposed to if I left you alone."

Ah. He should rectify the situation in regard to trust. It wouldn't matter what he told her, so much as how he acted on his stated intent. Things like trust, respect and integrity took a much higher priority when he held each of those for another person. And he did for her.

"I would be disingenuous if I tried to claim you were incorrect in your suspicions. The temptation to go out and attempt to take control of the course of events would've gotten to be too much if I'd had to wait long." The admission cost him little to say out loud and he was still amused as he continued to walk at the pace she set. Ahead and around them, the tour group walked along overtaking other people on the street here and there.

"We need to know more." It surprised him when she commented, but she kept to a conversational tone. "Coming after you is one thing, but investing in retrieving your family from Korea? The news coverage? That's more exposure than I'd thought they'd be willing to risk. Knowing why is going to be key to making sure you all come out of this okay."

The group stopped at a street corner, waiting for the traffic signals to turn.

Kyle started forward and had to gently tug Lizzy along. Her gaze was raised upward and she appeared to be a tourist enjoying the city skyline as they walked. Once the group reached the opposite corner, they paused again for a bit of history and a witty story from the tour guide. Lizzy's attention seemed to have been caught by a storefront.

He leaned close and made sure to brush his lips ever

so slightly over the shell of her ear. "Are you studying your reflection or the store?"

Her hand tightened on his arm as she huffed out a laugh. "The reflection and it's not mine. I'm checking out the area around us for potential issues."

"Is there anything I can do?" An itch developed between his shoulder blades. He rolled his shoulders uncomfortably.

Her gaze remained on the storefront. "Not really. If you spend time trying to spot dangerous people, you'll look suspicious. It's better if I keep an eye out. You keep your head down, turned toward me or looking at things in storefronts. Makes it harder to get a good look at your face."

As much as he'd wanted to get out of the confined space of the hotel, she wasn't making this outing enjoyable. Then again, he appreciated it. "I am very glad you don't let me forget myself."

"It's what I do." Her simple response was reassuring and unsettling at the same time.

Nervous, he studied the reflection in the glass pane and only saw buildings. Then he looked through the glass to the goods displayed. "Do spare a moment to admire the designer shoes too."

Silence.

He glanced at her and butterflies tickled his throat. Dusky rose spread over her cheeks. He coughed to cover his laugh. "I'm partial to the nude pair with the dusting of crystals across the heel. I think it would lengthen your already very shapely legs."

She bit her lip, then tugged him to continue forward with the tour group. "I liked those and the strappy red ones too."

More and more fun. "Not the pink ones with the silk rose over the toe?"

She wrinkled her nose. "Not so into flowers on the shoes. Maybe a bow once in a while if they're simple and elegant. The flowers, not so much, and I definitely don't like fur or feathers."

This time he did laugh. He had noticed those set in the corner of the display. Meant more for wear with lingerie than for going out, he'd bet. "I'm surprised you have this much of an opinion on heels."

There was a pause. "Okay, I have a thing for shoes. I don't get to wear them often, but when I do, I like pretty shoes."

He was delighted.

"Enough with the frilly stuff." Her tone turned brusque. "I need some critical thinking. We're missing something about your former employer and the projects you used to manage. Is there anything you didn't mention before?"

Kyle hesitated. He had resolved to testify and expose his mistakes in order to expose greater wrongs. It was one thing to do it in court. The testimony involved facts and documented proof. Telling Lizzy was a much more personal confession.

Her opinion of him mattered.

But she'd asked, so he would try to give her more. It was important for her to know in any case, because he was more and more certain he wanted to continue whatever this was between them.

The tour group around them burst into laughter at some joke the tour guide shared via their headphones. No one else was listening.

Before he could think harder on it, he took the plunge.

"Part of my responsibilities was to oversee portfolio management for a subset of their drug products." It'd been a challenging, interesting position at first. But as with any project management, departmental politics and personality conflicts had gradually numbed him to the good the drug products were actually meant to do. "The company had shipments of biological materials coming in by sea from Korea and other places. It was standard procedure to have those supplies tested to find out if they had expired due to various shipping delays."

The traffic light turned and Lizzy tugged him forward when he didn't move. He wanted to drag his feet the same way he wanted to delay in telling her his story. "If the supplies had expired, the shipping containers were illegally dumped at sea and reported as 'lost' so our company and our vendors could collect insurance without worrying about proper disposal. Those materials were potentially biohazards."

He watched her face, looking for a sign of judgment somewhere. But her face was serene, a study of polite attentiveness. A mirror to the tourists around them. "You went over that pretty fast earlier, so I hadn't thought about the premeditation involved. The way they went about it demonstrates an established procedure. There's a lot of proof of forethought there."

"All of that, into our ocean, and I knew," he confessed. "I've never been overly interested in environmentalism. It all seems very much removed from day-to-day living. It didn't seem wrong to me until I was faced with the idea of family coming back into my life. Then suddenly, smart business wasn't as important as doing the right thing. When I was approached to provide testimony to corroborate the evidence, I agreed. I gathered what documentation I could. The manifests, especially, are suspect. They don't match up well with what should have been in those shipments. I mentioned smuggling before and I refused to be even tangentially involved. I wanted my nephew to be able to trust and respect me when he came to live with me here."

He fell silent then, letting the babble of the tourists cover over the silence between them.

Finally, Lizzy spoke, "What I think about what you did isn't important right now. There's still a piece missing. They could be smuggling drugs but that's a stretch. There are much closer suppliers. It doesn't add up yet."

She continued her train of thought. "The level of effort they're putting into flushing you out into the open is way beyond that. Something about what you're going to prove in your testimony is worth a whole lot more."

"Yes." He paused. "And once we find out, it will be helpful in getting my family to safety, I hope."

"The trick is figuring it out, not waiting for it to become obvious. Timing and context are everything when it comes to intel." Lizzy pulled him into the chocolate store with the rest of the group. "You need to think harder. Beyond you and exactly what you're going to testify. What could you be tangentially related to?"

Her hand was still firmly on his arm. There was no rejection in her touch, her posture. She was still focused on helping him. Admittedly, he'd been afraid she'd pull away from him right out there in the open. But she hadn't.

And he was grateful.

As the crowd pressed them together, he ducked his head and pressed a kiss against her temple. "Biohazardous materials dumped in the ocean repeatedly and there's something worse. What could be worse?"

The store was small so space was tight once they stepped inside. As the tour group gathered around the counter, she led Kyle past to the chocolate bar at the back.

The employees were all occupied but her package wouldn't have been left with any of them. A human could get confused, give it to the wrong person, or worse, get curious all on their own.

Lizzy passed her hand under the customer-facing side of the bar, far enough from the edge that a random hand wouldn't encounter it. She found what she was looking for stuck to the underside, almost against the base behind a disgusting couple of pieces of gum.

"Ugh." She grimaced. Nguyen had his own ways of sticking it to a person when they gave him attitude. She had to give him that.

"Not the usual sound you make in relation to drinking chocolate." Kyle leaned casually against the bar next to her, studying the daily specials board. "So this is where you get your drink of choice."

"Recently, yes." She studied her prize.

Not a flash drive as she'd expected. It was a package wrapped in waxed paper.

"We'll be with you in just a moment!" one of the employees called over from the main register. They were still buried under tourists as they handed out samples of chocolate truffles.

Kyle flashed a charming smile and gave them a wave in acknowledgment.

Lizzy huffed out a laugh. "You've got the cool and calm covered. But you've got a handicap."

"What do you mean?" Kyle's brows drew together in his confusion. "And what is that?"

"I mean it's great to put people at ease, be immediately likable. But you're too memorable. We're not going to come back here again." Keeping the package under the counter, out of view, she unwrapped it. "And this stuff is something a friend uses to line boxes when she's packing sandwiches or candies.

"Maybe whoever left that for you is a baker." Kyle was trying to be all sorts of helpful.

She scowled at him.

He raised his eyebrows. "What?"

She opened her mouth, closed it, then opened it again. "I guess, it's just a weird idea."

"People have lives outside their day-to-day jobs," Kyle said. "They have hobbies, things to take their minds away from their work."

"Sure they do." She was barely paying attention to their conversation at the moment. She'd finally gotten past all the waxed paper to reveal a microSD card. Clever Nguyen—she didn't need to wait until she had access to her laptop.

She pulled her smartphone out of her pocket and pressed the tiny memory card into the reader slot. Thank goodness she didn't have to pop the back open and yank the battery to get to the microSD access.

"Okay then, what do you do?" Kyle's question cut into her thoughts. "Aside from collecting cute sunglasses, hats and scarves, what do you do in your free time?"

"I don't have free time." She didn't like the direction this conversation was going.

There were multiple files on the memory card. First was the ballistics report she'd requested. Skimming through, she looked first for the particular piece of confirmation she needed. She'd read in more depth when they were back at the hotel. The report told her the key thing she needed to know.

"How is it you don't have time to yourself? Or would it be called off duty?" Kyle persisted with his questions.

"I've been with you 24/7. This is the way contracts work sometimes." She lifted her gaze and scanned the room.

Still full of tourists, all the same faces she'd noted as they'd entered. Nothing on the street to be seen out the windows. They'd leave around about the same time as the tour continued on its way unless another convenient grouping of passersby turned up.

"What about between contracts? What do you do for you?" A hint of concern had entered his voice.

Anger sparked, flared up. "Look. I don't have hobbies. Not normal ones. I maintain my firearms. I spend time on the firing range. I make sure I'm always on my game."

"You work, even when you're not working." He studied her for a long minute and then looked out at the tourists. "You do other things, if you think about it. You have your indulgences."

"So why do you keep asking?" They were lingering too long and she wasn't thrilled about the current conversation.

It felt too much like the idiot small talk guys used when they were hitting on her at a bar. They always wanted to know what she did for a living, what she liked to do in her spare time, where she came from. Anything to give them an opening to ask her out and try getting into her pants.

She opened up one of the other files and started to skim through the data.

"Because you had a hard time imagining a person with something else to do besides their work." Kyle chuckled. "You are so confident in your area of professional expertise, so focused on work. I'm fascinated with the way you shy away from imagining people in their spare time."

She sighed. "It's not that I can't, I prefer not to."

He opened his mouth but she held her hand up.

"Don't ask why. It's just weird. And the only time I need to get into anyone's head that way...it's because I need to do a lot more than meet them in the light of day for a job."

She'd already said too much. It was something she could be very good at. But she didn't like who she was when she was getting inside someone else's head. To find them. To get ahead of them. Possibly to take them out of the picture.

He shook his head, still not getting it. "Why not get to know—"

"Because if I'm getting to know someone in their spare time, it's probably because I'm hunting them." Fine. She'd tell him directly. "I'm a sniper, Kyle. If I'm not providing cover for my team from a distance, I'm working on my own and I have a target. Getting to know someone is research for me. It's still work and generally, my target ends up dead. Because I'm good at what I do."

Kyle shifted his weight, turning toward her as he leaned on one elbow on the counter. "I see."

Boom.

Chapter Eighteen

The world exploded.

Well, not the world, but *something.*

Kyle ducked instinctively, but it was Lizzy who grabbed him by a handful of his shirt and yanked him down under the partial shelter of the bar. People screamed. Bars of chocolate fell off the shelves and bottles of wine fell from the rack along the one wall, crashing on the floor in shattered glass. Pieces of plaster came down from the ceiling.

She yanked a wig down over his head. "Get that straight."

With shaking hands, he did his best to tuck his hair under the skullcap of the wig, changing his hair from black to brown.

Lizzy's gaze passed over him and then she was reaching into her bag. A moment later, she jammed a cap down over his head.

After another few seconds, Lizzy's voice cut through the din. "Now. With everyone else. If we're going out, it has to be with the group."

He scrambled to stay with her as she pulled him into the panicking group of tourists. They poured out of the store to see equal chaos on the street. Sirens filled the air, getting louder.

"It wasn't this store and it wasn't a large enough charge to bring the building down," Lizzy was saying urgently. "Stand and stare like everyone else. Keep your head down though. Don't look all the way up. We'll wait until the emergency vehicles get here."

He swallowed, staring at the apartment building on the corner. It was all too familiar. In fact, he'd barely been gone from it for more than a couple of days. Several floors up, there was a hole in the side of the building billowing smoke.

His stomach twisted with sudden nausea. "That's…"

"Yes." Lizzy's whisper was grim. "It is. They still think we're in the city. They're trying to freak us out. Letting us know they found the actual apartment we were in."

"Did they just search it?" He had an insane moment to wonder if they'd found the excellent sandwich-making supplies in the refrigerator.

"Maybe. They could be watching to see if anyone leaves the building now, or one of the other apartment buildings nearby." Two or three people had their smartphones out, taking pictures or video of the destruction. Lizzy was doing the same. "Or maybe they're watching the hotel registers to see if anyone checks into a hotel somewhere downtown immediately after this. Someone who didn't have a previous reservation."

More and more people were gathering. He wanted to look around wildly, see who might be watching. Who might find him.

Lizzy's hand clamped on his arm like a vise. "Keep watching what everyone else is watching. It's another tac-

tic. They don't know if we're here. It's an act of desperation. They're trying to startle us into running. Otherwise,
we'd already be dead."

Desperation.

There was a tickle at the back of his throat. Maybe it
was the dust from the explosion. He wanted to cough.
He wanted to laugh hysterically. "I'd be dead."

"We. We would be." Lizzy put her phone away. "They
have to know you couldn't hide for this long by yourself.
They'd drop who was with you too. But this tells us a
couple of interesting things."

Concise was one thing. A dislike for stating the obvious was completely understandable. Her propensity for
being vague and understating the situation was giving
him anxiety issues.

"You must be kidding." He would've started walking
up or down the street—for God's sake—in any direction, but she held him in place. They continued to stand
among more and more people as they gathered to gawk
now that the initial panic had subsided.

"Breathe," she advised.

Fine. In through his nose, out through his mouth,
with his hand half covering the lower part of his face
to fend off the worst of the dust still hanging in the air.
Like everyone else.

"This is crazy." He looked at her, stared at her. She
was vibrant to him. Alive in this situation. This was her
element, handling a situation he'd previously only ever
imagined via television or movies. Through every moment they'd been together from the night he'd met her,
she'd taken in everything without a hint of uncertainty.
This was her work.

"This is wrong." Her jaw was set. "It's a danger to bystanders. It's a jackass move."

"You wouldn't do something like this. Nobody sane would." He was incredibly relieved when she didn't correct him. Sometimes you said something so the person could prove to you that your assumption was correct.

"Sane people have done awful things. Insanity isn't a thing somebody either is or isn't." Her response came out flat. She turned, catching the crowds in the video on her phone before returning to the smoke pouring from the gap in the side of the building. "I haven't done this, here. No. But don't go thinking of me as a good person either. Don't."

He'd wanted to know more about her. Now it was coming too fast to absorb, comprehend. It was more than intimidating, coming to grips with so many revelations. He'd known she could kill. He hadn't considered just how much her career choice required actively doing it. But as she hadn't withdrawn from him, the least he could do was absorb what she'd shared. Process the truth of it. He wouldn't react without thinking. So he backtracked to steadier ground. "You're sure we shouldn't be at least making our way to the edge of the crowd?"

"Nope. In the crowd, we're as safe as we can be. They're probably above us. They can't take a close look at people's faces on the street level. Otherwise, they'd have taken a shot at you by now, or at least sent more thugs to get you isolated. Muscle can snag us from the edge of the crowd in this kind of panic. It'd be a lot harder with us in the middle."

She didn't need to tell him not to look up. He'd already absorbed that lesson earlier. The sirens were getting closer, different kinds. He wondered if she could tell the difference between police and emergency response vehicle sirens.

"Any chance they don't know my face?" Amazing he hadn't asked her yet. She'd constantly made him wear sunglasses of varying shapes and sizes whenever they'd been outside. But they were here, out in the open, and he had a wild hope.

"They know it. It's easy to find as part of a background check." A pause. "Most biotech companies require photo ID on employee badges. They'd have the picture from your employer at least. Could get it from the DMV too, assuming you have a driver's license.

Fear wrapped around his belly and squeezed tight. "Do you ever lie to make someone feel better?"

"You can hold your shit together." She sounded sure. He wasn't. "You've never had to before. Not like this. But you can. Just another couple of minutes and we walk away with the other rubberneckers. Wait for the police to come and secure the area. When they tell people to move along, we will."

He wanted to run down the street, indoors, go anywhere. "Can't we just get in a police car? Let them take us someplace safe."

"What if they've paid off some of the police?"

Cold ran through him with Lizzy's question. He kicked himself for not having thought of it before, especially when she so obviously had.

"You're safe in the crowd. Don't make eye contact. Don't bolt. Go with the flow of foot traffic."

Police arrived, finally. They got out of their squad cars and started waving people on by. Lizzy kept her hand on his arm and led him away.

As they walked, she raised a mobile phone to her ear. It wasn't the smartphone she'd been using earlier.

"What are you doing?"

"I'm making a call while we're on the move." Lizzy was amazingly calm. "We're taking a big loop around the block."

"Seriously?" He mentally scrambled trying to see how any sort of phone call made sense when she had insisted on no contact until now.

"Part of the info we just received is enough to shock me and I've seen a lot of horrible things in my time. We're going to want to keep walking if we're going to talk about this."

"Hello?"

The man on the other end of the call sounded both disgruntled and eager. Then again, she'd balanced her brief chat with the administrative assistant to both bully the poor girl and bait Kyle's former employer into taking her call.

"Mr. Douglas, I'm glad I was able to reach you." She kept her tone pleasant, bland. Next to her, Kyle missed a step as they walked and glared at her.

"Who is this?"

Lizzy allowed her smile to come through with her words. "An interested party. I was able to uncover your contact information in conjunction with the trial coming up shortly involving a certain biotechnology company."

There was a pause. "I don't speak to the press."

"The press doesn't have access to you, Mr. Douglas, and you know your administrative assistant wouldn't have connected the call to you if I was a journalist." Lizzy chuckled. "I'm an independent contractor aware of the very sloppy work some of your current associates have been leaving all around downtown."

"I don't know what you're talking about." Douglas harrumphed.

"You do." Okay, she'd managed nice for enough of this exchange. Victoria would be proud of the practice she put in. "You're looking for Kyle Yeun and I have him. You want him bad enough to dangle that woman and her kid on TV for him. I think you've got deep enough pockets to pay me for this phone call and my help."

Another silence as Douglas obviously considered. "How much do you want?"

"Ah, ah." Lizzy glanced over at Kyle and rolled her eyes. The gesture took a fraction of tension out of his shoulders and he continued to walk and occasionally pause so she could look in the reflection of the glass storefronts. "I have a reputation to maintain and he believes I am on his payroll at the moment. I can convince him that I've arranged for a trade. Him for his family. Once the trade is complete, I'll simply fail to rescue him from you. In terms of compensation, I want double the fee you're currently paying your sniper from Edict."

"Done." Douglas answered too quickly. "How did you know about Edict?"

"I have a former colleague in the organization, you can check with her as a reference if you'd like. Her name is Jewel."

Douglas let out an impatient huff. "Not someone I'm familiar with but I'll put in an inquiry."

"You might want to provide feedback about the lack of finesse your current man has while you're at it." All right, that wasn't necessary. She had a mean streak to her and she also didn't have the opportunity to taunt her opponent directly. But she was both irritated and appalled by the explosion and the collateral damage it might've incurred.

And she was also sure now that she wasn't going to be head-to-head with Jewel.

"Have Yeun come get his family at 2:00 a.m. on Harbor Island," Douglas growled. "B-Two Ten on the lot."

"Will they actually be there?" Lizzy took her pitch back to a sweet lilt. "I'd really prefer if he believed everything was going the way I said it would."

"They'll be there. We'll deal with everyone at once." He was sure of himself.

"Pleasure doing business." Lizzy ended the call before the guy warmed up to his super villain role. Really, could the man get any more predictable?

She and Kyle stepped into Post Alley, making a show of cuddling in a doorway. "Seriously, how did you stand working for that man?"

Kyle's arms tightened around her waist. "I'm overjoyed not to have to report to him any longer."

She sighed. "I've arranged a time and a place for a theoretical trade to get them back. You have about thirty seconds to decide whether I'm actually going to hand you over to him."

He'd be stupid not to consider it. But they didn't have much time for him to decide whether he was going to trust her or not and he definitely didn't have time to seek out other alternatives.

"Well, when you put it that way, how can I possibly doubt you?" The amusement in Kyle's voice tickled her.

He was a smart man and she'd had the discussion right in front of him. So maybe she wanted to hear him say he trusted her. Especially considering the way she'd gone harsh on him directly before the explosion. The weight of his arms around her, the twinkle of mischief in his warm brown eyes and the upturned corner of her mouth were all reassurances.

At least one of them liked the person she was.

"Tonight, I'm going to prove your confidence in me isn't misplaced." But first, she needed to acquire some additional reinforcements.

Chapter Nineteen

"I'm going to need to make contact with Safeguard." Lizzy tossed the disposable cell phone into a streetside trash can and took out her smartphone, scrolling through screens with her thumb.

"If we're going to walk all the way to the offices, we're headed in the wrong direction." Kyle was not thrilled about traveling the distance. It would take hours. Perhaps she could be convinced to hail a cab. Or they could walk into any nearby hotel lobby and have the bellmen get one for them. It would satisfy Lizzy's insistence on staying inconspicuous.

"No. We're staying in downtown." Lizzy glanced up and around for a long moment before going back to consulting her phone. "Safeguard is managing security for a charity a few blocks from our hotel this evening. Specifically, it'll be my teammates on duty. We can contact them there."

"Coincidence?" He had trouble accepting it. It was very convenient.

"Maybe," Lizzy said slowly, slipping her phone back into her pocket. "Or Diaz wanted to make sure he and the team were close enough to provide support if things got dicey closer to the trial. He'd do it for any of us. The man's instincts are freaking amazing sometimes."

Her team was her family, he realized. They trusted each other to stand on their own and they were on hand in case they were needed. It was a far cry from the cutthroat corporate environment he'd been in at Phoenix Biotech and closer to the family business his father had run until they'd been bought out early in his career.

"They'll be providing private security for a charity event tonight." She had them pause as she pretended to fix her hair in the reflection of a storefront. "I can slip in and connect with any one of them. It's just a question of getting in, blending and then walking out again. They'll be able to finish up the event and meet with us afterward."

"And we need them?" He didn't want to spend all night arguing his cause to more people. His family could die while they all told him how important his testimony was.

Lizzy came to a stop and pulled him close, making it look like they were taking a selfie. He complied and assumed a silly pose. On the screen of the smartphone was a horrific image.

He swallowed hard as Lizzy used her thumb to swipe the screen, showing him another, then a third. They were photos of dead people, laid out next to a shipping container. Bloated, discolored, rotted, they weren't recognizable at all but they were *people*.

Finally, Lizzy tapped the screen and switched to a text document with several names accompanied by contact information, including his employer.

"They found what was inside the shipping containers," Lizzy whispered. "You thought they might be smuggling something, drugs, whatever. But it was much worse. This is definitely worth your life."

Even when she released him and tugged him back into a walk, he had trouble shaking off the shock of it.

"Look, it's a lot to absorb and I don't blame you for worrying. This is your family we're talking about, and your life. I've done okay on my own but to make sure this goes the way it needs to, I need reinforcements." Her gaze caught him up and held him with soul-deep sincerity. "We're not military or police, tied up in red tape, having to follow procedure. The Centurions will do the right thing. So once we do this tonight, we'll make sure your family is safe, and then you need to do the right thing too."

She wanted him to testify. This was the first time she'd expressed her opinion of whether he should or shouldn't. But this news, those dead people, mattered to her. If he didn't testify, they'd have died with no one to take responsibility for their deaths.

So far, Lizzy hadn't led him in the wrong direction.

"Best chance to make the trade and get all of you out safely." She didn't make him a promise. He was glad she didn't try to give him hollow reassurances. "You can't do this by yourself and I'm not enough to keep you safe and your family too."

"I've seen you do some amazing things all by yourself." He smiled and was rewarded by a small return smile from her.

"I can do a lot of things solo. I like it that way." She huffed out a breath. "But this requires a team."

They continued down the street, stopping in the shelter of a fountain to sit and watch people walk by.

After a moment, Lizzy spoke. "If I wanted to stick to

the exact letter of my contract and only keep you safe, I'd have to tie you up or sedate you until the trial. It'd be for your own good."

"I'd never forgive you." Even the thought of it made his stomach clench and he considered running down the street, away from her. But worse than not knowing where he'd go, he wouldn't know who to ask for help.

It would be stupid and he would end up dead.

"I wouldn't forgive me either." Lizzy leaned back as her gaze swept across the high buildings and rooftops. "So we step up our game and upgrade this to a team operation."

He was grateful. So much so, he didn't have the right words. Thank you seemed too simple. And it felt un-lucky to say it yet.

Lizzy gave Kyle time to work through whatever was going on in his head. Apparently, he was good to go be-cause he stood and tucked her hand into the crook of his arm, tugging her along a few feet. "Well, it looks like we're headed back to Pike Place Market."

"For what?" She lengthened her strides to match his, noting the pace of the tourists and businesspeople around them. It was the end of the workday and the streets were becoming much busier.

Good. Easier to get lost in the crowd. Though she was going to have to stash him someplace and go back for her gear at the other hotel.

"You wanted to slip into the private party tonight to talk to your teammates." Kyle didn't resist when she pulled him onto a side street to change their course.

"Yeah, there's not a lot of time for me to figure out what catering company they have and get hold of a server's uniform." She wondered if she could be so lucky to have Maylin's company catering the event. There was a chance. Maylin was one of the top caterers in the city.

"Ah, but that's your usual approach." Kyle made a *tch, tch* sound. "You said we needed to become harder to predict, blend in more. Be harder to find."

"Yes." For a man who'd almost died the other day, and been caught next to an explosion intended to flush him out today, he was sounding way too upbeat.

All right, she was being dramatic. Edict hadn't found him yet, hadn't realized he'd been so close.

Kyle nodded. "I'm done hiding and ducking for cover. From here on out, I want to outsmart our opponents. Walk right past their noses before they realize we've been there. Today, they threw a temper tantrum because they found where we were and didn't find us, based on what you told me. I wish to drive them into insanity wondering where we are."

"Don't get full of yourself. Today was lucky. If we hadn't been part of that tour group, you could've been spotted coming out of the store when the blast drove us all out into the street." He needed caution and a healthy fear for his goddamned life. Hell, she was afraid for his life.

"That's just it." He tipped his head back and studied the sky. "It's only a matter of time in a cat-and-mouse game. We need to change the rules because the longer we allow this to draw out, the more chance we have of losing. The game changer will be meeting up with your team and taking action."

As they crossed the street and entered the market area, melding into the press of people shopping in the tight hallways lined with goods, he laughed. "If we're going to do this, we'll do this the way I do things."

Lizzy stared at her reflection in the mirror.

"You're beautiful." Kyle was a dark shadow over her left shoulder. His words were simple, and when they first met a couple of days ago she'd shrugged his compliments off as meaningless. Candy offered by a man to sweeten her mood. She'd never believed it to be sincere.

But she knew Kyle a little better since their first, brief meeting. Even if the time had been short, it'd been intense. Or maybe she was willing to believe the words more. Either way, his comment brought heat to her cheeks and a pleasant warmth blossomed in her chest.

The tiny cocktail dress she was wearing had been his choice and was the epitome of the stylish "little black dress." A simple black sheath covered by a sheer layer of chiffon cut to accentuate her figure and fall in a handkerchief hemline just short of her knees. It was sexy and elegant, daring and modest at the same time. There was even enough swing in the skirt to more or less hide the line of her handgun, holstered on her thigh. She'd never have chosen something so perfect herself. Hell, she hated trying on clothes. For her, it was all about the accessories.

And the shoes.

He'd picked this dress out from a rack at one of the shops around Pike Place Market though. She had no idea how he'd spotted it or known how it would look on her. Then he'd found her the shoes. At first glance, they'd been simple black pumps. Then Kyle had lifted the pair to show the heel and the pale cream silk with black lace ribbons tied in a tasteful bow. They were elegant. Sophisticated. Feminine.

Everything she loved about a pair of shoes and exactly the opposite of what most people would assume she'd wear.

They were what he thought she could be when most people only saw what she did for a living.

"Thank you." She smiled at his reflection in the mirror.

He raised an eyebrow. "You're getting better at taking a compliment."

She lifted a shoulder, left bare by the cocktail dress. "You're getting better at giving real ones."

He stepped closer to the mirror, and her, adjusting the lapel of his suit. The man did clean up well. Good suits had something in common with military uniforms. They could make a person look sharp. But it took a certain kind of man to put it on and own it. He might not be a soldier by her terms of experience, but he was a man of action and having him at her side tonight was actually a welcome comfort. Her nerves were steady and she didn't have the itch between her shoulder blades urging her to constantly look around to see who might be creeping up on her.

"Why the sudden frown?" Kyle placed a hand on her shoulder, the heat of his touch seeping through her skin.

Her nipples tightened slightly in response and she firmly told her libido to rein it in for the next few hours.

She looked at her reflection in the mirror again and blinked. Her face had gone neutral. Blank. It was one thing to know you wiped your expression to hide your thoughts and it was a completely different thing to catch

a glimpse of yourself doing it. Not bad. Just…a learning exercise.

Turning up the corner of her mouth she gave a slight
shake of her head. "A girl could get used to the idea of
having you around. It's a dangerous concept."

He gave her a playful leer. "Am I that distracting?"

Turning to face him, she flicked an imaginary speck
of dust off his shoulder. "Maybe. Not the issue though.
You put people at ease. It's a hell of a skill. But I can't
afford it."

His expression faded slightly. "It's not my intention
to distract you or take your edge away."

"You don't." She wanted to reassure them both. "I
won't let you."

Somehow the silence after her statement echoed in
the hotel room. *Awkward* wasn't the word for it.

"I'll make sure I'm on point." She wanted to clarify.
Wanted to take away the words that sounded too much
like a rejection. But it wasn't as if he'd made a long-term
offer. So why was she suddenly stumbling over her own
words? "You be sure to follow the instructions I gave
you. No horsing around."

He chuckled. Of course he'd get up to a few things.

It was a risk, taking him along. But Kyle had a couple of good points. He was safest with her and he also
helped her blend into the kind of crowd this social event
was expecting far better than if she went in there alone.
Definitely less predictable than her trying to infiltrate
the catering staff. Their pursuer probably didn't know
her face. Since this was a masked gala, they wouldn't
recognize Kyle's behind the solid black domino he'd ac-
quired, and there was a low likelihood they'd anticipate
him making an appearance in any case.

To be on the safe side though…

"Let's get some of the gray streaked into the sides of your hair."

Kyle scowled. "Is it really necessary?"

"It's about stacking the deck in our favor." She waited. "The people after you have you pegged for midthirties. They won't be looking for a silver fox."

"That might be the closest you've ever come to saying you find me irresistible." When she only huffed at his statement he sighed and shrugged out of his jacket. "I probably should've anticipated this before I got fully dressed."

"True." She reached into her duffel and came out with the hair chalk. Easy application and it did wonders to change a person's look in seconds. Just as easily removed for another quick change later. She tossed it to him.

"It's a good thing this is one of my older bespoke suits." Kyle caught the package of hair chalk neatly. "I've lost a few pounds over the last few days. Otherwise, the bulletproof vest would mar the fit of my suit noticeably."

"Fortunately, not a primary concern for tonight." He'd looked very good as far as she was concerned and she felt better having him wear the vest all the time. Wouldn't save him from a head shot, but it was protection from most shots taken at him.

"Perception is always a primary concern." He tossed the argument back over his shoulder as he stepped into the bathroom. "Sometimes you don't want people to notice you, sometimes you do. There are times to be recognized as the center of attention and others when it's more advantageous to skirt the sidelines. The point is, you always want to have optimal control over how you are perceived."

True. A skill some people worked on for years and one she hadn't gotten the hang of yet. "You have a point there."

"Controlling perception is fairly challenging. I've found the game to be an interesting mental exercise over the years." His voice projected well even from the bathroom and she made a mental note not to let him talk her into having sex in there.

If they had sex again.

And damn it, the man had her thinking about bedding him when he wasn't even trying.

"In my line of work, I'm mostly trying to stay out of sight." As a sniper, she'd been in many situations where both her mission and her own life depended on remaining undetected.

"Perception is still applicable to the situation, arguably." He came out of the bathroom combing his fingers through the sides of his hair. The gray streaks were heavy, beginning to look more natural as he blended them into his hair. "I guessed you wanted me to apply generously in this case."

She noted and crossed the distance between them to help him blend just a bit more. The chalk changed the texture of his hair a little too. The strands were a touch more coarse. "Good news is, now you have an idea of how you'll look in a few decades when you actually go gray."

He left off finger-combing his hair, surrendering to her ministrations, and placed his hands on her hips instead. "I'm rather curious as to whether you'll still find me desirable around then."

She laughed. No answer for him though. She'd never thought ahead more than a few weeks, much less decades. Plus, he was fishing. She wasn't entirely certain what he was hoping to hear in response but she didn't want to make an ass out of herself if she was misunderstanding.

Instead she straightened his collar and didn't quite meet his gaze. "Let's get through tonight, then survive tomorrow. One day at a time."

"Lizzy." His voice had dropped from his playful conversational tone to a deeper, rougher sound. "Too many uncertainties are between now and tomorrow. I want you to know these last few days have had an impact on me."

Her too. But just saying so would sound flippant, at least to her. Of course, her mind was going into overdrive so she was imagining all sorts of directions this conversation was going.

Give her a target and a rifle. Make life simple. Then she only ever had to have the right timing to hit her mark.

"Whatever happens, I would like to be able to find you again," Kyle continued. "I would like to continue to explore this thing between us."

She bit her lip and finally met his gaze. "I'd like that too."

Kyle's dark brown eyes were serious. Sincere. "Will I be able to find you?"

She owed him absolute honesty. And she didn't have a good enough answer for him, not right now. "I don't know."

There were decisions outstanding. And to make those, she needed to think ahead more than a few weeks.

After a long moment, Kyle put his hands on her hips and turned her so she was looking into the full-length mirror again. "After tonight, it will be different. You change your hair, your accessories, your appearance at a moment's notice and it is easier than a children's game for you. I will not catch up to you if you don't want me to."

She studied the two of them in the reflection. They looked good together, she thought.

He used one hand to brush her hair off her shoulder, exposing the nape of her neck. Leaning in, he breathed deeply against her skin, his hot breath sending delicious shivers through her as he exhaled. "We have now."

"We have like fifteen minutes before we need to get going."

He chuckled, the sound coming from deep in his chest. "We can be quick and still make a lot of things happen. We'll make the most of now."

And he kissed her neck as he set his hands on her hips to hold her steady. He pressed his own hips into her ass, making her very aware of his hard erection. She let her lips part, and didn't argue.

His gaze lifted and met hers in the reflection. "Watch us."

Chapter Twenty

Kyle ran his hands up her sides then, lifting her arms and encouraging her to place her hands on the wall to either side of the mirror. As she complied, he kissed the smooth skin of her shoulder and the soft curve of her neck. Something about the spot where her neck met her shoulders was his favorite. He wanted to breathe in the scent of her there and kiss, even bite ever so gently.

Then he ran his hands back down her arms and over her back, around her torso and up her belly to cup her breasts. The tempting weight of her breasts filled his palms and he squeezed briefly. She rewarded him with a soft gasp, letting her eyes shutter closed.

Oh yeah, this mirror was going to be very useful.

He pressed his hips into her ass, rolling them to be sure she felt the hard ridge of his cock. "Eyes open, Isabelle. You don't want to miss this."

Long lashes lifted to reveal those liquid dark eyes, and the desire he saw there made him want to be inside her right away. He pressed himself against her again and struggled for patience.

He had a few other things he wanted to do first.

Releasing her, he stepped back just enough to reach under her skirt and hook the sides of her panties with his thumbs. He knelt then, drawing her panties downward and caressed her legs all the way to her ankles. When he reached the floor, she stepped out of the delicate underwear without prompting. Balling up the tiny bit of silk, he tucked it into his pocket so they didn't lose track of it.

Looking up under her skirt, he enjoyed the sight of her shapely behind and lifted his hands to grip her just at the tops of her thighs. He squeezed once and she groaned in response, spreading her legs a little for him.

"More," he told her. "I want you open for me."

She shifted her weight, spreading her legs to a wider stance.

He smiled, looking up at her in the mirror's reflection. "These shoes are incredible on you."

Her eyes flickered as her gaze darted to the shoes and back to him. Color rose up in her cheeks. He wondered if she'd ever admired herself in a mirror before.

"You're beautiful," he told her. Because it bore repeating, even if she'd heard it a hundred times.

Then he angled his shoulders between her legs, further encouraging her to open to give him access. Steadying her with one hand on her thigh, he used the other to spread her with his fingers and he flicked his tongue against her clit.

She cried out and her thighs trembled, squeezing together, but his shoulders kept her open for his pleasure. And he took it for both of them, licking and exploring, finding her most sensitive spots and learning how to tease the best response out of her. He swirled his tongue and heard her whimper. Then he licked in a long sweep, pressing hard as he did.

Oh, his Lizzy liked that.

He did it again, gripping her thigh to hold her in place as she squirmed.

Pausing, he looked up at her. "Hold your skirt up for me, so I can see you."

Her breath came out in shallow pants as she removed one hand from the wall to gather up the front of her skirt and held it to her chest.

He kept his gaze on her face as he tasted her again. She moaned and closed her eyes. He feasted. Licks and suckles, even a tiny nip here and there. All of it drove her mad and he enjoyed the way she moved her body, simultaneously trying to respond to him and encourage him.

He wanted to see her come apart in his hands, under his mouth, so he fastened his mouth over her clit and slide a finger inside her. A sharp cry escaped her as he did it and her inner muscles were wonderfully tight around his finger. Slowly, he set a rhythm, moving his finger in and out in time with the way he flicked the tip of his tongue against her clit.

She clenched her thighs even harder and froze, every muscle tensed.

He didn't stop, instead sucking at her clit as he continued to slide his finger inside her.

"Kyle!" Her orgasm took over and her body shook with it.

He withdrew his finger, stroking her through it and prolonging it as much as he could. When she was still, both her hands bracing her against the wall again, he rose to his feet behind her and undid his pants.

"Ah, Isabelle. You are irresistible."

She raised her head to look at him in the reflection.

Her lids were heavy over her eyes and a pleased smile played over her lips. "You are a very. Bad. Man."

He chuckled. "May I continue my bad, bad ways?"

Her lips parted. "I can't wait to see what you have in mind."

He grinned. It took only a few moments to retrieve and put on a condom. He returned and set one hand on her hip, pulling her toward him. He placed the other hand on the small of her back, encouraging her to bend over just a bit more. Then he slid inside her.

She moaned.

"Good?" He rocked against her, filling her.

"Yes," she whispered. Then she drew in air and repeated it louder. "Oh, yes."

Watching her abandon herself, the sheer pleasure on her face, almost undid him. He gritted his teeth and struggled to make this last, withdrawing slowly from inside her and plunging back into her. She called out, spreading her fingers wide on the wall and bracing herself more securely. "Harder."

He drew back again and obliged, thrusting into her hard and deep.

She nodded, barely coherent. "Do it again."

He took hold of her hips and did. And again. He started slow, rhythmic, to make sure he gave her what she wanted without hurting her. And she was making him work to keep his own control but his own pressure was building. He picked up the pace, his balls tightening as the sensations shot through him.

Her inner muscles tensed as she crested into another orgasm and he couldn't hold himself back any longer. He drove into her once, twice, and came inside her with mind-blowing release.

* * *

Lizzy's vision cleared while she was still trembling from the second orgasm he'd given her in...yup, less than fifteen minutes.

Whew. He hadn't been kidding.

In the reflection of the mirror, she watched Kyle walk into the bathroom and emerge a minute later with a hand towel. She appreciated the consideration.

Cleanup took a minute or so in comfortable silence. He stayed close, brushing his lips over her shoulder or helping steady her with a hand at her waist.

Finally, she turned to him and held out her hand.

He glanced down at her open palm, at his own groin, and back up to meet her gaze. Oh, another night, she was going to make him unbutton and do exactly what he was implying. Definitely.

"Panties." She raised an eyebrow at him.

He blinked at her in mock innocence. "You want them?"

There was an interesting idea. She'd never gone out to dinner without them, especially not wearing a dress like this. With him, it could be all sorts of dangerous.

"Yes. I will be wearing panties tonight. This is business." She would hold firm. She was not going to let him talk her out of it.

Even if he'd already coaxed her out of the panties anyway.

Gah. He was all sorts of bad things. He made her want to entertain so many ill-advised little ideas, she wasn't ever going to manage to remember them. Until he looked at her with those naughty eyes and that suggestive grin.

"Seriously." She gave him a scowl, even if she was giggling inside. "Hand them over."

He sighed. Then he made a production of pulling them out of his pocket ever so slowly. Staring at her, he kneeled down in front of her and held them so she could step into them.

Had she ever been so turned on by a man putting her panties on her?

Nope. But it was a great new experience.

Chapter Twenty-One

"Relax." Kyle gave the hotel bellman a wink as he held out his hand for Lizzy.

She set her heels on the ground before standing up out of the cab, the hem of her cocktail dress whispering around her thighs.

"I can't believe I let you talk me into this dress," she murmured.

"I thought you liked it." He definitely did.

"It looked fine when I was standing in front of the mirror." She let him transfer her hand from his own to the crook of his arm so he could lead her inside to the ballroom. "I didn't realize how short it was going to be when I sat down."

"I did." He grinned as she freed her hand and swatted him across the shoulder.

"You're…"

"Incorrigible." He supplied a word for her since she seemed to be having trouble deciding on a descriptor of her own. Reaching out, he adjusted the delicate lace mask she wore to better show her eyes. "And you are beautiful."

She sighed. "I should've gone with my original idea."

Anyone overhearing her in the somewhat crowded

lobby might assume she was still talking about choice of wardrobe. But Kyle thought she was referring to the idea of slipping in with the catering staff.

"I like this idea better." Hotel personnel directed them toward a set of escalators leading to the mezzanine level and the ballroom. "Besides, would anyone who knows you anticipate this as your method of arrival?"

There was a moment and then she responded. "No. And they're never going to let me hear the end of it, either."

He might be going to hell for it, but he was enjoying her discomfiture. "You're acting as if this were prom and you were one of the teens that planned not to go."

"I didn't go to my prom." She smoothed the layers of her skirt against her right thigh.

She had a small gun strapped high on her thigh. He was torn as to whether it was incredibly cliché or irresistibly hot.

For the time being, he'd go with the latter and figure the former was a cliché because it worked.

"Why not?" They worked their way past the coat check, and they were not the only ones without outerwear, then joined the line to get into the ballroom.

"I was one of those teens who decided it was fine if I didn't go." Her response was flippant.

"I was joking." He regretted it too. Events like prom meant something to any teen growing up in the US, he thought, whether they went or not. It was iconic.

She shrugged, glanced at him, then smiled. "Hey, don't feel too bad. I didn't go because my brothers had a rule that anyone who wanted to take me had to ask them first. Only, they beat the sh—the bejesus out of anyone who got near me, so no one ever asked."

"I see."

"Your mouth is still twisted up in a frown. Let it go." She gave his arm a squeeze.

Ah. That explained how she read him so easily even with his own half mask. Thinking about it now, he schooled his expression to what he considered his usual half smile. Polite. Not overly impressed. But inviting someone to surprise him.

It worked with most people.

"I'm going to need to walk around the perimeter."

When she would have let go of his arm, he tightened his elbow against his side and covered her hand with his opposite one. "Going about things differently, right? You're a guest. If you want to blend, then you mingle."

She blinked. "You're kidding."

"I'm right." He snagged a wineglass off the tray of a passing waiter and handed it to her, then procured one for himself. "This sort of social function is my element. You're still thinking like security. Leave the security to someone else and enjoy the ambience instead. Even if someone is looking for me here, they'd have had to get past your own team. If I understand the situation correctly, this could be the safest we've been outside the hotel room."

He couldn't see her brows behind the mask but the corners of her mouth were drawn down in a frown.

"Blend. Yes?" He lifted his wineglass to her.

"I don't know how you talked me into this." Finally resigned, she lifted her glass to his and then joined him in taking a sip.

"It's fun to go against what's expected of you." At least he thought so. "Perhaps I'm a bad influence on you."

She huffed out a laugh. "I'd still be mad at myself because I'm the one who's letting you affect me."

They wandered the area for a few minutes and he greeted a few people. Ladies responded well to his compliments and men studied him, wondering if he was someone important.

In the past, he'd always been sure to have a lovely lady on his arm. He enjoyed the impression it presented. People were predictable and in these settings, he knew how to prompt the reactions he wanted. It was a mental exercise and an entertainment.

And people glanced at the lady he was with, just as they always did. The difference tonight was that everyone took a second look at Isabelle, and a third. For once, the lady at his side was more than an accessory.

Isabelle projected charisma and confidence even when she wasn't entirely sure of herself. She was lovely and entirely uninterested in catching anyone's notice. So of course they wanted her to notice them.

But her focus was still on the outer edges of the room and it was becoming obvious.

In a room full of people, she was the kind of person who drew the eye. Exactly what she didn't want.

As far as he was concerned, there was only one thing to do.

"Dance with me."

Dark eyes turned toward him. "Excuse me, what?"

He led her toward the dance floor. "You want your teammates to spot you and it's drawing the attention of everyone here. It's impossible for you to be inconspicuous, as gorgeous as you are right now. So everyone we talk to is wondering who you're looking for. Anytime we move on to talk to somebody else, the people we just left keep watching you to see if you've found who you were looking for. I'm both impressed and wondering how I can acquire the same quality."

"You're kidding." She sounded horrified.

"All of my fantasies of you as a super sexy spy have been shattered." As they reached the dance floor, he turned to her. "There're plenty of people with us on the dance floor. You don't have to be self-conscious. But since everyone looks at the dance floor once in a while to watch people dance, it'll make it easy for your team-mates to notice you."

She pressed her lips into a thin line and let him pull her against him, placing one hand in his and the other on his shoulder. "You could be right."

"I know I am." He grinned.

"I could also suck at dancing."

He laughed then. "I'm a strong lead. Trust me."

Dancing was an art. Done well, dancing could be sex of the socially acceptable kind. The first few steps were simple, patient, giving her time to get over her hesitation and let him lead. As she grew more comfortable, he coaxed her into a turn or two and took the opportunity to pull her back in close. He liked the feel of her in his arms, liked the way her lips parted slightly as he pressed his hand into her lower back and encouraged her hips to press against his.

Her eyes widened as he stepped forward, toward her. She was forced to step back in response or end up with his thigh between hers. Once she did step back, he con-tinued for a few more steps then took her in a different direction. When he did it again, she'd caught the hang of it and let them travel backward.

"Not many people dance anymore. You're a quick

learner." And too many women thought they were better than they were. He preferred not to count how many times a woman tried to anticipate what he was going to do and forced him to let her look awkward. Not Lizzy though, she was reserved and cautious, but she didn't misstep.

"How do you keep us from bumping into the other people on the dance floor?" She craned her neck a bit, trying to keep everything in sight.

"It's my job as the lead," he answered, turning her to avoid a slightly tipsy couple as they stumbled past, off-beat. "You don't have to watch the people immediately around us. You can look over my shoulder at the people beyond the dance floor. Let me worry about the immediate surroundings."

He knew better than to tell her not to keep watch around them. Despite his early assurance regarding the security of this event, he was glad she was still vigilant. It felt wiser to have someone literally keeping watch on what was behind him.

It wouldn't kill her to admit she was enjoying this. "This…doesn't suck."

"I'm glad." He looked down at her, the corners of his mouth turned upward in a sexy smile.

God, she already tended to look at his mouth a lot and with the mask hiding half of his face she pretty much had to focus on his mouth or his eyes.

Her breath tended to catch and her heart rate kicked up when she lingered too long on either.

Kyle was the best dancer she'd ever been with. Explained a lot about how good he was in bed too. What had he said before? Incorrigible.

Yeah, he was an incorrigible flirt.

Whenever she started to relax in his arms as they danced, he'd press his thigh between hers or slide his fingers up her spine, or do something else to make her completely aware of his body against hers. He was sort of torturing her.

She had never been interested in jumping a guy's bones in the restroom.

But there were other secluded spots in even the public parts of a hotel she'd be tempted to sneak away to.

"You are definitely a bad influence on me," she informed him.

He blinked, then his grin widened. "Care to share what naughty thoughts you have?"

"No." She considered. "Not yet."

Oh, she was not going to regret sleeping with him, but she absolutely was going to make sure to keep her mind on the current mission.

"Well, we've been dancing for a few songs now." He slowed, their steps carrying them to the edge of the dance floor. "Care for a drink, and maybe a bite to eat?"

"Sure." Actually, she really could use a drink. And seeing as the food tables had been set up on the outer edge of the ballroom, it was a good direction.

He tucked her left hand into the bend of his right arm again. She wasn't sure what proper etiquette was, but she was glad he was leaving her right arm free. If something did come up, her gun was on her right thigh.

She could shoot with either right or left, but when it came to handguns she was better with her dominant hand.

As they walked toward the buffet table, she recognized some of the staff. "Huh. My idea would've worked out after all."

"Hmm?" He had snagged another glass from a passing waiter. This time it was champagne.

She took it from him and they continued. "The caterer is a friend of mine."

"How many caterers do you know?" He sounded amused.

"Only the one. I know a couple of restaurant owners too." It was how she picked up food downtown when Maylin wasn't within easy contact. Knowing where you could get food prepared by people you trusted was a part of the reason she'd decided to stay downtown and not elsewhere in the Seattle area.

"So this is the person who cooked the excellent Korean meal." He picked up their pace a little.

She smiled. "Yes."

"I'd like to thank her."

"Maybe not tonight." It could come out odd if anyone overheard. "But from what I gather, the best way to thank her is to enjoy more of her food."

Maylin loved to cook for people. And as awkward as Lizzy was with people, it was easier to do things that made Maylin happy than it was to try to express it in words. Diaz didn't get why Lizzy was so hesitant to try telling people things, but Maylin got her.

Besides, everything Maylin made was good. More than good. Amazing.

"Unusual food selection." Kyle brought her attention back to the table. He handed her a small plate.

Rather than have both her hands full, Lizzy let go of his arm so she could carry the plate in her left hand. "You think so?"

"A lot of catered buffets have 'safe' food choices. Roast beef, chicken breast prepared with a white sauce and a choice of pasta." He ticked off the list on one hand before taking up a plate of his own. "This has variety and smells phenomenal."

The buffet was set up with a selection of grilled foods. There was beef and chicken, as he'd mentioned, but there was also lamb and pork. There were also a few types of sausages. All of it had been prepared Brazilian barbecue-style, seasoned and presented with a few of her favorite side dishes.

"I'm not familiar with this." He had stopped by a dish of rice and black beans.

"*Feijoada con arroz.*" She supplied the name for him. "Next to it is fried polenta."

"Ah." He took a small amount of each.

As he did, she snagged several small round puffs of bread.

"I take it you like those?"

"I never miss out on *pão de queijo* if I can help it." She popped one in her mouth.

There was no way Maylin had done this for her. The coordinator of the event chose the menu. But if anyone ever wanted to lure her somewhere, Maylin's *pão de queijo* might do it.

When they reached the end of the buffet, Lizzy caught sight of an empty table. The raised tabletop meant people had to stand to eat there. Considering most women were already in chairs, probably regretting their shoe choices, it wasn't odd for this one to be unoccupied.

Plus, Diaz was standing near it looking intimidating.

She went ahead and claimed the table for herself. Kyle was a step behind.

"Some party," she said to no one in particular.

Diaz didn't respond but he did manage to loom closer.

Kyle looked out onto the dance floor. "Should I wander away?"

"No," Diaz said at the same time she did.

"Ah, I wondered when we were going to start talking then. I guessed this sort of thing was supposed to be kept brief."

Diaz groaned. "This is overly dramatic."

"And yet, not as bad as it could be," Kyle replied.

"There's a few complications." Lizzy took a sip of champagne.

"We saw the interview when it ran on the news." Diaz sighed. "Combine that with two explosions on the same street and the police calling us demanding to know where you were, I figured."

"Yup." Not much explanation required. "Shooter was Edict, but not our old friend."

A pause. Then Diaz responded, "Good to know. I'm also curious as to why the US Marshals aren't asking me where you are."

She lifted a shoulder delicately instead of shrugging. Victoria would be so proud. "I met with Nguyen once before the shit hit the fan, once after. He's trusting me to handle things for now."

"Okay," Diaz said slowly. "I should be happy to hear it but I'm wondering why."

"A question for another day." She meant for it to come out lightly, but it really was something to worry about later. They had more urgent tasks. "We've got an appointment at oh-two-hundred hours and I'd appreciate help."

"Where?" Diaz asked.

She told him, plus the rest of what had been on the microSD card. It took a split second for that bit of information to sink in, even for Diaz. They'd all seen a lot and this kind of thing, innocent victims, hit hard. It wasn't more than a moment, but it was still there, because they were still human.

Kyle, for his part, remained silent during the exchange. He listened and idly sipped champagne. Once in a while he smiled as if in response to something said.

He would be a better spy than she would be.

"This is a tough scenario but it can work out." Diaz said finally. "You'll need to get to the area as soon as possible and pick your position."

Her sniper opponent might've already gotten there. She'd need to find a vantage point without running into him. Or take him out if she did.

"Marc and Victoria will make sure Mr. Yeun arrives safely, ostensibly alone," Diaz continued. "And they will oversee extraction. I will provide cover at the ground level. Keep your comm with you and turn it on at the meeting time."

It was a plan, elegant in its simplicity. Straightforward. Diaz would flesh out and handle the details on the ground. If she needed audibles, he'd make sure to call them out when the time came. "Copy."

"Huh?" Kyle asked.

"We have a plan." She smiled at him. "You'll be in good hands."

The best, as far as she was concerned. And she'd worked with a lot of professionals over the past several years. This, the confidence she experienced with the barest of discussion required, was what she wanted as

she continued to work. Puzzle pieces came together and
fit when she coordinated with Diaz and their fire team.

"Where do you want Victoria and Marc to meet you?"
Diaz paused as a few couples walked by. "Or do you
want to just check in here?"

"Might be best." Now that they were planning, she
figured it would be perfect.

"Victoria will meet you."

"Okay. Once Kyle is secure here, I'll need to head
back to get my gear."

Diaz raised an eyebrow when she referred to Kyle by
name but didn't comment. Instead, he turned to Kyle.
"Once your family is out of harm's way, we'll arrange
for a safe house for them until the trial is over. It will
have to be separate from you."

Kyle raised an eyebrow and glanced at Lizzy. She
shrugged. It'd ripped Diaz to shreds a few months ago
when they'd wanted to take action to rescue Maylin's
younger sister and had to stand by. The two full squadrons of resources, weapons and ammunition plus communications and technical support it required was more
than any single person could fund. When it came to a
temporary sanctuary, they could provide that and work
out the budget later.

There would always be tough decisions to make,
when doing the right thing wouldn't be this doable. Diaz,
and all of them, tended to help where they could and
when they could.

"All right." She slipped her hand into the bend of
Kyle's arm. "Let's get through this."

Tonight's outcome was going to determine whether
or not he'd have the chance to build the life he'd been
planning for his family, and for himself. He'd made the

past couple of days…fun, more than fun. He'd become someone important to her.

She wanted him to have his future.

Chapter Twenty-Two

"That's it?" Kyle was almost making her drag him across the ballroom. At least he was keeping his voice down.

"That's what we needed." Lizzy exchanged smiles and nods with a few of the people they'd chatted with earlier.

Nothing to see here, moving along. Yeah, hello. Smile and nod.

She waited until she could speak to him again without anyone overhearing. "Diaz will set up the key details with the rest of the fire team. I'll go ahead to scout. We'll make necessary adjustments at go time."

"I thought there would be a lot more planning." Kyle sounded unsure.

She didn't blame him. "Regardless of whether our former colleague is directly involved, Edict as an organization knows the Centurion Corporation and Safeguard in particular. They've had time to research personnel profiles and get to know strategy and tactics used in the past. Now that they know we're at least tangentially involved, they'll be looking to encounter us again even if they don't exactly know when. One of the most effective ways to remain unpredictable is if we ourselves don't all know the entire plan."

It required relying heavily on each team member as an individual with a key task. Not all fire teams could manage it. But theirs could.

"You've done this before, then, so it's not necessarily unpredictable." He was reaching for arguments now.

She wanted to reassure him but this entire job had all the aspects of having gone down the rabbit hole. "We've never done it to this extreme, no. But we can still make it work."

Kyle choked back a panicked laugh and picked up his pace until they were comfortably walking together, rather than her pulling him by the arm. "And we're headed where now?"

"A leisurely walk." She fluttered her eyelashes at him. "Ending at the front desk to reserve a room."

He gave her a long look. "This is a fairly large charity event."

"Yes."

He cleared his throat. "You're trying for a last-minute reservation."

"If I have to coax somebody into checking out, I will." Not the nicest thing she'd ever done, but hell, it'd happened in the past.

He rolled his eyes. "You could always offer to share a room with someone. I think we encountered at least two different couples who'd be interested."

"Unnecessary exposure for innocent bystanders." He was teasing, she knew. Though, looking at the smile playing around his lips, he might not be joking about the interested couples.

Hey, to each their own.

"Are you the type to…have fun in groups?" Fine.

She was distracted. Momentarily. But she did want to know the answer.

He leaned over her. "Are you?"

She shrugged. "Never occurred to me. I like my fun intense and personal."

He chuckled. "I've had the pleasure of entertaining a few close friends in the past, I'll admit. It can be an experience of a lifetime with skilled partners. But for the most part, I've satisfied my curiosity on the possibilities. I'm inclined to agree with you."

"Huh." No idea what to say to that. She took the time to scan the room again, noting familiar faces in contrast to new ones. Mostly, it was to buy her time. Unfortunately, he seemed to be waiting for a response. "Okay, I asked because I was wondering about your history again. I don't know why I keep asking. It's not like I think you having an active lifestyle is wrong or anything."

He pressed his elbow tighter against his side, squeezing her hand briefly without being obvious. "I am delighted when you ask anything about me. Your interest is flattering and your lack of jealousy to accompany it is a relief. I wish I could return the favor, but to be frank, the idea of someone else touching you brings out a very ugly side of me."

She was caught without an immediate comeback. Hell, she almost stopped in her tracks.

Kyle cleared his throat. "I realize I don't have the right to the sentiment, but it's there."

Her stomach flip-flopped and a tightness unwound in her chest. "Since we're being honest, I have to admit that I don't mind. It actually makes me feel wanted."

She was alternately appalled and amused by her own reaction. This was definitely headed into relationship territory, something she'd avoided for as long as she could remember. Relationships were like missions. The more complicated they got, the more likely they were to end badly.

"And I'm also not immune to being jealous." She tipped her head so she could look up at him. "I don't get my panties in a twist over your past adventures because it's done and before you ever met me. Random flirting is what it is. But the minute you're seriously tempted by someone else, we're going to find out how well I actually handle jealousy. It'll be a new adventure for both of us."

And wouldn't that be fun.

No, it wouldn't. Her stomach churned.

He blinked, then chuckled. "Your thought process is singularly unique."

He stopped and stepped around to face her, right there in the middle of the hallway. "Here and now, I am singularly captivated by you. I am very glad I haven't had to share you with anyone for the past few days and I hope very much to keep this going." He placed his hands on her shoulders and leaned in for a kiss.

She gave it to him, and along with it, a piece of herself.

"I don't even know what to ask for," he murmured. "So I'll enjoy this. Time with you."

His lips were hot against hers, his breath mixed with her own in a dizzying combination. With effort, she stepped back and took in enough air to clear her head. Stepping forward to take his arm again, she pulled them back into a stroll.

Time was about the only thing definable in this whole situation. They had a very little bit and there was no way to know what would happen in it.

"Glad you're enjoying it." She made a quiet, rude noise.

He outright laughed. "Thank you for sharing it with me."

And she *was* sharing with him. Not her usual behavior with any man, either on a mission or casually on a date. Communicating any more than the bare minimum was usually an awkward, conscious effort. But Kyle Yeun had a way of inviting her to confide in him by offering himself. He'd been open with her about his lifestyle, his wrongs, his intentions to make a better life, his family. All of it.

They did make their way to the front desk, after a pause in an alcove off the main hallway for some judicious kissing. She let him request the room, then coax the desk manager to find one for them when the initial response had been disappointing. Kyle not only turned on his charm, but also took on a sharp business edge too. In a few minutes, the desk manager was handing over hotel room keys with assurances of a late checkout noted on the room.

Nice touch.

But Kyle withdrew as they got in the elevator and farther away from people watching them. By the time they stepped out into the hallway, he was passive and thoughtful.

She led him down the hall and to the room, using the key to gain entrance and clearing the hotel room as she'd done with him in the past.

"You should be pretty comfortable here." It was a spacious room, decorated with a modern touch. "No Frederick to keep you company, but Victoria and Marc should be here in a few minutes."

"They watched us check in." Kyle was undoing his tie as he walked around the room. His words were given in a distracted, half-hearted attempt to keep up his side of the conversation.

She narrowed her eyes and waited until he stopped and met her gaze. "Is there a reason we should stop right now?"

"No!" Anger, temper, something flashed in his eyes. "This is…damn! I need my family safe. And I need to testify. You and your people are helping me. I'm thinking about all of that."

"Yeah? What's with you now? You're not you."

"Do you know me? Really? Why do this for me?" He sat on the edge of the bed, shoulders slumped.

It was a good question.

"Because you're doing a good thing." There'd been a lot of answers she could give him but some, having to do with her personal feelings, were too tangled up to say yet. Instead, she gave him the simple ones. The ones she'd have even if she didn't feel so much. "And your family doesn't deserve to suffer in order to hide the wrongs in all of this. Because this isn't a difficult decision to make. I can help, so I will."

Her fire team, Diaz in particular, had been faced with harder decisions and challenges to overcome to do the right thing. In this, her path forward was clear.

"Do you always do what needs to be done?" His question was laced with a hint of annoyance but the sharpness was hiding a more vulnerable note of hope.

Isabelle kept her gaze steady on his. "It doesn't matter if a thing is scary or dangerous, disgusting or boring. No matter how onerous a task is, it still remains to be done by somebody."

His scowl deepened as he listened to her but he didn't offer one of his usual teasing comments. He was having trouble holding on to the humor he used to keep his uglier emotions at bay.

Damn it, she wanted to give it back to him. As annoying as he was, rage-inducing sometimes, he was funny. He had a way of pulling a smile from her when she least wanted to give it to him. She ached for it a little, and for him.

So she gave him a small smile and imagined it was a sad offering as compared to the happiness he could spark in people, in her. "When I was young, my mother said it was often best to let those who are good at doing a thing complete the tasks. Because it will be done quickly and well, and hopefully not need to be redone."

It was about time for Victoria to check in with them. Lizzy stepped to the door and opened it, scanning the hallway. Victoria stood waiting at the far end. Her teammate gave her a nod and disappeared around the corner. She'd wait until Lizzy left, then come to the room.

Anyone who took notice would think Kyle was just having a lucky night.

"And this thing, the man who needs killing. You will do it." It wasn't a question. And the hope was there, shining through more clearly in his tone.

"I am very good at killing." A light inside her, the tiny flame he'd lit, died. And again, she was the cold, simple, clean killer she'd taught herself to be. It was part of why she was very, very good.

He was a civilian. There was a pretty high chance it'd sink in after all this was done and he'd try to get as far away from her as possible.

"Thank you." The words came from him as the corners of his mouth turned up. "For saving my family. No one else would've helped us."

Isabelle swallowed past the lump in her throat. She hadn't looked at it that way. Hadn't even tried.

She wasn't special. She didn't want to believe there weren't other people in the world who would do this. There had to be. It was faith in human nature and all that. For all the truly despicable things humans had done to each other through history, there had to be people to inspire the happy endings.

Legends and all that shit.

She wasn't a legend. She was a person trying to do something because she cared.

"Victoria and Marc will be ready with a car. Make sure you get to the car."

"Your instructions are burned into my brain." He tugged at the pristine white cuffs peeking from beneath the dark fabric of his suit sleeves.

She shook her head. "Every plan goes to hell. Plan A, plan B, whatever. Things never go as planned. Keep the objective in mind and just do what it takes to get there."

He was silent for a moment, absorbing what she'd implied. "I'll get my family to the car."

She nodded, accepting his prioritization. "All of you would be best case. Go for best case. You're wearing your Kevlar vest?"

"Yes." Kyle tapped two fingers against his chest. The sound confirmed the presence of a layer beneath the fine fabric of his suit still.

She'd checked before they'd started this evening. It wasn't like he would've taken it off. But it felt better to check again.

Victoria and Marc would be at the ready to pick up

Kyle, his sister and her son. They'd get the Yeuns to safety. Her teammates were very good at what they did too.

"What about you?" Kyle's gaze had become more intense.

Truth? She didn't have a spotter. The person who could murmur observations and distance measurements. Wind direction and speed. Their help increased the chance of an accurate shot exponentially. But she'd done very well without a spotter in the past. No. She wasn't worried about making her planned shots. She was more concerned about the other sniper.

She'd have to find him before he found her.

A spotter would've also been watching her six. They'd have been able to warn her of any direct attackers and given her cover as she scrambled into a position to defend herself.

She'd be vulnerable in her shooting position. From what she'd scouted using satellite images earlier in the day, there was no alternative. She'd know better once she was actually there.

"I'll make the best of what I've got to work with out there."

Chapter Twenty-Three

The moon was hidden beyond a low ceiling of clouds but it wasn't unusual for the Seattle area. It wasn't even going to be much of a problem. Live in or near a city of any decent size and there was always going to be a certain amount of ambient light no matter how late at night.

Lizzy was dropped off by the cab at the Harbor Island Marina. Theoretically, she worked there and had left her car in the parking lot. So the nice cabdriver, who'd kindly offered to wait for her, drove away with a wave once she'd jingled some keys at him and assured him she would get home just fine.

The evening had been full of smiling and waving. Her cheeks hurt.

She'd traded her cocktail dress and gorgeous shoes for a simple black T-shirt and pants with dark combat boots. Now that the cabdriver had driven away, she slid on urban fatigues over her close-fitting clothes. It'd be warm but at least the patterning on the fatigues would break up her shape, make it harder to spot her.

Leaving the rest of her gear in her duffel, she slung it over her shoulder and headed north toward the shipping container areas covering the majority of the small island.

The cranes were visible in the night, rising up over

Harbor Island and looming against the immediate sky-line. Given the choice, she'd have made her way to the upper parts of one of them to choose her vantage point. But she'd had a party to get to and reinforcements to round up. Chances were, her opponent was already here and tucked into his own perch.

Damn the bastard for getting out here before her.

She kept as quiet as she could approaching the outer perimeter, sticking to whatever cover was available to her. The other sniper could take a shot at her at any time if he spotted her. She needed to find him first and neutralize him.

It was close to midnight and there wasn't a lot of time for this game. The two of them could sneak around for hours trying to get the higher ground and clear shot on the other. If he knew she was here.

Hell, she'd done this before and it had taken days before she'd managed to take down her opponent in the middle of nothing but dust and rocks and sand mites. And there'd been the goddamned camel spiders too. At least here the worst she had to worry about were roaches. Maybe.

Circling, she searched the shadows for him. Slow is smooth, smooth is fast. She continued to sweep her gaze systematically across the terrain as she let her training regulate the speed and rhythm of her blinking to keep her eyes fresh despite the strain of trying to see in the dark. After a short time, she began to search more efficiently as her eyes adjusted even further to the lower light.

Minutes ticked by and she worked up a sweat searching the outer rows. Finally, she waited for a facility lamp to flicker out and climbed a stack of shipping containers before the light stuttered back into brightness again.

Sucking in huge lungfuls of air once she got to the top, she struggled to keep as quiet as possible. Damn, running was fine but her ability to climb quickly but quietly could use some additional training.

Lying flat on the storage container, there was no higher point in the area with the exception of the cranes. From here, she hoped she'd be able to find him or else she'd be climbing the cranes one at a time to try to sneak up on him.

But she was betting he wasn't in the cranes. Based on his previous perch, the one she'd investigated with Kyle, he liked a sheltered nook with multiple choices for a hasty retreat. They were also susceptible to significantly greater influence by the wind coming up off the waterway. It'd make any shot more complicated. He was more likely to be on the shipping containers, tucked into a hidey-hole with a clear line of sight on the meeting place.

As her breathing normalized and her heart rate recovered, she shimmied farther along the top of her crate alligator-style to avoid unnecessary noise. At the edge, she waited until she recognized each of the night sounds. The splash of water against the edge of this industrial island out in the waterways. A random seabird or two. The dull roar of distant engines as planes left the nearby airports and flew past Seattle. She took each sound, identified it and disregarded it as she searched for the sound that didn't belong.

It was the scent that helped her locate him first. The sweet smell of bubblegum wafted to her as a light breeze picked up. She turned her face quickly into the wind and studied the area ahead of her.

She eased her own rifle and scope out of her duffel.

First she checked that the scope shade tape was still in place to be sure no random reflection of the scope would betray her location, then using the scope, she took a closer look at both the far stack and the near. Of course he wasn't lying directly on top the way she was. But she'd hoped to see some hint to give her a target. She had to find a way to identify where he was and get her shot.

At this point, she needed to do something unconventional to flush him out.

Leaving her rifle out, she slipped it into place across her back. Tightening the three-point harness hard against her body, she made sure it wasn't going to flail at all while she climbed. She shimmied back down off the high stack she'd been using. Reaching back into her duffel bag, she came up with a flare and a flash grenade. Neither of them was particularly quiet and both of them were about to ruin his night vision.

Hey, even ninjas require some help to go unseen.

She uncapped her glorified road flare first and closed her eyes as she lit and tossed it along the edge of the nearest container, aiming for the darkest shadow in the aisle. As it flew and skittered noisily across the ground she jogged toward the first stack, keeping far enough away to keep the top edge in sight. As she put distance between her and the flare, it began to burn brighter and brighter until a hundred new shadows danced in the red light.

There was a brief flash, catching her eye. She froze and slowly crouched down as she peered up at the first stack. There, the short end of the container, second from the top, had tarp stretched over its end instead of two closed metal doors.

A puff of white vapor slipped out from the edge of the

tarp. Hard to see, definitely. If she hadn't been watching for it she'd have missed it.

Gotcha.

She crept in close until she was pressed to the side of the bottom container of the stack. The metal wall of its side was cold and rough with rust. It smelled metallic and salty and she wondered how many times this particular container had traveled the Pacific.

Hefting the flash grenade, she considered her options. Flash grenades were heavier than they looked and made a decent amount of sound in conjunction with the blinding flash. Once it detonated, the light from the flash grenade would sear his retinas and potentially do permanent damage.

Which was why she was going to lob it someplace else and not be looking anywhere near its direction when it went off.

There wasn't much time before the rest of the team arrived with Kyle. This sniper needed to be neutralized and she needed to be in her own perch well before they arrived.

She yanked the pin, drew back her arm, released the handle, counted slowly to one-Mississippi and threw the flash grenade. Without waiting, she turned and began to climb as soon as it hit the ground and began to clatter along the asphalt. The tarp above her flapped slightly.

She definitely had the right location. Good. Otherwise, she'd end up shot in the back.

The flash grenade went off less than a second after bouncing, casting the metal under her hands in brilliant white light. She kept climbing, scrambling furiously now. As she reached the edge of her target container, she gathered her legs under her and launched herself into the tarps.

Heavy fabric parted for her and she plunged into darkness, hearing more than seeing the man inside. He'd been lying on the floor, close to the edge and she'd managed to land partially on him. As he rolled away from her, she managed to kick his trigger hand. His rifle fired and she kicked again, sending the rifle out and over the edge.

His knee connected hard with her cheekbone as he cursed.

She rolled onto her back and pivoted on her tailbone to bring both her legs together between them. Her two-footed kick contacted with the soft portion of his torso and she was rewarded with his grunt of pain.

In the dark, she heard the telltale click of the safety coming off his secondary weapon. Question was whether he could see her or not and how much time she had to disarm him.

She could see his faint form as a darker shadow against the black. He was in reach, she could do this. In two seconds, this would be over either way.

"It's five to two." Kyle stared at his watch. "Why aren't we getting out of the car?"

Marc sat in the driver's seat, dressed as a chauffeur. "Technically, we were just waiting here until it came time to drive out through the shipping container lot over there."

Lizzy's teammate was a genial man and tended toward a bit more easy conversation than either Lizzy or Gabriel Diaz. Despite using more words, Kyle was finding that Marc didn't actually answer his question any more than Lizzy did until he was ready to.

Tricky conversationalist.

"All right, why are we waiting?" Kyle was trying to be patient but he was reaching his limit.

Marc was looking around them, studying the other cars and surroundings. "Surveillance cameras are all disabled, as far as I can see. Doesn't look like Lizzy's work though."

"No? Is that bad?" Kyle leaned forward to peer through the tinted windows.

"Not necessarily." Marc tapped a small radio set against the dash. It wasn't a part of the car and didn't look like a model Kyle had seen before. But then, he didn't spend a lot of time noticing what was in the front of most car service vehicles. "We all break silence in a few minutes. There'll be a set of orders and we'll have confirmation about whether we're proceeding as planned. If Lizzy doesn't check in at that time, then we worry."

Two minutes never passed so slowly.

At exactly 2:00 a.m., the radio came to life.

"Diaz here."

Marc lifted a handset and spoke into it. "Lykke here. We're in position."

"Scott here."

Kyle sat back, relief flooding through him. Everything was going to be okay if she was out there.

Diaz's voice came across and it was grim. "We've run into a delay here closing up the charity event. Edict decided to pay us a visit. Guessing they anticipated you'd try to meet up with the team but they missed you. Ash and I are a minimum of thirty mike out. You're going to have to stall."

Kyle tried to swallow past a hard lump in his throat. Could they? "Who or what is Mike?"

Marc turned his head to answer over his shoulder. "Mike is minutes. Radio protocol tends to have us use 'mike' for minutes and 'sierra' for seconds. It's a military thing."

"Negative." Lizzy's voice was low and urgent. "They're here. I have eyes on one older businessman, three bodyguards and our two targets. This situation will not remain stable for thirty mike. It's going to be over in ten or less."

Diaz was for a moment. "Scott, are you in position?"

"A-firm." Lizzy was getting quieter or Kyle was having trouble hearing past the rush of his own blood in his ears.

"Can you provide cover?" Diaz asked. "We're en route. Will cut the time as much as possible."

"Copy that. Break," Lizzy responded again. "Lykke. Proceed with the exchange."

The semblance of a trade. Kyle for his family. Once they were safe, Lizzy would provide a distraction so he could get back to the car too. Marc would drive them away.

Marc put the car in Drive. "Affirmative. Diaz, confirm your position. If we have to, we'll reroute to rendezvous with you."

"Copy." Diaz responded. "We'll provide support as soon as possible."

Marc turned his head to speak over his shoulder again, suddenly dead serious. "Slight change in plans."

Kyle took in a deep breath and let it out slowly. "Lizzy said nothing ever works out the way it's been planned. That's why you don't make complicated ones."

That surprised a chuckle out of Marc. "Well, that's close enough to truth. We're very practiced at making field decisions. Too much can happen too fast and everything has to be done on the fly. I wouldn't try this if Lizzy wasn't out there."

"She's good." Kyle was certain of it.

"Very." Marc confirmed.

Then Marc was putting the car in Park again. "Let me get out first, then you. We'll hear the man out and make the exchange. Just don't get into their car, and try to stay clear of their people. Don't let them get hands on you if you can help it. Let us do the rest."

How did they live their lives like this? He took the wild thought and jammed it in the back of his mind. He could think about it later, if he survived. It was time.

The car door opened as Marc leaned in. "Ready for you, Mr. Yeun."

The man's voice had taken on a diffident tone and his demeanor had changed. He was suddenly very much a hired driver. Yeun kept his expression neutral as he stepped out of the vehicle. After a moment, he moved forward and stopped a few meters closer to the waiting group but still in easy reach of the car.

Huge shipping containers rose up in stacks on either side of them. The metal boxes were sized to be moved directly from the ocean barges to 18-wheeler trucks if necessary. Lined up as they were, they were intimidating and he felt closed in despite the wide expanse of asphalt all around them. There were dim utility lamps spread throughout the area, but the light they gave off was barely sufficient to see by.

"Yeun, I told you to come alone." His former boss

stood approximately four meters away, flanked by two thugs. One of them had his sister by the arm.

Diaz had asked them to buy time if they could. Kyle didn't doubt Lizzy's assessment that this would be over in less, but he could do his best to play things out. Besides, it would be odd if he didn't approach this the way he approached his corporate dealings.

Straightening, he spread his hands, palms out. "We live in a very crowded city and I prefer to maintain a certain level of fitness. I neither own a car, nor do I have a driver's license."

His old boss snorted. "Goddamned fresh off the boat. Don't you know anyone can get a driver's license in this state? You don't even have to be a fucking citizen of the United States of America to get a license to drive in this state. How do you not have one?"

Kyle raised his eyebrows. "I was not aware."

His boss could go on for a while, given the opportunity. The man loved to vent.

"How do you get through security at airports, then? We've sent you on so many business trips, I've fucking lost count."

Kyle shrugged. "I have a US passport."

His boss barked out a laugh. "Yeah. You are a citizen at least. Been here long enough to have a green card, become a citizen. Good for you. Look, your family is damned proud."

His sister and her son were frightened. They were clean, appeared unharmed, but both had dark circles under their eyes from lack of sleep. They were also unable to say anything as duct tape was securely fastened across their mouths.

"Your hospitality is not one of your strong points."

Kyle hoped he could set his former employer off on another rant. But he did not want to push too hard. He'd have to rein in his usual sarcasm and keep it light.

"Hah." The man wagged a stumpy finger at him. "You know what was never right about you, Yeun? You can tell English isn't your first language. You're always so proper about how you speak. So fucking formal. I'm a strong believer in not trusting anyone who doesn't curse."

Everyone had their pet peeves. For Kyle, he enjoyed language and conversation. In particular, he tried to be engaging so he could enter into more of both. In this case, he kept his mouth shut.

"Okay. This has been a shit show." His old boss wiped sweat from his brow. "You've caused way the hell more trouble than you're worth and dragged me into this. I didn't need to be involved. But of course, you go squealing to the police and I have accountability. I gotta get this cleaned up. Best thing is to make sure you don't go to trial tomorrow."

Kyle swallowed hard. This wasn't unexpected but it definitely could have gone better. "I thought the intent was for me to change my testimony. Wouldn't that be much safer for everyone?"

His boss laughed. It was an obnoxious sound, the echo of it bouncing off the huge containers around them. "Do you think I'm going to trust you after you got us here in the first place?"

Kyle didn't have an answer. He could try for reassurance but they both knew he'd say anything at this point.

"And these two. They've seen you and heard us both discuss this." The man waved vaguely at Kyle's sister and nephew. "It's much cleaner to deal with this mess now instead of letting you all run loose. Can't rely on you being grateful for your lives. People forget to be afraid after a while. It just doesn't work out."

Well, the man had a point. A good one.

"We've got you all here and we can make sure you disappear. Don't make this harder than it has to be." His boss let out a gusty sigh. "Even if you run, I won't even have to try to come after you. There's no place you can get to where you won't be shot down like a dog. Trust me."

No trade then. No chance of getting his sister and nephew away from the man who had them.

Lizzy hadn't updated them to reveal whether the other sniper was out there. She'd only confirmed she was in position. He wasn't going to doubt her. No. He was going to have faith. Since the very beginning Lizzy had shown him she followed through with what she said she was going to do and she made things happen.

He'd have to do the same.

"Do you think you can play with people's lives this way without consequences? This trial is highly publicized. Eliminating me will only draw further investigation. You've only made things worse for yourself and the company. Idiot." He growled, putting all of his anger and frustration into it. "I won't forgive you for bringing my family into this."

Then he charged his former employer.

The man paled, caught unprepared.

The two bodyguards drew their weapons.

A strange noise sounded somewhere above him and the bodyguard holding his sister jerked and fell backward, almost taking her down with him. His nephew reached out his hands, bound by duct tape at the wrists, and grasped at his mother. The two of them stumbled back a few steps and Marc suddenly appeared there, rushing them smoothly back toward the car.

Kyle reached his old boss then. Keeping the portly man's body between him and the other bodyguard, he slowed a fraction as he drew his right arm down and back. Then he punched the man hard in an uppercut, high in his gut, hoping to get past the extra baggage and hit him in the solar plexus. He followed with a left hook to the jaw. The man cried out in pain and raised both hands to his broken face.

As his old boss staggered backward, Kyle looked past him at the bodyguard pointing a gun directly at Kyle. Fear spiked fresh in his chest but the man's face was frozen in a look of confusion. The bodyguard stared down at his hands as the gun dropped to the ground. Then the man toppled over, bleeding from a shot to his shoulder.

"Get down. Get back to the car!" Marc was there again, roughly grabbing hold of Kyle and spinning him around. Marc gave Kyle a hard shove toward the open car door.

A gunshot rang out, close. Kyle saw his sister and nephew huddled down in the backseat wells of the car, their eyes wide with fear and horror.

He half turned in time to see Marc falling. Without thinking, Kyle skidded to a halt and doubled back to grab Marc. Stumbling, they headed to the car.

Shoving Marc in the backseat through the still open door, Kyle dived into the driver's seat of the still-running car. Throwing it into Drive, he sent it careening out of the parking area.

"Scott here." Lizzy's voice came over the radio.

"Kyle, you're safe. All targets neutralized. You're safe. Ease up on the gas pedal."

Lizzy. She was still back there. He yanked the steering wheel to the side.

"No need to do celebration donuts, just circle around to the other aisle. I'll meet you on the ground there. Ease up on that pedal."

"Marc's been shot."

Silence. Then, "Hurry. I'll do the assessment in the car and we'll get him medical attention."

Kyle put his faith in Lizzy and headed back to go get her.

"Nice and easy. I'm watching over you. We'll handle what comes next together." Lizzy's promise settled deep in his chest and he breathed.

Yes, one thing at a time. By tomorrow, this would be settled.

Chapter Twenty-Four

"Your contract is finished, you know."

Lizzy didn't bother to acknowledge Federal Marshal Nguyen's comment, but she did give him a nod. Respect between colleagues and all that.

"There's an investigation underway at Harbor Island." Nguyen sounded unconcerned. "Apparently, there was an altercation before dawn this morning. Maybe smuggling. Security system was bypassed but someone reported shots fired in the area. Blood was found, but no bodies."

Not surprising. Phoenix Biotech might've sent in a cleanup crew after Safeguard had left the vicinity. Or Diaz had gotten a detail in to sweep the site. She'd been focused on getting Marc, who was still in surgery, to medical care, then getting Kyle's sister and nephew tucked away in a Centurion Corporation safe house east of the city. They'd barely had time to get Kyle showered and back to the courthouse to be transferred directly back into the custody of Marshals Decker and Nguyen.

She hadn't had to worry about the sniper though. Her shot had found its mark. He was dead.

"Any reason you're on edge today?" Nguyen stood next to her, but didn't crowd her. It wasn't just out of social politeness. It was professional courtesy. Both of them wanted to have room to ready their firearm if the unexpected occurred.

"The days leading up to this trial have been weird." She didn't mind being candid. "For a man testifying to being aware of illegal dumping, he's had a lot of shit go on around him."

Nguyen's shared information had been the leverage she needed to gain access to Kyle's ex-boss and she was grateful but she wasn't officially supposed to have knowledge of it. She also still didn't know why Nguyen had shared it.

"He has." Nguyen's agreement was far too pleasant. "Some perspective might help, if you listen to hearsay."

Meaning anything the US marshal was about to share was never said.

"I'm always open to general gossip." No she wasn't, but this wasn't gossip.

Nguyen grunted. "Could be, an investigation turned up one or two of the shipping containers supposedly lost at sea."

"Huh." Imagine that.

The images she'd seen in the file probably weren't the only ones. They'd still been enough to join some of the saddest nightmares she had. This had to be an incredibly costly investigation for the US government. It was a big ocean out there.

"What was in those containers was a tragedy." Nguyen's tone turned grim. "This joint investigation was established once it was determined a lot of people supposedly coming to the United States on visas never arrived."

People. Trying to cross an ocean to get to the United

States. Horror twisted her gut anew. Those shipping containers were huge and the pictures had been zoomed in to make the victims identifiable. She still had no idea how many had died but those containers could accommodate dozens. There was a goddamned company in the Seattle area turning those things into actual homes.

How many desperate people could be crammed into those for the chance at a new life?

Goaded into fresh shock, Lizzy actually looked at the marshal. "Seriously? What you found can be summed up as a joint investigation, huh?"

"Every one of the missing people had applied for visas and been denied." Nguyen didn't meet her gaze. "The Korean authorities started matching the missing person's reports from concerned families with the trend for visa applications and determined they must have tried to find another way to the US."

Illegal immigration was a major problem. In the Seattle area, being a major seaport, there were actually a lot of immigrants from Southeast Asia, Africa and other regions around the world. The Canadian and Californian borders had their own issues too. It was a complex, difficult situation to address.

Lizzy wasn't even going to begin suggesting a solution for it. But the reality of it wasn't something to pretend didn't exist.

"So Kyle's testimony proves more than the civil and federal charges listed publicly." Lizzy hated stating the obvious, but she had to say it out loud. Otherwise, her brain wasn't going to be able to process it. And she'd seen some horrible things with her own eyes. "He's confirming mass murder."

"Premeditated," Nguyen confirmed. "Those people

paid money, were hoping for a better future. And they died."

"I don't even want to know the international repercussions of this trial." She should, but she didn't want to.

"Mr. Yeun will only need to testify this one time, in this federal court." Nguyen sounded like he was trying to be reassuring. The result made her wary. "His recorded testimony will ensure that Phoenix Biotech can't do this to more people."

One battle at a time. This one, at least, would save lives that would have otherwise been lost. There was no shortage of people trying to leave one life for a chance at a better one.

"What about his family?" Since Phoenix Biotech had been responsible for bringing them to the United States, there was every possibility Kyle's family would have to go back to Korea to wait until Kyle could make arrangements for them to get green cards. It could take years.

"They've already been awarded their visas." Smug. The US marshal was definitely proud of himself at the moment. "We ensured those would remain valid. The boy's scholarship is also independently funded so he won't lose that either."

Relief flooded through her. Not that Kyle wouldn't have been able to work through it, but the man deserved a break.

"It's been a positive experience, working with the Safeguard Division." Apparently Nguyen had decided on a change in topic. "I'm impressed."

Now she definitely didn't believe him. "Two police officers injured. I went missing, with your witness, and refused to tell you how to find us the one time I did contact you."

Her own fire team had taken damage. Marc was still in surgery as they spoke, with Victoria at the hospital with him. It was taking a long time to extract all of the fragments from the bullet he'd caught in the back.

Marc was a tough bastard. He was a Centurion. He'd pull through.

"Decker just about lost his shit trying to locate you." Nguyen agreed. Then he chuckled. "The man is the steadiest, by-the-book deputy I have ever encountered. Trying to locate you had him completely unhinged. It was a learning experience, for him, and for the US Marshals in general. We didn't expect you to manage to stay off the radar for as long as you did. But since you were so good at staying off the radar, I took advantage of the situation to toss out a few fake leads. If we'd had a leak, they would have been exposed going after those and it would've thrown them further off your trail. As it was, no bites either within my organization or the Seattle PD. It was very reassuring."

Huh. At least he wasn't angry with her. It could be a lot worse. Plus it was good to know they'd been doing their own work keeping the pressure off her and Kyle.

"I believe in maintaining positive relations with organizations like Centurion Corporation's Safeguard Division." Nguyen cleared his throat. "Keeps us all on our toes. Doing things differently. It's good to make sure we don't get too full of ourselves."

Not a bad perspective to have. It was something she imagined Diaz and Harte thought about all the time.

"We'd like to continue working with you in the future."

There was an emphasis on the pronoun. It did her ego some good to hear it. But if anyone was going to hear her decision first, she owed it to her commanding officer.

"Contracts go through Diaz," she responded automatically. People were starting to fill the hallway. There must be a break in sessions.

"All right." Nguyen was still amiable. "We'll want to debrief though, once the trial is over."

"Where?" She was not going to be thrilled to be stuck in an interrogation room down at the police station. This smelled like a potentially bad situation. "And do I need my lawyer?"

Nguyen held up his hands, palms out. "I meant it when I said we want to maintain positive relations with Safeguard."

She'd talk to Diaz and have the Centurion Corporation legal team on hand anyway. It never hurt to be prepared.

"I'm more interested in the explosives set in the city while you and Yeun were missing." He tugged at his suit and rolled his shoulders. "Obviously, there's more than the usual criminal element in town."

Edict was definitely not the norm in terms of private contract organizations. Most of their contracts were valid and legal, as far as Lizzy knew, but they'd definitely crossed the line with anything having to do with their current main contract holder.

"Talk to Phoenix Biotech about that." She didn't know whether it'd be the time to discuss the events around Maylin's sister's disappearance.

There'd been some discussion with the federal government but she hadn't been a direct part of it. She'd only given reports on the day Edict paid a visit to the Centurion Corporation's Training and Recovery headquarters outside Seattle, and the following incursion on Phoenix Biotech's facility.

"We intend to," Nguyen assured her. "We want to know the right questions to ask though and the Centurion Corporation seems to have clashed with the people Phoenix Biotech has hired twice now."

True.

"Talk to Diaz." She was done.

Nguyen was being friendly. He could definitely take a harder approach and she'd have stood her ground anyway.

It wasn't that she didn't want to cooperate. To her, Diaz was the head of Safeguard. She wasn't going to decide what was and wasn't said to the US Marshals or any other potential partners. Not her pay grade. Not her issue to be worrying about today.

"You're closer to this than he is." Only a slight edge betrayed Nguyen's frustration. "You're also more personally invested in the situation."

He was wrong there. Diaz had every bit as much reason to be watching Phoenix Biotech and Edict very closely.

"I'm not permanently assigned to Safeguard." Generally not something the man needed to know. But she figured it wouldn't hurt to give him the heads-up. He came across to her as a man who would continue to pursue every lead until he found out what he wanted to know. That'd include showing up at the Safeguard offices looking for her. "I was retained for this contract, but the decision is still outstanding as to whether I'll be reassigned to a new fire team for Centurion Corporation or permanently assigned to Safeguard Division."

That was about as far as she wanted to go with the sharing though. The man did not have any reason to know the decision was hers. Both Harte and Diaz were waiting on her answer by end of business today. She'd come to the courthouse to keep an eye on proceedings even if she remained outside the actual courtroom because it'd given her something constructive to do while she wrestled with the pros and cons.

Stay or go?

Nguyen sighed. "Fine. I'll talk to Diaz. Do I need an appointment too?"

"Probably not." You know, she could probably be more diplomatic here. She was supposed to be working on her interpersonal skills. Kyle's charming smile came to mind, the one he used on people when he was about to talk them into doing something they didn't initially intend to do. "But it'd be appreciated as a professional courtesy. Once you've got the date and time set, I can try to be in the office too so you can talk to the both of us if it's appropriate."

Nguyen grunted, somewhat mollified.

She needed more work on the circumspection, probably. Could consider the way she worded things. Maybe.

Sometimes simple meant clear communication.

Sometimes getting things done meant it was impossible to keep it simple.

Well, she'd have to grow past using Post-it notes if she was going to stay in this line of work.

There was a crush of people heading out of the courtroom. It'd been one of the longest days of Kyle's life and he wasn't sure it was over yet. A few steps outside the courtroom, he saw two men waiting in the hallway. Hard to miss them.

Diaz and another man weren't standing together, per se, but they were next to each other. Both of them had a rock-solid quality about them, an air of confidence and capability that was intimidating. As eager as people were to leave the courtroom and head to wherever they were going—home, dinner dates, restrooms—they gave both men space and sort of flowed around them.

Kyle glanced about, looking for a similar void of people where Lizzy might be waiting for him. She wasn't.

His belly felt heavy and hollow at the same time. He was too drained from the day's testimony and line of questioning to burn more energy in wondering where she was. Instead, he closed the remaining distance and came to a stop in front of Diaz and the stranger. He would go looking for her once he'd completed his responsibilities here, and to family.

It wasn't just about him anymore and it might take some time, but he wasn't going to forget about her.

"Mr. Yeun, I'm US Marshal Nguyen." The man held out his hand and Kyle took it in a firm handshake. "My colleague Deputy Marshal Decker sends his regards."

Ah. Kyle imagined Decker was not pleased with the turn of events. "I hope Deputy Marshal Decker is well. The past few days have been unpredictable and there were few choices when it came to avoiding certain threats."

Nguyen raised a hand to forestall additional commentary. "Deputy Marshal Decker was definitely challenged to provide support in the effort to keep you protected, Mr. Yeun, but Mr. Diaz and I agree the actions taken were the best possible under the circumstances."

"Good." Some of his accustomed assurance returned now that he had this damned testimony behind him. Just because the other man had his hand up didn't mean Kyle was finished having his say. "I wouldn't want Decker, or Officers Austin and Weaver for that matter, to suffer unfortunate consequences as a result of my going into hiding with…Miss Scott as my primary protection. As far as I'm concerned, it wasn't any of the protective detail team's fault and it wouldn't be fair for them to be reprimanded for it."

Diaz cleared his throat. The big man had a quirk about his mouth. His lips were turned up at one corner and he might have been smiling. Possibly. The rest of his face was a study in stoic seriousness, so it was hard to tell. "Miss Scott has expressed similar concern. Marshal Nguyen and I are in agreement with you both."

Kyle settled in to the conversation at hand. "Well then, I imagine the two of you have something to discuss with me then?"

Nguyen looked at Diaz and backed away slightly, perhaps a few centimeters, ceding the floor to Diaz.

Kyle had spent significant time bringing together project teams, facilitating executive steering committee meetings and managing people in general. These two men had authority and they were new to working together. Their cues were obvious and they were still establishing a rapport.

There was a collaboration in the making here and Kyle found it somewhat reassuring.

Diaz turned to face Kyle completely. "According to the terms of the contract you signed with Safeguard, Miss Scott's services are complete."

Ah. So Lizzy was indeed gone. And her absence might be indicative of whether he'd ever find her again. Or if she even wanted him to. "I'd like to speak with her."

"You can look for Miss Scott at the Safeguard offices for the time being. If she's not on the premises at the time, you'll be able to leave a message for her there and we'll make sure it gets to her." Diaz didn't miss a beat in his response. It was very well practiced and delivered smoothly.

"I see." Actually, he did not. He was tired and irritable and wanted to check in with his family then rest. He wanted to hold Lizzy in his arms again.

"Considering the complications leading up to today's trial, I'm here to see if you are in need of Safeguard's services for extended personal protection," Diaz continued. "We've got a few options for you and while the part you've played in this trial is complete, you and your family may feel better for the added assurance of safety while you put this all behind you."

Nguyen nodded. "You also have the federal witness protection plan, Mr. Yeun, but that was extended to you specifically and didn't take your sister and nephew into consideration."

The US marshal appeared genuinely regretful about the situation. His brows were drawn together and his gaze showed concern.

Kyle had been thinking about it. "My nephew has a scholarship and his education is a priority. I'm told by the legal team that the threat to him is considered to be minimal at this point. His mother will want to be close by but she also was hoping to give the young man space. It would be difficult to take all three of us and reestablish a plan for their life and his education."

But not impossible. He would do it for them if he had to. And then there was finding Lizzy.

Diaz was watching him. Waiting.

"Mr. Diaz, I would like to explore some of the personal protection options you have available in further detail." Because Kyle could trust Safeguard, Lizzy in particular. And they were driven by practicalities, logic and money. Kyle understood them. Whereas the government was a completely different animal.

"Drop by as soon as you're ready, Mr. Yeun." Diaz glanced around and then returned his attention to Kyle. "Your sister and nephew are currently at Safeguard's Training and Recovery facility outside of the city. You're welcome to come out to the facility and have dinner, see to their needs. Or if you'd like, we can bring them back here to any accommodations you had in mind."

"I appreciate the offer, Mr. Diaz. I'm not certain if I'll be entering protective custody again…" Kyle glanced at Nguyen. "…or if it is safe to return to my apartment. It's a bachelor's home but I'm sure we can make do."

He hadn't been expecting his sister and nephew so soon. Hadn't made the more practical arrangements yet.

Sympathy was there in Diaz's eyes. "Why don't we take you to see them, Mr. Yeun? We're planning to move them from the current location to accommodations more suited to an extended stay. The three of you can spend the night on Centurion Corporation grounds and make long-term arrangements tomorrow morning."

Nguyen nodded in agreement. So much for protective custody. With his part in the trial over, that must be complete, as well.

Diaz was generous, but Kyle was a businessman first and foremost. No offer was without its hidden assumptions. "Thank you, Mr. Diaz. I am grateful to you and your team for the exemplary services provided thus far. But to be brutally honest, I no longer have employment. While I have significant savings set aside and I was willing to sign a contract with your organization to get me through this trial, I will need to take the time to assess my finances and seek out a new position before I know what further services I can afford."

"Understandable. I think if you do come back with me to the Centurion Corporation facilities, I may have a few ideas to discuss with you regarding those concerns too." The man leaned forward slightly, enough to make Kyle eye him warily. "All professional considerations aside, my partner has extended the invitation for you and your family to join the Centurions for dinner. She intends to ask you where you found the pair of shoes you bought for Lizzy. I've been informed I'm not allowed to come home without you. Please consider it a personal favor."

Chapter Twenty-Five

"Isn't it early to be drinking?" Lizzy studied the pair of glasses on the small table in Diaz's office. They were new, she thought. Like brandy snifters but slightly taller and narrower. A new bottle of Macallan single malt scotch stood next to them. "What's the occasion? And is Harte here?"

Diaz wasn't usually into the whiskey, whether it was single malt or blended. He kept some on hand for when Harte was in town.

Chuckling, Diaz came around from his desk. "No. Not today. He's due in soon though. This'll be out again."

"Okay," she said slowly. "Is this out for me? Seems kind of fancy."

She wasn't picky about her drinks. Oh, she liked good cocktails if she was drinking but she wasn't particular about what kind of vodka she was served when a cocktail called for vodka as long as it was decent.

"Not really." Diaz nodded at her feet. "What about you? You're dressed up kind of fancy. What's the occasion?"

She was not going to blush in front of Diaz. Nope. "Nothing. I just wanted to wear the shoes."

Because the black heels Kyle had chosen for her were

her new favorites and she hadn't gotten to wear them for long. Sure they'd been picked to pair with a cocktail dress, which she'd gone back to the hotel to retrieve, but the shoes went well with business casual too. The effect was a dressy business casual.

"What? Not used to me going for the dressy look once in a while?" She knew it was defensive body language but she allowed herself to cross her arms over her chest anyway.

Wouldn't hurt for the guys around the office to start acknowledging she had a feminine side.

Diaz held up his hands, backing away from the topic.

"How's Marc after the surgery?" She'd gotten the update from Victoria that he'd come through and was resting but she needed to catch up on the long-term impact.

"Alive and already bored." Diaz didn't waste time with niceties. "Lost a lot of blood though. Took a lot of time to hunt down the bullet fragments in him. Fragments tore him up inside and did a lot of damage. They're keeping an eye on him now for infection. It's going to be a long recovery."

Ah, shit. Their fire team was well and truly a mess.

"Going to need a new person on our fire team, then?" she asked, then bit the inside of her cheek.

Diaz's stared her. "Yes. Pending some structural changes to the way this division is organized. Been meaning to talk to you about that. Glad you came in this morning."

"Figured you'd hunt me down if I didn't." She owed him an answer. It wasn't her style to run from it for too long.

"I'll listen first, then tell you what changes I'm considering." Diaz motioned to the two armchairs.

Uh-huh. Sure. Don't drop any bombs to make her doubt her decision. Only leave her insanely curious. Bastard.

She made herself comfortable in one of the chairs. "I joined Centurion Corporation because I wanted to work in the private sector for a team with the same kind of standards I hold myself to. It's been a good couple of years. I've learned a lot."

Diaz waited.

"Not going to lie, being in one place for too long made me antsy these last few months. I've still got to work through this need to be out there and blow off steam. I thought the personal security work was going to be boring. Didn't want to lose my edge."

"Valid concern." Diaz nodded.

"These last couple of days are probably not going to be representative of what Safeguard does. But I figure the situations will come up." Here, she was fishing some. Nguyen hinted at future collaboration. "Maylin's sister, then Kyle, neither of those contracts was what we'd normally anticipate."

Diaz only smiled.

Okay then, he was going to make her tell him her decision first. Probably reserving whatever he was thinking to change her mind if what she told him wasn't what he was hoping for. The old, contrary part of her would've wanted to do exactly the opposite just to prove he couldn't tell her what to do.

But she didn't want to be that person anymore.

"They were a challenge though. Both of them. And we did some good in a personal way." She tapped her heel against the floor. "You didn't like those sorts of jobs for us, and I agreed because they could get messy as hell. But, they have their moments."

Seeing Kyle hug his sister and nephew, spending time with Maylin and her younger sister... Those had been incredibly rewarding moments.

"I think dealing with the personal complications is a good thing. I don't want to lose touch with the people we're working to protect and I think there's a lot to learn about personal security." She met Diaz's gaze steadily. "I'd like to stay on with Safeguard, if you'll have me."

Leaving, even going back to Centurion Corporation, would take her down a path to become colder, more solitary. She'd forget how to laugh and Kyle had only just reminded her how much she enjoyed the feeling of warmth it gave her.

Diaz broke into a grin. "Like I was going to let you leave without a fight."

She rolled her eyes. "I could see you getting ready to talk me around. Trust me."

"Glad I don't have to." Diaz rose to his feet and crossed over to his desk, picking up a tablet. "I'll get a contract drawn up for you. Standard two year. A couple of perks added for your renewal."

"You mentioned organizational changes?" She figured he was planning to tell her, but wanted to draw it out a little longer. Torture.

"A couple." Diaz turned and leaned against the edge of the desk, holding out the tablet to her. "You're being promoted. I need a right-hand person to run this division and you're it. Salary to be increased along with the responsibility. In the field, we'll be partners."

"Partners." Interesting. "You're not rebuilding the fire team?"

"Ours won't be structured the same way, no. For Centurion Corporation, fire teams work. Safeguard isn't going to get as many contracts willing to employ four resources or more. Probably never going to need a squadron all at the same time. So I'm organizing us into two-person teams. We've got about two dozen resources either on contract or waiting for assignment at the moment. I'd like to expand us by another fifty percent. There'll be some future training, too, on working in pairs."

Ah. She liked the idea. Of course, some engagements like the bigger parties and private charity events could still require a larger set of personnel but they could still be organized to work in pairs.

"Makes sense." She studied the tablet. Victoria's name was at the top, her partner marked as TBD. "But Marc is going to be out for a long while."

Diaz sighed. "Yeah."

"You could have had me working solo." She'd leaned toward it before and was still probably the best in the division for it.

"Could have." Diaz shook his head. "But you're best qualified to be my second. Victoria is better at training up a new person in a team. I'm going to find her a new partner. Someone fresh."

"That'll take some shaking out." Victoria and Marc had been close.

"It'll be your responsibility to oversee it." Diaz sounded very happy to hand off that particular assignment.

"Joy." Maybe it wasn't too late to reconsider.

"I plan to have you get to know each of our new hires, make sure I didn't fuck up the hiring process. Confirm they're a good culture fit in the first few weeks." Diaz moved around to the other side of his desk. "You'll be in charge of intel in general, nothing you haven't been doing already. So this is sort of an expansion on those responsibilities."

She narrowed her eyes. Casual as his move was, was he retreating?

"We've actually got a new hire. Not going to be a field operative." Diaz lifted his chin to indicate the tablet in her hand. "Man's a project manager. He'll be responsible for keeping our in-progress contracts organized, draw up new statements of work or change orders, and build a finance team to handle invoices, expenses and all that. I figured you could get started with the on boarding process for him."

"And what's our on boarding process?" She tapped the tablet's screen to pull up the new hire files and froze.

"I figure you could establish that as you went." Diaz said quietly. "Maybe you could figure out which office is going to be his, for starters. He's over in one of the pods waiting."

Kyle was pacing when she walked into the pod. Turning to face her, he swallowed hard. She didn't look happy to see him.

"You're here." Her voice was quiet, neutral.

"Yes." Maybe she didn't want him to be.

"As a new hire."

He nodded, straightening. Funny how he had so much confidence and self-assurance, arrogance even, and facing her he wanted to apologize like a schoolboy who isn't absolutely sure what he's done wrong but saying sorry just in case. "Safeguard had need of someone with my experience."

"True." She set a tablet on the table. "I'm supposed to find you an office."

Well, fortune didn't favor the hesitant. "Will you be here for the day only or are you staying?"

"Would you have a problem working with me?" Her dark eyes were still unreadable. But he'd spent time with Lizzy over the past few days and he was sure he hadn't imagined the slight quaver in her voice. Her vulnerability.

Something she trusted to him.

"I was going to try to find you, regardless. Working with you is going to be a new experience." He straightened his tie and resisted the urge to fuss with his suit jacket. He would not fidget further. "It depends on just how much you can put up with me."

She lifted an eyebrow.

He grinned. "I'm impressed with the facilities here. Can I talk you into testing the opacity settings on some of the conference rooms?"

"No." Her response was immediate, sharp, but she didn't hide her smile.

He stepped toward her and held his hands out. After a moment, she placed hers in his.

"I won't work here if you feel uncomfortable." He glanced around through the glass and then returned his gaze to hers. "I can find another position someplace else."

She tipped her head to the side slightly. "You want to work here though."

"Yes." He nodded. "It's an interesting change. Challenging position. And I've learned this place does things that have a direct impact on people's lives. I'd like to reconnect with that feeling again."

"So what do I have to do with it?" She had stilled, waiting for his answer.

Everything.

And somehow, he needed to let her know because otherwise, she'd shut down and withdraw behind a professional wall. He could see her bracing for it. He didn't want her to.

"Meeting you was the last thing I could have anticipated." He wasn't exactly sure what he was going to say but he figured he would start and let it flow, unplanned. Sincere. And hope she didn't hate him. "I can't say if I'd have thanked you if I'd known how much I would change after meeting you."

He'd been a carefree bachelor living a shallow life. He'd thought he'd been happy. Now he was sure he wouldn't be if he couldn't at least let her know how he felt.

"Whatever way our stories end. However you choose." He closed his hands around hers and squeezed gently. "You've changed me for the better and I can actually say I am building toward being a good man. Someone my nephew can be proud to live with. Because I knew you."

Her fingers had tightened in his grip, returning his hold with her own strength. Encouraged, he continued, "Here. Now. I am grateful to have met you. And I can't imagine life moving forward without you. So please. Lizzy. Isabelle. Let me be a part of yours."

A small noise escaped her and tears welled up in her eyes.

Shocked, his mouth fell open. "I'm sorry, I—"

She kissed him.

There were several long minutes he lost in her lips and he didn't care at all.

"Are you certain about testing the opacity of the conference room?" When she pulled back and swatted him across the shoulder he gave her his best rakish grin.

"Let's go find you an office before more people try gawking."

Startled, he looked out into the office space. "There's nobody there."

She glared at him. "There's half a dozen people in cubes trying not to be obvious about peeking over the top. And Diaz is probably watching on video feed."

"Oh." He turned to the camera and gave it a jaunty salute.

She cursed and grabbed his sleeve, dragging him out of the pod. "Let's get you an office."

"Is it private?"

"No. All of them have glass walls."

"With opacity adjustment, I saw the control panels."

"You aren't allowed to use them."

He planted his feet and halted.

She turned. "What?"

"I've got a few things for the office." He'd actually discussed the job with Diaz the night before, so he'd made a stop in the morning at his flat and also at the hotel for a few special items.

"Seriously?"

He ducked into the pod to retrieve a box and then followed her down to the end of the office floor. It took a minute to pick an office at the end, then he set the box down on the desk.

"What did you…?" She peered into the box and fell silent.

Carefully, Kyle lifted out the fishbowl and peeled away the plastic wrap spread across the top temporarily to keep water from spilling out. "I couldn't leave Frederick behind."

Epilogue

Lizzy strode across the darkened office floor as indirect lighting came up at intervals to provide her with just enough to see by.

It was late and while she and Kyle were both guilty of working long hours, they usually made sure to leave the office together. Managing this thing called work-life balance was a tough concept. It hadn't been much of a consideration for either of them until they'd met each other. So far though, it'd been an adjustment they'd both taken to. Easy enough when their time off was spent exploring fine dining hot spots around downtown Seattle and taking active day trips around the Puget Sound. They had fun together. A lot of fun.

Tonight was the third time this week he'd managed to work late enough for her to come seek him out at the Safeguard offices rather than in bed at his condo. But to be fair, her hours were odd too. The important part for both of them was the flexibility to make their days off count.

This was Monday night, essentially her equivalent of the start of a weekend since she generally had assignments from Friday through Sunday. Kyle usually arranged his office hours to match and they made a point of spending their two days off together, away from the office.

Their most recent success had been an overnight kayak expedition around the San Juan Islands. The sights around the islands and the wildlife had been incredible, highlighted by cooked-to-order gourmet meals for breakfast, lunch and dinner. It'd been a foodie adventure and she was eager to see what they could come up with next.

They'd been talking about an extended vacation but they'd also both taken up their new responsibilities at Safeguard with enthusiasm. Plus, he'd been making sure his sister and nephew were settled in an apartment near his nephew's university. The past few months had swept by in a blur.

Which made the time they spent together something they both made the most of, whenever they could.

The glass walls of his office were dialed to opacity, tweaking her temper up a notch. He wasn't supposed to limit his line of sight when he was working alone. It made him vulnerable to oncoming danger.

Like her.

She covered the last few steps to his office door and stopped in her tracks.

On the desk was a dinner spread set between two pillar candles in hurricane glasses. Savory scents teased her and her mouth started watering just a little, but not just because of the amazing meal.

Kyle sat behind his desk with his feet up, his suit jacket open and his tie undone to hang down on either side of his collar. His perfectly tailored dress shirt was unbuttoned and left open to expose his chest and deliciously sculpted abs. His dark gaze found hers over the candlelight and he gave her a slow, sexy smile.

"Happy birthday, Lizzy."

Slowly, he lifted his hand from behind the desk to set a pair of absolutely stunning shoes of creamy white lace accented by delicate crystals. They were open-toed and on the front of each balanced a sparkling butterfly.

Caught without words, she crossed over to the desk. Picking up a *pão de queijo* and popping it into her mouth, she chewed slowly and savored the cheesy Brazilian bread treat.

Unruffled by her lack of response, Kyle took his feet down off the desk and stood smoothly, pouring her a glass of wine and holding it out to her.

She took it and had a small sip. "Thank you, for all of this."

Especially for the amazing shoes.

He came around the desk and reached out, his hand brushing her jaw in a light caress as he slid it behind her head and grasped the nape of her neck. He pulled her close for a scalding kiss, his lips hot on hers as she opened for him. He tasted of wine and spice, his breath mingling with hers until she set the wineglass down and spread her hands over his chest.

When she tilted her head back in a gasp, he pressed a trail of searing kisses along her neck and whispered, "We could celebrate right here."

She growled and set her teeth against his shoulder, not hard enough to break skin, then licked the same spot. "Negative. Cameras everywhere and this is already way more than any of them need to see."

He chuckled and straightened without protest, the

hunger still in his gaze, promising the night was going to be a long one once they got back to his place.

She gave him another quick kiss and then turned her attention to the slices of skirt steak with garlic butter. There was just enough here for a light meal.

"I figured you might enjoy a snack." He leaned against the edge of the desk. "There's another dinner waiting in a basket back at my place."

She raised an eyebrow at him. "Does Diaz know you're the reason Maylin's catering company is expanding this winter?"

He shrugged. "The food is unparalleled."

No argument there. "Why a basket?"

"Well, if things go as I hope they will, we'll be heading out as soon as we stop by to pick up the luggage I've packed." A twinge of uncertainty had crept into his tone.

"Packed?" Her heart did a little flip. "Where are we going?"

"I thought you might trust me. The first flight is to Hawaii." He gave her a heart-stopping grin. "You can find out the next stop after a couple of days and I give you the boarding passes to our next destination. All cleared with Diaz already, no worries about any contracts. Just a well-deserved vacation."

Together.

"What about Frederick?" She glanced at the goldfish in question, still swimming around happily in his fishbowl.

"Diaz even agreed to come in and feed Frederick every day."

Lizzy huffed out a laugh as she touched the water's surface. The goldfish swam up to the surface to kiss her fingertip.

Kyle opened his arms in invitation and she stepped into him without hesitation.

"You keep surprising me," she whispered. "Not just with what you do, but the way you get me to react. I'm all sorts of things I forgot I liked being when I'm with you."

"I love you." He made the statement simple, his voice almost cracking with the emotion behind it, then pressed a kiss against her hair. "I love everything about you. I'm looking forward to discovering more."

She swallowed hard. "You're a complicated man, Kyle Yeun."

"Yes." And she saw through all of his posturing to the person he'd evolved into over the past few months and who he could be.

Even better, he looked at her and saw her too.

"I love you too." Her mouth had gone dry but she'd gotten better at saying what she felt, out loud, to him. "I might not say it often or even admit it again anytime soon. But I do. So I'll say it now because I have no idea what's going to happen tomorrow or even later tonight and you have a tendency to have explosives go off near you."

"Let's survive to tomorrow together, then." He bent his head and kissed her.

* * * * *

Read on for a preview of
CONTRACTED DEFENSE,
the next book in the SAFEGUARD series
from Piper J. Drake.

Chapter One

"The Dalmore, neat, with a water back and a straw, please." Victoria Ash settled at the bar with a tired sigh. The evening was only half over, and already, she was at loose ends. Of course, being at an engagement party for two of your closest friends with neither your husband nor your working partner made it even more uncomfortable. The two situations were unrelated, at least.

The bartender gave her a friendly enough smile though. "The 12 year or the 15?"

She considered a moment. "The 15."

"Anything to eat? I could bring you the dinner menu."

"No, thank you." Victoria shook her head. She planned to have a quiet drink, then return to the event held in the adjoining hotel before any of her teammates missed her.

It was a special night, and for once, she wasn't overseeing security on the event. Tonight she was the guest of her longtime teammate and employer, Gabe Diaz. He and his fiancée, Maylin Cheng, were celebrating their engagement. Any event hosted—and catered—by Maylin promised to feed the guests well, with exquisite innovation. There was absolutely no room left in Victoria's belly for the dishes this establishment had to offer.

Victoria had honored her hosts, eaten Maylin's fine cuisine, and had her fill of champagne. The last tiny dessert bite had been a delicate pear tart topped with impossibly thin shards of dark chocolate. With the decadent taste lingering on her tongue, the Dalmore was her choice to savor and then cleanse her palate. Perhaps after she'd finished a glass, or two, she'd have identified why she was in such an abominably irritable mood and be able to head back to the festivities in a better frame of mind.

Her drink was placed in front of her with the accompanying glass of plain water. She used the straw to transfer a drop of water into her scotch. Lifting the glass so she could enjoy the aroma from the amber liquid, she smiled as the tiny bit of water opened up the scotch to give her notes of winter spices and orange citrus along with richer hints of dark chocolate.

Yes. Given a few minutes to enjoy this and she would be in a much better mood. Her ex never did give her a moment's peace to enjoy her scotch. He preferred shots and chasers. Savoring a drink, enjoying the complexity a good scotch could offer, wasn't a preference of his. Now she needn't take his hurried tendencies into consideration.

Wasn't that lovely?

"Why're we here?" A belligerent voice interrupted her enjoyment.

There'd been a handful of customers scattered through the establishment. These three had walked in from the street as she'd been ordering her scotch. Dressed in jeans and tees, they were probably looking for a different kind of bar. This one was a quieter place, enclosed on three sides with brick walls and hardwood shelves lined with

real books. It invited people to come, sit, savor a drink
and even enjoy a book. There'd been one or two people
tucked into corners reading on e-readers. Besides being
attached to the hotel hosting the event she'd been attending, the laid-back atmosphere of this bar had attracted
her in the first place.

"You wanted good hard liquor." One of the noisy trio
defended his choice at volume. "My app says this place
is the best for scotch and whiskey. Good food too."

Belligerent Boy let loose a rude noise. "You know
what, forget your stupid phone app. I saw The Five Point
on TV. They've got drinks and food, plus we won't have
to worry about them closing early. We can stay till breakfast. That's the kind of night I want."

Victoria kept watch on the trio without turning toward
them. She could see just fine in the reflection on the
floor-to-ceiling glass windows of the bar's street front.
With luck, they'd take themselves out to the sidewalk in
a minute and she could return her attention to her drink.

"I dunno. This place has something going for it. Saw
some familiar faces maybe." The third pitched in at a
more reasonable sound level, but he was still completely
audible even from across the bar. "Gabe Diaz is here tonight for some event. You heard of him? Where he is,
his team is too."

Sipping her scotch, she kept her glass raised to ob-
scure part of her face. If she could see them in the reflection, they could turn and see her. Despite their careless
words, they had been slowly turning to take note of the
people in the room. None of their gazes had lingered
longer than a second but they could've recognized her.
Most people in her line of work made it their business
to recognize another person in the private contractor

field. It wasn't easy, but if they were familiar with Gabe then they'd have a chance at identifying her. She'd been with Gabe's team longer than any of her previous stints in the business.

She wasn't dressed for work though. It'd been a good time to wear the rose gown with the subtle golden shimmer, so sheer, it required a nude silk sheathe beneath. It fit her perfectly, the fabric poured over her torso to fall from her hips and pool into a fuller skirt around her ankles. She'd left her hair down for once. It hung free of the severe knot she kept it in for when she was working. A few soft curls worked well in her golden blond hair. Nothing about her shouted private security or former military.

"Ah, Diaz and his Safeguard experiment. Whatever." Belligerent Boy flopped his hand around in mockery. "Word is they aren't worth the contract fee. Clients aren't happy. If they're here, it's going to be a clusterfuck. Guaranteed. There are better companies to do the job."

She kept her expression neutral, but she filed the tidbit of information away. It would be wise to follow up and see if the comment had any validity to it at all. At the very least, Gabe would want to know it'd been said out in the bar.

His companions snickered. "Like yours?"

"Hey, I work for the best." Belligerent Boy raised his hands. "They appreciate good work and don't get their panties in a twist when a man heads out for well-deserved time off."

This was starting to sound like a badly scripted commercial. These men had walked into this bar on purpose. There was no way it was a coincidence. Yet, it had to be to pick a fight or stir up some similar ridiculousness. Real clients with serious contracts wouldn't be getting their information from bar gossip. On the other hand, journalists had been hanging around the Safeguard teams ever since Kyle Yeun had stood trial to testify against Phoenix Biotech. The trial had been right in the spotlight of public scrutiny, and Safeguard, specifically Lizzy Scott, had been his bodyguard. Perhaps Belligerent Boy was trying to score an interview with some journalist trying to get dirt. Either way, she'd best get them out of here before they cast a shadow on Gabe and Maylin's special night.

"Excuse me." The nice bartender had approached at this point, quite possibly at the worst moment. "If you gentlemen aren't going to order a drink or food, I'm going to have to ask you to head on to your next destination."

"Yeah?" That was a challenge. Belligerent Boy cocked his head to one side and threw out his chest. "You think so? You one of Diaz's wannabe real mercenaries, on watch at the perimeter? Maybe we should head inside and see how good Safeguard's security really is."

Actually, no. The bartender was simply doing his job. Since this event wasn't a contract, Safeguard wasn't maintaining high-level security. There shouldn't have been any need to. As far as anyone else was concerned, this event was a simple engagement reception. Victoria set her glass down, promising herself another scotch after this was resolved.

"Yeah nah bro, I reckon we take this outside." Another new voice had entered the mix, and this one had a wonderful accent. It wasn't British or European, closer to Australian but not a match for that continent either. Perhaps New Zealand?

"Who're you?" Belligerent Boy did seem to be looking for a fight.

"Does it matter?" The newcomer wasn't much taller than Belligerent Boy, but he managed to look down the few inches he had on the other man in a genial way. Truly, his broad shoulders and chest cut an impressive figure, and there was a strength of presence that filled available space in a way normal physicality could not. He took a few steps through the other three, forcing them to step aside before they thought to stand their ground, and headed outside.

The newcomer was ballsy.

Victoria would've been infuriated but she'd have been wary. The trio was the former and not the latter. They swarmed out after the man, probably as he'd intended. She followed at a more leisurely pace and gave the bartender a pat on the shoulder. "No need to worry for the moment. They'll all get this out of their system and move along."

Unless the four of them came through the glass, that was. The entire front of the bar and the adjacent hotel lobby was window front or glass door. Watching the three range out in a semicircle around the single man, they all appeared fairly capable to her experienced eye, a step above the average bar brawler at least. Someone could very likely come through the windows since it'd be better than throwing a man into the street where things could become much more fatal. First Ave wasn't the busiest of streets, but it still had traffic at this time of night.

A commotion on that scale would definitely require police and potentially disturb Gabe and Maylin's party. It wasn't something Victoria was willing to allow if she could help it, so she stepped out of the bar too.

They hadn't gone far, just out onto the sidewalk to stand under the nearest streetlamp. Unfortunately, it was one right in front of the lobby entrance to the hotel. Victoria sighed inwardly. Though perhaps it wouldn't turn out as bad as she was anticipating. The newcomer had turned to chat amiably with them, offering a pack of cigarettes.

Ugh. She truly disliked smoking. She could if she had to play a particular role for a mission, but she'd never taken up the habit of her own accord. However, it seemed to be an effective way to de-escalate the situation. She'd give the newcomer extra points for charm.

Belligerent Boy had shuffled forward as they chatted though, closing the space between him and the newcomer as they'd been lighting each other's cigarettes. Belligerent Boy turned to mutter something to one of his companions, bringing his hand near his mouth in an overly dramatic gesture of secrecy. They were all laughing but Victoria narrowed her eyes. His posture was awkward. His upper body twisted and his hips still squared up with the newcomer.

She pushed open the door and headed out of the bar. "Oy!"

The newcomer dropped his cigarette as she came out and bent to retrieve it. Belligerent Boy unwound at that moment, his upraised hand tightened into a fist, throwing a wild haymaker punch at the newcomer. Already low, the newcomer deepened his crouch and lunged at Belligerent Boy. He caught Belligerent Boy around the thighs, driving forward with his head and shoulder and hoisting the man in a considerable show of strength.

Belligerent Boy fell to the side, knocking one of his companions off balance as he went down. From Victoria's perspective, the collision might've saved Belligerent Boy from getting his skull smashed in on the corner of the lamp-post. As it was, Belligerent Boy had the breath knocked out of him and hit the sidewalk.

It was still two on one, and this needed to end before hotel staff or someone on the street noticed the scuffle and called the police. Yelling again wasn't an option. Better to end it with as little noise as possible, and miraculously, the men had only uttered grunts in the few seconds since it'd started. She started forward toward the drunkard closest to her with her fists up, letting her heels clatter on the sidewalk with enough noise to get his attention.

Turned out, her target was a capable man in the middle of a fight. He heard her coming and turned to face her, taking a competent fight posture. She could slow down. Her gown and heels weren't optimal for confrontation, and he had a longer arm reach on her. He blinked slowly in the fraction of a second it took for her to consider, probably deciding the same thing about her appearance.

Screw it.

She rushed him instead, bending at the last possible moment to hoist her skirt and let loose a front kick instead of the punch he'd thought she'd been about to throw. She caught him in the chest but he had twisted slightly and managed to deflect some of the kick's force. Letting her momentum carry her into a turn, she pivoted low on both feet into a crouch and kicked out her other leg. He hadn't been prepared for her change in elevation, and her leg sweep caught him at the ankle. He fell flat on his back on the concrete with a whoosh as his breath left him.

In the meantime, the newcomer had managed to take

the third man to the ground. With all three men groaning and gasping to catch their breath, her new friend grinned at her and stepped clear, offering her a hand up.

She reached into the front of her gown and pulled out a money clip. Tossing them a twenty, she sighed. "Why don't you boys go have a drink someplace else? It wouldn't be advisable to continue this...discussion. Police could be here any minute."

The newcomer at her side chuckled.

The three men scrambled to their feet, Belligerent Boy still dazed. Maybe he'd hit his head on the sidewalk after all. He paused, then grabbed the twenty. The trio headed down the street and around the corner.

"Well, that was less than subtle." Victoria slanted a look at the man next to her. "Your pack of cigarettes are crushed."

He glanced at the crushed pack where it lay forgotten on the pavement. "I hate the things anyway. Grabbed them up from one of the outdoor tables over here."

"Ah." She eyed her new ally as he straightened his clothing. "Are you all right?"

"All good, Queenie." Dark eyes twinkled with good humor, and the creases at the corners of his eyes spoke more of laughter than bad times. He ran his hand through his hair and managed to reestablish himself as quite presentable in fairly short order. "Thank you for the assist."

Come to think of it, she was in a much better mood after their brief scuffle. A workout, however unplanned, had done wonders for the tight ball of brooding she'd been carrying around recently. "I'll buy you a drink for defending the honor of Safeguard, if you'll leave off calling me Queenie."

"I don't know your name yet." He grinned, holding

his hands open in a conciliatory gesture. "I only know you fight like a warrior dressed like a dream."

Pretty words delivered in a wonderful accent. She smiled despite herself. He noticed her give in and his grin widened. Oh, he was going to be the incorrigible type.

"Adam Hicks, at your service."

"I can wait outside, if you'd feel more comfortable." It was still early in the night, and while Adam was very interested in Victoria's company, he wasn't about to assume her coming up to his hotel room meant he was getting laid.

Of course, he wanted to. Very much. It'd been a long while and she was an incredibly attractive woman. He just wanted to give her every opportunity to give him clear signals. He'd invited her up here, though, on the premise of cleaning up her shoes and the bottom of her gown. They'd gotten messed up when she'd helped him encourage the other men to leave the bar downstairs. Apparently, she hadn't booked a room in this hotel for the Safeguard party.

"It was generous of you to offer the use of your sink. I wouldn't want to keep you out of your own room. It won't take me long to clean up." She gave him a sweet smile. Her face was striking with high cheekbones and an angled jaw. Her mouth was small, her lips plump. The effect was captivating.

He couldn't help but focus on those lips for a moment, wondering what she'd taste like. When he tore his gaze away and looked back up at her eyes, they were a steel blue and sparking with amusement.

Giving a relaxed smile in return, he held the door to

his room open for her. He'd given her enough space to get by, but she brushed against him as she walked in anyway. A hint of warm, spicy perfume with a note of sweet teased him as her passing touch sent ripples of heat through his body. He swallowed hard and willed his cock to stay in his pants. He'd had the tuxedo fitted a few days ago, and he'd give the tailor points for having done the fitting to allow for good movement. He'd not torn a single seam in the fight earlier. But the cut and fabric of the pants were not going to hide the way he was responding to her.

Victoria paused, taking in the small but elegant hotel room. Her gaze noted the open closet and every nook and corner as she visually cleared the room, something he'd done as he'd opened the door and before he'd let her in. Her shoulders, bare in her lovely gown, relaxed a bit. She was in peak physical condition, without the sleek look of those who might remain slender by controlling diet. Muscles slid under her smooth, porcelain-white skin in subtle definition. He'd not noticed earlier because her glorious blond hair had fallen in soft curls down her back. Now though, she'd pulled it over her shoulder.

She turned toward him, her gaze trailing as she took her time enjoying the look of the room. There she stood, framed in the light of the bedside lamp he'd left on, all rose and gold in the middle of an impeccably decorated room of creams, pale blues, and soft brown accents. He could be looking at a high-end magazine, really, or a dream. But he was awake and a very lucky man.

"I'll only be a few minutes." She crossed the room to the bathroom and left the door partially open.

He stepped inside and let the door close. This had been an unpredictable evening. He'd come on the last-minute invitation of the lead of the Safeguard Division. He'd had a chance to introduce himself to Gabriel Diaz, wish him and his fiancée well, and then have a few bites to eat as he'd circulated. The guests had been people both from Safeguard and the Centurion Corporation as well as close partners, including one or two representatives from local law enforcement. It'd been swank, the food was delicious and the space somewhat crowded. He could blend in fine in those events but they drained him. He'd thought his cheeks would be sore from all the smiling.

Then he'd stepped out to the quieter bar for a drink and found himself a refreshing brawl, a little one, a breath of evening air. Ah, he was rough around the edges, what could he say? It'd been fun. And he'd met Victoria.

Who was now in his bathroom.

"Do you happen to have a safety pin or sewing kit?" Her voice was low-pitched and had a husky quality to it, but it carried well.

He headed for the closet and pulled his duffel off the floor. "Probably have both."

The duffel was more of a go bag containing enough clothing for the next few days, and he kept it equipped with simple travel necessities as well as spare ammo and extra blades. He was a private military contractor now— best to have whatever he might need on hand. Pulling out a small travel kit, he approached the bathroom door and held it out. "Here."

Victoria glanced up at the mirror, using the reflection the same way he was, to see around the edge of the door. "Thank you."

She opened the bathroom door a bit wider and took

the kit from him. Her fingertips brushed the inside of his palm as she did, tickling him with the shock of their contact again.

"This gown was made to allow for dancing, not sparring." Her tone took on a wry flavor. "It's fine through the torso and the lower skirt, but the back, right at the bottom of the zipper, gave at the seam some. If I don't at least pin it for now, it could pull open even more, and I'll end up with unexpected air-conditioning in this dress for the rest of the night."

He chuckled. "Did you need some help?"

She stopped twisting to see her back in the mirror and lifted her gaze to look at him via the reflection. "I guess that depends."

Her lids were at half-mast and lips pursed in a half smile. He stilled, waiting.

"How much longer am I going to be wearing this?"

Message received. He pressed the door to the bathroom the rest of the way open, and she watched him enter, giving him her back. He moved with care, not wanting to damage her dress and wishing he could tear it off her at the same time. It was slow torture for him to find the tiny zipper and pull it down, revealing more and more of her. She let the lace and silk slide to the floor in a puddle of pink-and-gold shimmer at her feet and sighed as he coasted his hands back up her sides to her shoulders.

She turned to him, lifting her face, her lips parted as she paused. "Just this, tonight, for fun. No strings attached. No surprises?"

He let his lips spread in a slow smile. "This is plenty surprise for me, Queenie, and I plan to keep my attention on exploring the adventure at hand. No strings. No ulterior motives. I'm just a very horny man right now."

Laughing, she smoothed the fabric of his tuxedo jacket, then grabbed the lapels in her fists. "Good. Let's have fun."

Don't miss CONTRACTED DEFENSE
by Piper J. Drake,
available in ebook now,
wherever Carina Press ebooks are sold.

www.CarinaPress.com

Acknowledgments

Thank you to Angela James for your understanding and incredible patience. Every chance I have to work with you is a fantastic learning experience!

Thank you to Courtney Miller-Callihan, for not only putting up with my random insanity but accepting me in all my madness.

And countless thanks to Matthew Beckerleg for reading through the rough parts and helping me get to a better working draft, reminding me to eat and giving me space to get the book done without distractions.

About the Author

Piper J. Drake is an author of bestselling romantic suspense and edgy contemporary romance, a frequent flyer, and day job road warrior. She is often distracted by dogs, cupcakes and random shenanigans.

Play Find the Piper online:

PiperJDrake.com

Facebook.com/AuthorPiperJDrake

Twitter @PiperJDrake

Instagram.com/PiperJDrake